EMPIRE *of the* SENSELESS

To Dana:
The world where we
live? Probably not.
But a great coffee
read nonetheless!
Love ya!
Katherine

Other books by Kathy Acker
Published by Grove Weidenfeld

GREAT EXPECTATIONS
BLOOD AND GUTS IN HIGH SCHOOL
DON QUIXOTE
LITERAL MADNESS
IN MEMORIAM TO IDENTITY

EMPIRE *of the* SENSELESS

Kathy Acker

GROVE WEIDENFELD
New York

Published by Grove Weidenfeld
A division of Grove Press, Inc.
841 Broadway
New York, NY 10003-4793

Library of Congress Cataloging-in-Publication Data

Acker, Kathy, 1948–
Empire of the senseless/Kathy Acker.—1st ed.
p. cm.
ISBN 0-8021-3179-4 (pbk.)
I. Title.
PS3551.C44E47 1988
813'.54—dc19 88-19154
CIP

Manufactured in the United States of America

Printed on acid-free paper

First Edition 1988
First Evergreen Edition 1989

10 9 8 7 6 5 4 3 2

Illustrations by Kathy Acker

This book is dedicated to my tattooist.

Table of Contents

Elegy for the World of the Fathers

MY FAMILY FORTUNE

I Rape by the Father

(*Abhor speaks through Thivai*)

This is what Abhor, who's my partner, part robot, and part black; told me was her childhood:

My Grandmother

She's my father's mother. He came out of her. And she came out of a German-Jewish family which was real wealthy.

But when she was still a kid, cause of all the pre-Nazi nationalistic shit murkiness in Germany, you know about that one, her family had to leave Germany. Not exactly political exile. Voluntary . . . political exile. In order to escape from those pre-Nazi ghettoes the family had to pay, with its wealth. Wealth was the price and cost of political escape. Wealth was the price and cost of capitalism. But now there're multinationals. Nana (my grandmother) arrived in Paris with her mother and father penniless.

Like a lot of poor people do, her parents put her out on the streets to pasture. To make them money. She was the right age, about ten. At that age my grandmother was beautiful. Almost as beautiful, even as a child, as she was stubborn and determined to make someone of herself and something of her life. She wasn't going to prostitute her whole life. As my grandmother got older, she got more stubborn and determined.

I'm stubborn and determined.

There was a young boy, a teenage worker. He looked like a shy fox; his eyes almost came together while a thin mouth stretched from huge ear to floppy ear. This boy, almost as beautiful as a strand of my grandmother's cunt hair, from a distance and in fantasy loved my grandmother. He watched her go from John to John.

After some time, the time it takes for desire to overcome shyness and distance, since there is always time, the boy and Nana would walk down the streets, hands tightly clenched, so that in that heat sweat dripped on to the ragged street, in between her jobs of walking the streets, in between her bloody periods of hard labour. According to Karl Marx, this continent opened up a hundred years ago. What continent? The continent of the end of the capitalistic or teleological world. In the nineteenth-century Western world the people who ventured into this new continent were the militants of revolutionary class struggle. Knowing this the Vice-Squad Captain who patrolled these streets thought that both Nana and the boy, since he was her pimp, were terrorists.

Actually Alexander, the boy, was innocent. When he had been about six, he had naturally fantasized that his great-great-great-great . . . grandfather had been Alexander the Great. He loved snakes. His mother, a real snake, had been a lousy mother. She had mistreated him by alternately screeching everywhere and as loudly as possible whatever she felt at the time, a thoroughly narcissistic bitch, and by smothering Alexander as if he had just died with all the weepy affection which he didn't want. Just as two warriors fight to death, he had to adore her to death. He grew up in this war. He grew up in war. He grew up or, rather, refused to grow up both totally suspicious and as unformed, as open as a wild animal. This was why Alexander resembled a young fox whose I's are permanently crossed.

Being simultaneously unable to perceive anyone other than himself and overly romantic, Alexander loved my grandmother by hating her. He loved her by wanting to kill her: to carry her out of the slum which is prostitution.

Nana and this kid walked through the sun-burnt, brain-burnt streets, holding hands tightly. If they could have, they would have killed each other.

The Vice-Squad cop did it first. One night, since he needed that day to fill his arrest quota in order to keep his creepy job, he busted my grandmother. And busted what, not whom, he thought was her pimp. Bust the whole lot. Scum. Get poverty off the streets and back where it belongs. Dead.

Now Nana was in business: her real pimp got her out of jail. After twenty-four hours, just so that she remembered her place in the scheme of things. If there is a scheme of things. My grandmother never forgot anything. Since Alexander was innocent or not a businessman, there was no pimp to buy him out of jail.

Alexander was innocent beyond the point of real innocence to that of stupidity. For he believed that he was innocent. Perhaps he was, but he had this world wrong. He believed that since he was innocent of pimping and the courts were just, he didn't need to give a lawyer money. He believed that lawyers earn money only off of guilt. The court forced a Legal Aid lawyer on the boy. But since the Legal Aid never showed up in Court, or for that matter never anywhere else, Alexander was able to plead his own innocence. Then the Vice-Squad swore whatever the Vice-Squad swears in order to maintain the scheme of things. Which might or might not exist.

The whole thing, case, took exactly five minutes: the judge said numbers to the prosecution; the prosecution said numbers to the judge; back and forth for five minutes. Finally the judge said some numbers. A man who should have been more than an extra in a monster movie ushered, to put it politely, Alexander through several doors and into an empty prison cell.

After several weeks he was ushered out of the prison cell and on to the street. On another street he bought a sawed-off shotgun off a pawn, then stuck some sharpened kitchen knives in his belt, and walked back on the street. He went for the whole Vice-Squad. He tried to kill every Vice-Squad. He was nineteen years old. A romantic. He managed to kill four of them. Literally the cops had to nail him to a wall in order to keep him: madness had made his strength so great.

They (the courts) condemned the boy to death.

It was one of the final nineteenth-century revolts of the non-existent against their economic controllers. In a sense, Nana when she was a whore had been one of its final causes.

Parts of the police's duty has always been to combine against all who aren't them and their own. For a cop, duty's nature. The flics made sure that the judge, who was one of their own, condemned the boy to as an immediate death as possible.

The light on the night of the boy's execution, the only light, was pink chair light green violet violent flesh. All the people haunted by crime and misery, living in the Section of Desolation, converged upon that spot: the jail in which they made their electrocutions. On two sides of the jail, bourgeois houses, unable to see with their eyes anything which wasn't on television, were holding their eyes tightly shut. They said: 'What you don't see, you don't know.' Beyond the prison's other two sides, walls reached up into the centres of the god's eyes. If there are gods when there are poor people. Beneath the walls, the cripples and the mentally crippled, the lonely, shuffled their huge feet.

Cops sitting on monstrous black horses forced the desolate back against the walls. But the mass was too pissed-on and pissed to be controllable. Neither black beast nor human beast could break through the throng of human filth.

When the light was the water, at dawn, there was no water, when instant electrical waves cursed and coursed like water through the boy's body: the mass like a tidal wave roared. 'Murder. We are murdered.'

The cops moved in on them like a wall which moves. Everything becomes something else. In blood and change, my childhood began.

Being poor, Nana had learned that society is only a filthy

trick. Being totally stubborn and determined not to become a filthy trick of the rich, dead, for death is not a human life, according to her own lights Nana succeeded. She married a rich man who owned part of the garment district. The poor can reply to the crime of society, to their economic deprivation retardation primitivism lunacy boredom hopelessness, only by collective crime or war. One form collective crime takes is marriage.

I think that because I perceived what marriage was for my grandmother and because I love her, I am not able to sexually love another human being or accept another human being's love. If I have to love, out of desperation or desperately, I know love only when it's allied with hate.

Daddy

Thivai. The beginning of any person must be the beginning of the world. To that person.

That's how it is for me.

First, Thivai, there were no animals. That is, no wild animals. Oh there were cats and dogs who are somewhere between humans and real animals. The cats were so thin they looked like knives. Predatory knives ran down the streets. Just like in Detroit. No human could walk on the streets without blood covering her limbs.

The streets were really one street, a bit of pavement running parallel to the coast almost all the way down its bay.

Behind broken bits of pavement, shrubbery dense from being all different shapes without any possible passageways for humans, twisted out of the rock which was the only earth and harder than anything: this rock-earth occasionally rose right up into mountains, and then to and into air.

Rock became sky.

The first light which was air sat on the sea. It appeared to be weird. Or a haze which resembled human nausea. Then the tops of the water, as if they were and there were waves, but there weren't, were light. These tops were dapples of changing colour; there was no other light.

Not in the way rock had become sky, the light moved into water.

The tops of the water were valueless jewels. In the distance the risen rock was haze. All was hazy and resembled human nausea.

The day after the beginning of this disgusting world, the rock formed a cave. The cave was big enough for lots of people. There were several large black worms and their feet were white. They crawled into the holes at the ocean floor's bottom. In the full late sun, a burro had fallen asleep. His large head lay next to a sleeping dog's larger head. The bees were bigger than horses.

Daddy was Nana's only kid. She adored him. She gave him everything she could. He, in turn, turned to her as a mother turns to her child. They formed a closed world.

By the time daddy was born, Nana was very wealthy. He was a beautiful boy: his hair was thick black and his eyes were big black. Since he had turned to grandma rather than outward to the world, he had no morals, for any morality presumes a society. Since my grandmother loved him, she saw no reason to teach him anything or that he should learn anything.

This substitution of *primitivism* which must be *anarchic* (in its non-political sense) for *morality* gave my father his charm. His charm blinded not only his parents but even every old farty schoolteacher to both his complete lack of social awareness and of education. Politics, for my father, was, always, a hole. Parents and teachers scolded him only in the way a child reprimands a favourite fat cat; when my father was being punished, he knew he was really being praised for being unlike other humans. When he was ten years old and unlearned, my grandfather, who everyone considered a saint, and Nana together killed themselves: they couldn't live without each other.

Daddy was coming into puberty. He inherited six million dollars. These two – money and sex – must have had something to do with each other, cause from the night he lost his virginity, daddy never had trouble finding lovers. Lovers were men and women to whom he gave gifts, not love or need. Daddy, being daddy, needed no one. He wouldn't consider, just cause of sex, being tied to any other human being.

As he got older, he got even better looking. When he was forty, he got married because he wanted to propagate himself once. Sex was joined to money. She married him because her mother desired this marriage because his family was wealthier than theirs. She was fifteen. Like my father, she worshipped her mother.

The only man she ever worshipped was my father. He didn't care about her. He married her to have me. He cared about me. By him. His. He educated me. I was educated the way he had been educated.

I looked like him. I smelled like him. I learned like him. My father had propagated.

As a result of this education I don't know anything about politics and I never read newspapers. As a result of this education I just like trouble. As a result of this education I don't know anything about the world. As a result of this education I'm dumb.

My mother hated the way I was. I felt she hated me. I felt she wanted to kill me and I felt since she was my mother she must love me.

Out of confusion which resembled nausea, I complained to daddy that my mother didn't love me and was a cold. He informed me coldly, in front of her, that she loved me of course because she was my mother. Since he was glaring at her, she had enough intelligence to know that she should never open her dumb mouth again.

Daddy played all sorts of games with me. He taught me how to throw a real football. He taught me gymnastics. He trained me into total physical perfection.

Then he taught me a final trick. He showed me how to insert a razor blade into my wrist just for fun. Not for any other reason. Thus, I learned how to approach and understand nature, how to make gargantuan red flowers, like roses, blooming, drops of blood, so full and dripping the earth under them, my body, shook for hours afterwards. During those afterhours, I fantasized my blood pouring outwards. This was relief that there were no decisions left.

Daddy left me no possibility of easiness. He forced me to live among nerves sharper than razor blades, to have no certainties. There was only roaming. My nerves hurt more and more. I despised those people, like my mother, who accepted easiness – morality, social rules. Daddy taught me to live in pain, to know there's nothing else. I trusted him for this complexity.

Otherwise I was innocent. I actually thought a man and woman got a baby by rubbing their asses together. What this looked like I didn't actually know. The woman would do something like shitting. Dong this or having a child was something I certainly didn't want to do. Ever. The only person I wanted was my father.

One day daddy said he had something to tell me.

'What do you have to tell me?' I was so quiet, I was dead. My nerves were as sharp as razors.

'You know your mother?'

I didn't want to know my mother.

'Your mother isn't your real mother.'

I didn't care. 'Who's my mother?' I asked without caring.

'You don't remember her. As soon as you dropped out of her cunt, she gave you to the hospital. Nana and I took you. She never tried to see you. Ever again.'

'We don't talk about her,' said my mother who was now fake.

'We don't talk about her because she was mad, Abhor. She was the only woman I've ever loved. You look exactly like her. You remind me of the woman I loved, Abhorra.'

This mother who was fake no longer existed. I existed.

I realized that my father hated and loved me because he had to. This mixture of total attraction and disgust calmed my natural fears and drew me more and more toward him. I was his mirror. I was his knight. I was strong daring loyal questioning. I would do anything to be loved as long as love or adoration didn't involve closeness. The fake mother had long been banished to her bourgeois summer house.

When did I start to fuck? Oh, I started to fuck, Thivai, when I was fourteen. At that age I didn't give a damn who I fucked cause any boy who fucked me loved me. Fucking was love. Since I don't think it is anymore, I don't fuck around anymore. Now I know that we, all of us, know more than we know we know, this is human knowledge, cause I still didn't exactly know what fucking was and I didn't know how my parents felt about my fucking and yet I knew I was evil cause I was fucking. So I knew daddy would kill me if he caught me fucking. I don't know how I knew this.

I was in the bathroom, fucking some boy. Daddy came home. I heard the front door close. I threw on my clothes and ran up to daddy. 'Hi! Hi!' I kissed him. There's only one picture I have left of me as a kid. I'm three years old. My arms close around my father's thighs. 'Shall I get you some Jack Daniels?'

Daddy wasn't an alcoholic. He drank the usual six martinis at night and mommy, she was a moralist, kept telling him he was an alky.

I knew he'd say 'Yes'. Daddy could never reject Jacky Daniels. They were a bunch of homosexuals. When daddy went off to his bedroom, I opened the front door and snuck the boy I'd been fucking out.

I returned to their Parisian apartment with the J.D. I handed it to daddy. He was holding up a boy's tie which he'd found in the bathtub. He didn't believe my lies. He sat down on his bed where he always sat. My daddy was almost crying.

'Abhor.'

My limbs were frozen with tension.

'Abhor, I know what you've been doing.' Lies never work except as lies. Like language and love. My mother taught me this. Like love. 'These men don't respect you, Abhor.'

How could I explain that I cared neither if they respected me nor who they were.

'Abhor,' daddy explained, 'I'm the only man who'll ever

take care of you properly.' His hands were reaching for my breasts while tears were coming out of his eyes.

'Why don't you do it with mommy, daddy?'

'We're too old. We don't do it anymore.' His right hand was rubbing my breast.

'I'm going to phone mommy.' Over the phone, I told her that her husband was trying to do something to me. I didn't use the word 'fuck'.

She said, 'Let me speak to him.'

'Daddy, mommy wants to speak to you.'

I don't remember if his hand left my nipple. I don't know what they said to each other.

After he put the phone receiver down on the table, he put his cock up me. There was no more blood than in a period.

Part of me wanted him and part of me wanted to kill him.

So I stayed in their apartment and that night I dreamed that the blood lying over the ocean in front of my eyes was light. The light by which I could see. The fishing boats sink or stink.

The German Romantics had to destroy the same bastions as we do. Logocentricism and idealism, theology, all supports of the repressive society. Property's pillars. Reason which always homogenizes and reduces, represses and unifies phenomena or actuality into what can be perceived and so controlled. The subjects, us, are now stable and socializable. Reason is always in the service of the political and economic masters. It is here that literature strikes, at this base, where the concepts and actings of order impose themselves. Literature is that which denounces and slashes apart the repressing machine at the level of the signified. Well before Bataille, Kleist, Hoffman etc., made trial of Hegelian idealism, of the cloturing dialectic of recognition: the German Romantics sung brazenly brassily in brass of spending and waste. They cut through conservative narcissism with bloody razor blades. They tore the subject away from her subjugation to her self, the proper; dislocated you the puppet; cut the threads of meaning; spit at all mirrors which control.

I knew that pleasure gathers only in freedom. For I was soaring through the sky, my huge white and grey wings stretched out to the horizontal limits of my vision. I was alone. In the sky. I was almost white.

I flew downwards, hollering with pleasure, swoop as if into the slate of water. But I didn't. Then swooped directly into the cold of that ocean, it was the light of morning, as directly as if I was going for food. Out of the tunnel my body had carved in the water, a fountain of light burst upward.

The city awoke. Bursting. Angels sat on its head. Everything burst. Carolled. There is only glory. Because I know there are angels and visions, there is freedom. Only in real living human life. After years of regular torture, boredom replacing all other mental activity, continuous fear, forgetfulness of all dreams to the point of inability to dream, to have visions, after years of being driven into the corners of rats, of garbage cans filled with plague, of cut-off limbs, driven into every form of living which is death: suddenly the people in this city were free. They were free to experiment.

This is what the people said to the sky. 'Now the mad bird has won. Now even criminals can fly.'

But (in my dream) thousands of tiny fish were translucent and looked like worms. They leapt, with their tiny sharp teeth, out of the water at me. The teeth bit through the thin feathers into my flesh. From me the little teeth were red. One baby fish leaped so high, he bit through my rotting teeth with his teeth. Then through my tongue tip. Many fish tore my wings off of me out of hunger. Me actually courageous I tried to keep my life by screaming swooping dodging. Nobody and nothing came to my rescue. There was no such thing as rescue. There could have been no reality. I had only myself to save myself. I couldn't save myself. My wings were more torn than dishrags, they were sick, and the tongue was so torn it couldn't speak. I could neither fly nor cry. Nor could I stay alive.

Inside my mind I scream aloud; inside my mind, the world, I scream aloud. Somewhere I am a female and I have long hair and that hair is floating over the soil so dry, for centuries, that nothing ever grows in it. Here there is only emotion. I scream when I die. Then I sink into black. The rest of any living is nights. The cities have died. The cities are full of rats; the rats are bored; people seem as lonely as they are bored.

After that night I was so unsure of myself, I desperately made love with anyone. Since lots of boys fell wildly in love with this double material sex and mental lack of me, daddy was jealous. 'If I was a young boy, I'd knife a boy who fucked you.'

'I don't like knives.'

'We've hit bottom.' Daddy knew how low love had brought us. 'We're downwind from even from where the rich spit. Any man would do anything to prevent our joy. But they'll all be sorry for their rules which are crimes. If, by any chance, there isn't any real justice, if we have no rescue: I hereby invoke all the gods or Energies who sanctify our love or so-called crime to make these men suffer the horrors of hell. May their suffering equal God's.'

'I didn't know God existed.'

Not only did this monster to whose force I had, by force, yielded hate even the notion of my fucking a boy. He also, was, even more, frightened that other people, society, would notice his ridiculous restrictions of me and question why. He realized he had to give them, society, a reason why he was shutting me up.

All daddy cared about was what society thought about him. He didn't care if he was really evil because he didn't have any morals. He was free to do whatever he wanted as long as he was secret. He was a moralist. He just didn't want society to think him evil.

So he gradually let it be known I was a cripple. For this reason, he was shutting me up for the rest of my life. I was a genetic cripple: I was weird. Also I was dyslexic and autistic. I was too crippled for anyone to love me.

My mother knew I wasn't a cripple. She was real dumb. So daddy gave her the one reason for my life imprisonment which could penetrate her thick skull. He, he explained, was saving me from marriage because marriage is the worst life any woman can have.

My mother agreed.

'Marriage,' my father said, 'turns woman into whining passive-aggressive liars while the men become narcissists. Whatever good is possible between any man and woman marriage destroys. For the woman becomes lobotomized and the man acts like a bad actor acting the part of President Reagan. My one goal in life, darling, is to allow your daughter to be as intelligent and fully realized a human being as possible.'

'Yes,' my mother dared to open her mouth, 'males are creeps.'

But as soon as her husband walked away from her, *my mother*, I hated those words, reverted to her usual inability to accept the truth. For the truth, being complex, always hurts. She whined to her mother, because she always turned to her mother, what her husband had said.

At the moment my mother was whining, daddy was smelling my cunt. 'I've reached my best moment now!' he explained. Now I was sure what he was referring to. 'This is the moment of truth!!! . . . I'm going off off off jacking it off!!! . . . my hands're gonna be broken from this one!!! . . . I don't even recognize my own body!!! . . . and it doesn't matter!!! . . . I know you're mine!!! . . . I made you!!! . . . I'm making you!!! . . . I swore I'd live for pleasure!!! . . . My tongue is fucking enormous!!! . . . feel it!!! . . . it's reaching down to my waist!!! . . . you're seeing your actual father in his moment of truth!!! . . . God almighty!!! . . . nothing matters!!! . . . you're my God!!! . . . my daughter: I worship you!!! . . . I beg you to do it, show I can please you!!! . . . now look at it, it's big, in my corkscrewing hand!!! . . . kiss it!!!'

My father explained again, 'I am fucking God and I made God!!! . . . Holy Shit!!! . . . all I have to do is look at God and God is happy cause I've made God come!!!

'God is in heaven I'm in heaven I've died the whole world in heaven!!! . . . I'm coming all over your face!!!'

I licked up his sperm.

My grandmother, unlike my mother, wasn't a dope. She didn't do dope. When mommy whimpered to her that her husband (whom she loved more than anything on earth), that this husband was keeping me in a private prison and privately whipping me, grandma replied that this couldn't be good for my welfare. This couldn't be for the sake of my welfare. My father couldn't be whipping me for my good. So he must be acting for his own good, because there is always Good. No one was sure what that might be.

My mother's mother was a dominating old bitch. With her shaking flesh she wobbled via taxi over to my father. 'Bud,' she asked him. 'What's this shit about you not letting my granddaughter fuck for money? I mean, get married?' Grandma always got her terms mixed up. 'Do you want your daughter to be a freak? After all, she carries our name.'

'I don't have enough money to let her marry, Florrie. Marriage's too expensive a business.'

'I'll finance it,' grandma replied.

'If you finance her fucking for money,' said my father whose IQ was 166, 'I'll let her do it.' My father knew his mother-in-law was the cheapest thing on earth, even cheaper than himself.

'I'll finance it.' Then grandmama huffed and huffed on to the uppitty hotel she called her home, but by the time she had walked into her grey red and black clown study, she had forgotten everything because she didn't have any middle-term memory.

For the moment my father and I were free to fuck each other everywhere, in every bathroom in town.

When daddy wasn't with me, he lived in a brothel. A sex-show was the brothel's front. Since the sex show actors had only fake sex, this sex show's legality acted a cover for the rest of the filth which went on.

The desperate voyeurs who sought their sexual gratification in the masturbatory contemplation of a remote object of fantastic desire and an array of attendant secret fetishisms; the exploitation of sex for commercial and assorted equally venial reasons; the way in which patrons of this seedy burlesque house fell prey to its psychotically disturbed perverts; the degradation of the performers who not only put their flesh and minds on parade in the tradition of the Miss America beauty pageant but also were forced to watch this deterioration, this deterioration of themselves, so that they, like the other objects, were simply objects of scorn to the 'fans' . . . Their buyers . . . This sex show had nothing to do with pornographic voyeurism. None but the most callous of males was unconcerned enough to be voyeuristic. Most humans felt totally disgusted by and repudiated both what they saw, what they felt, and the whole system of values behind the sex show and the pornographic magazines and especially novels sold outside the 'theatre'. In other words, the primal urge of sex had become a revolting phenomenon.

Here language was degraded. As daddy plumbed and plummetted away from the institute of marriage more and more downward deeply into the demimonde of public fake sex, his speech turned from the usual neutral and acceptable journalese most normal humans use as a stylus mediocris into . . . His language went through an indoctrination of nothingness, for sexuality had no more value in his world, until his language no longer had sense. Lack of meaning appeared as linguistic degradation.

This is what daddy said to me while he was fucking me: 'Tradicional estilo de p . . . argentino. Q . . . es e. mas j . . . de t . . . los e . . . dentro d. la c . . . es m . . . indicado p . . . entablar g . . . amistades o t . . . tertulias a . . . es m . . . similar a. estilo t . . . : se c . . . la c . . . con l. palma de la m . . . y s. apoyan l . . . cinco d . . . se s . . . y s. baja l. mano, l . . . de e . . . manera y . el c . . . se h . . . hombre. origen e. profundamente r . . . y s. han h . . . interesantes t . . . en l . . . jeroglificos e . . . y m . . . Es e. mas r . . . para d . . . de l . . . comidas p . . . no c . . . la de . . .' He had become a Puerto Rican.

One night I dreamed my mother had a lover. She realized how powerful and addictive fucking is. Then I was free to be.

I told my father my dream. Even though he despised her, he cared so much for me, he determined to find her a lover.

He picked up a young anarchist. Since this slut had problems with vermin, fleas and crabs, the slut needed money to delouse himself so he could be a successful slut. He was too poor to buy any medicine. The parasites were so numerous at night he often dreamed that he was attacking a young girl. His right hand became a claw and tore at her face. Worms reared out of the skinned female visage. The anarchist, waking, wanted only to stick razors into himself. My father explained to the boy that it'ld give his wife only pleasure to take a lover.

The anarchist agreed to fuck my mother.

My mother, being weak, was so desperate to talk to anyone she let the anarchist fuck her. Then she became a nymphomaniac. My mother took one drink and fucked everyone in sight.

One account of the degeneration of language. Slut.

My father went to Greece. One night he was sitting on his yacht off the coast of the island of Ithaca, from where Ulysses had set off on his own to find out the truth. At night the water, the sky and the few buildings of the nearest town were many different colors of black. There was only black. My father saw a shadow on the other side of his yacht, took out his pistol, and shot. The shadow fell, dead, down to the deck. In the law court, my father declared that he hadn't recognized the young man who he had killed.

The blood lying over the waters was light. The fishing boats stank.

Pleasure gathered only in freedom. According to the law court, my father had murdered. My mother and I were unable to do anything. We wrote letters, pleading daddy was insane. Mommy thought he was insane. I was so scared I came from an insane family, I stopped writing. I had to. Insanity, in my blood, was poisoning me. I was going to spend my adult life screaming to the moon.

The family wealth succeeded in getting daddy six months in the looney bin on a lunacy charge. Then daddy, desperate to find out what had happened to me, escaped from the madhouse.

He wandered through streets he didn't know, looking for a cab. Six youths who were armed stopped him and looked through his body for money. Daddy grabbed one of their knives and got three of them before the others stuck it into him. They left him without money and bleeding over the sidewalk.

Desperate, daddy began to pray. But he had no one to whom to pray. Meanwhile my mother had killed herself cause, though she hated daddy, she was unable to live without him. Once his restraining hand had been gone, she had blown all her money. She faced poverty and took sleeping pills instead.

I saw my mother's dead body in the morgue on Christmas Day. It was the first dead body I had ever seen. The two cops there were anxious to return home to their warm Christmas meals. They told me to identify her.

I wanted to kill myself just as my mother had killed herself. This is my madness.

Meanwhile daddy realized all he had done, all he had destroyed through lust. He began to cry. Two tears ran down his cheeks. He raced to his only possession, his yacht, which moved, and moved off. Into the bloody sea. No one's ever seen him again. I don't know what happened to daddy. I decided to keep on living rather than kill myself.

II Raise Us From The Dead

(Thivai speaks)

Male

As long as I can remember, I have wanted to be a pirate. As long as I can remember, I have wanted to sail the navy seas. As long as I can remember wanting, I have wanted to slaughter other humans and to watch the emerging of their blood.

Insofar as I know myself I don't know either the origin nor the cause of my wants.

It was a dark night for pirates.

Winter had approached all of us on the ship. One night whose beginning was death, three pirates squatting on the deck just like fat cunts or pigs held a consultation which lingered, like death, without becoming anything else. For one human they had taken during their last battle remained bound and gagged near the bowsprit. Their discussion became more confused, then too confused, at least for the victim who could still hear; the pirates had become increasingly drunk. A fat slob waddled over to the victim who was a child and raped her again.

She didn't struggle as the other two did the same.

'Afterwards I'd like to do it to you,' the first pirate turned to the second pirate.

'No. I'm younger than you so it's possible for me to have a child. I don't want one. Just cause it's safe for you . . .'

'Not if I do it in your asshole. In your asshole you're safe.'

'Just stop what you're doing. Above all I don't want to be pregnant!'

'You don't believe me. You don't trust . . .'

'No.' The second one explained: 'Why should I trust you? You tell me why I should trust you. You tell me why I should trust you who can't get pregnant not to make me pregnant.'

The third pirate came in his pants. A round stain showed.

'Don't you believe I can fuck you and not make babies?'

Used to protecting his virginity like a girl, the youngest of the pirates capitulated. 'If you let me alone I'll let you do it tonight. But you've got to promise you won't tell anyone.'

Fatty replied 'I promise' since he never meant anything by these words. 'But you're going to spread yourself for me now. Otherwise I want that thin trigger that thin cock you're showing me so much, I'll cut off your head to get at it.' Among themselves, also, pirates're murderous. 'But after I come when you're dead, you can do whatever you want.'

Fatty dove in, ground and pounded his cock up into the so tight it was almost impenetrable asshole. He pound and ground until the brat started wiggling; then thrust hard. Thrust fast. Living backbone. Jewel at top of hole. The asshole opened involuntarily. The kid screeched like nerves. After a while the kid felt Fatty become still. After a few more minutes he asked Fatty if he had come.

'Shut up. Shut. Up.' As it dropped out the final bit of sperm enflamed the top of his cockhole.

Barely mumbling 'Now it's time for me now it's time for what I want', the pirate who had just been fucked bent over the child tightly bound in ropes, already raped. His hands reached for her breasts. While sperm which resembled mutilated oysters dropped out of his asshole, he touched the breasts.

The three pirates turned away from the child. They went back to their work of gnawing and gorging themselves on Nestle's almonds, Cadbury chocolate flakes, barbecued tortilla chips, green benas, toffeed vanilla, Lucozade, and Mars bars. They guzzled down can after can of swill.

The Captain, me, walked on deck. 'What a group of pigs! Didn't your teachers in all the nice boarding schools you went to, which you never talk about, teach you about nutrition?'

'This ship isn't a public school,' Fatty blurted out through showers of Coca-Cola mixed with beer. 'This shit is a pirate ship. And this is a philanthropic association.'

'Sure,' Captain Thivai, me, sneered. 'I'm a sweet socialist government so I'm paying you to sit on your asses in the sun and get suntanned just so that you are so happy you will not revolt against my economic fascism.'

Fatty dared to oppose me. 'No way. This ship is our philanthropic association, our place of safety, our baby crib. Since they have enough dough to be our charity donors, all the people outside it, all the people outside us here, are our enemies.

'Since we live on this ship, we're orphans. Orphans are dumb and stupid.' Fatty was epileptic. 'Since we're stupid, we don't know how to conduct ourselves in decent (monied) society and we kill people for no reason.'

'Historically, weren't some of the most violent political murderers,' the punk added, 'aristocrats?'

'Do all of you have parents?' I asked my crew, for I was astounded. 'Do you generally come from good backgrounds?'

'How can I answer a generality? So how can I answer any question?' Fatty obviously came from a superior background.

'Do you,' pointing my finger at the youngest therefore the weakest of the lot, 'do you, personally, have parents?'

'I don't have no parents.'

'Me neither.'

'Him also?'

'No one.'

'None.'

'No one has nothing anymore.'

'Then who'd you come out of and where d'you come from?' I wasn't going to be fooled by the scum.

'That's our business. Each one of us.'

The English pirate answered, 'We're not used to discussing private affairs. It's not your business on whom we piss.'

I had to agree with the English, for it was necessary for me to trust my crew about whom I knew nothing except that they were not the scum of the earth, they were the scum of the now scum-filled seas.

And the next day, when the ship stopped near a shore on which a bordello was stretching out its claws, I jumped ship. A cock cried on the top of a hill. Roosters' red crests jumped through the weighted-down grasses. A guard and his heavy gun descended. I hid from him.

Where there were buildings huge trees had showered dew on to their red roofs. My fear dried up my throat. My hands lay over my stomach for protection.

The sun . . .

Fear disintegrated my throat . . .

Stunned . . .

I woke. I was no longer free. Words woke me. 'It's me, Xaintrilles. This afternoon the General Staff'll interrogate you. Good luck 'n all that. I'm leaving for Ait Saada.'

I didn't speak.

Xaintrilles squatted down on his haunches and looked at the bars. He saw a young man spread flat on the floor, still, his knees apart, a sackcloth jacket over only part of his stomach. 'Thivai, aren't you listening to me? Maybe you can't hear anymore?'

I recognized despair enough to open my senses only inside me. Lice gnawed my cropped head. Xaintrilles carried this body inside, chafed hands and knees.

In the deep river firemen and convoy soldiers washed themselves. Mud scintillated around the decaying bath-house.

I lovingly rubbed my skull, the light wounds the hair-chopper had made. 'Shave me. To the flesh,' I said.

The gentle hair-cutter, as soon as his officer had left, positioned the straight razor at the front of the forehead. 'Thivai, I can't. There's not enough left.'

Upon returning, the officer looked at the prisoner and ordered the barber to shave him totally.

I smiled, I lowered my head, the barber trembled, my flesh peeled off my head and the tip of my ear, the officer by his red leather boot crushed my shoeless foot; the cutter wiped his fingers on the linen knotted around my neck. Then he went back to his cutting. My hairs dropped off like flies. As they were cut, they brushed by the ears, the holes of the nostrils, caught in the eyebrows, mommy, I only went to the hairdresser to cut off a lock of hair, my matchstick, mommy's sitting in the armchair, mommy's holding my knee, mommy's picking up a magazine, mommy puts it on her knees. Véronique's behind the mirror. Véronique stands upright. Then the hairdresser pushes her down while Véronique makes signs which the mirror reflects. The cut hairs brush past the beehive I've hidden in my shirt; mommy leaves, forgetting her purse. She walks through the rain along the river. Am I dreaming? The haircutter looks around him, he puts his hand on the hot flannel of my pants, his hand climbs up my thigh, I look at Véronique, it's she who's raping me it's she who's touching me, mommy's screaming out loud and crying in the rain. Dock workers drag barbed wire sheets through the slush. Mommy bites her soaked scarf. The haircutter's hand sinks between my knees; again I push it away; his other hand travels down my stomach; my knees hit the marble washbasin which nevertheless maintains its balance; the haircutter's hand rests openly on my obviously palpitating stomach. The hairdresser looks behind him.

Under the door, mommy's drying her shoes. She enters the room. Night fell. Her wet hands hold my small ones, I fall into the armchair; mommy pays the hairdresser; he presses me against the door.

Mommy drags me out, down black streets until we reach the river. The dock workers're trying to warm themselves by standing as close as possible to a fire made out of charcoal dust. Mommy, holding me in her arms, jumps into the thicker mist. She mounts the jetty and runs over the rocks. Snow is covering the rocks. I try to writhe myself away, but she's pressing me into her hips. So I bite her hand, while a tug-boat whose bright port dead-lights are throwing glimmers on a black oily sea, moves down the estuary; mommy throws herself, . . ., I bite her hand, as her arms let go, I fall down the rocks, rolling down the rocks, mommy falls into the sea (my mother's suicide), the foam finds and recovers her, I twist my body round toward the rocks. There a wave carries my mother's head. Her palms slide along a sleek, slightly glittering rock. The tug-boat bears the other way, then stops; a sailor runs on to a bridge; he unfastens a yawl, runs back on board; they row toward the jetty. Between the clouds the stars're shining. My head's bathing in a small abandoned puddle. A sailor jumps on to the jetty, lifts me in his strong arms, up, and strokes my forehead and left cheek. The other sailors ship their oars and, lifting up my mother's body, bear it over a huge flat rock. The sailor puts me to bed. From the tip of the tent's main peg a lantern was barely balancing. My blood flowed into my hands. The sailors telephoned, held my hands in theirs, covered my face, They tore the khaki posters and bills open . . .

After the jeeps and the lorries left, wounded on the forehead now by the rising sun, I placed my sackcloth jacket over my face. The rest was naked. The flies in the toilet and the wine-press the soldiers had for their own convenience were gnawing at the barrier wires' edges; they darted forward, leapt over my cock, sunk into the mop of hair below, scurted over the curly locks, so I trembled, opened my thighs. The morning breeze cooled down the thighs and the sexual mass. The flies stole . . .

Again Véronique tosses her hairs behind her; I take hold of this hair and throw my face into it; Véronique turns around and places my head in her hands:

'Xaintrilles wet-kissed me in the garden.'

I throw my arms around her waist, then I eat at her mouth; revolving her thighs rub and press themselves against my stomach; though she's pushing back my arms, I kiss her eyelids; her hand rubs my back my waist; her eyelids taste of mud; the sweat wets my opened shirt.

As soon as she laughs, I turn her over under me on the armchair.

The wind bangs the books on the table shut. My hand burrows like a mole in her clothes. Over a teat. Trembles. Under my hand the teat is hot. I stroke the other teat. With the second hand I unhook the dress. And tongue the teat's tip. 'And me,' she pants. She crushes my mouth by her breast. Wide open the windows look over the park. Xaintrilles walks through the thick grass, his gun erect.

'Don't be so hard,' he tells me. 'You're breaking my legs.'

I crawl over him. Sirens stain the distance.

Today there's no more pirates therefore I can't be a pirate. I know I can't be a pirate because there're no more pirate ships.

In 1574 there were pirate ships.

By that time the total halt of legal, or national, European wars forced the French and German soldiers either to disappear or to become illegal – pirates. Being free of both nationalistic and religious concerns and restrictions, privateering's only limitation was economic. Piracy was the most anarchic form of private enterprise.

Thus, at that time, in one sense, the modern economic world began. In anarchic times, when anyone could become any one and thing, corsairs, free enterprisers roamed everywhere more and more . . .

Murderers killed murderers . . .

Human beings are good by nature. This is the credo of those who are liberals, even pacifists, during times of national and nationalistic wars.

But in 1574, when regular, regulated war, that is, national war, which the nations involved had maintained at huge expense only via authoritarian expansion, ceased: the sailors the soldiers the poor people the disenfranchized the sexually different waged illegal wars on land and sea.

War, if not the begetter of all things, certainly the hope of all begetting and pleasures. For the rich and especially for the poor. War, you mirror of our sexuality.

I who would have and would be a pirate: I cannot. I who live in my mind which is my imagination as everything – wanderer adventurer fighter Commander-in-Chief of Allied Forces – I am nothing in these times.

Nightmare City

1. The Psychosis Which Resulted From Gonorrhoea

My life began when I had gonorrhoea. I was eighteen years old. Or rather, it began when the gonorrhoea ended, if such things ever end. For the foul disease had completely incapacitated me: I became dependent on other people even for the necessities of life.

I'm now not only useless, as are all human beings and as most human beings, the ones who aren't rich, believe they are. I'm also physically and mentally damaged because my only desire is to suicide.

I'm living on Chiba. My current fuck is always telling me that I ought to kill myself but, more significantly, that everyone wants to kill me.

'Who in particular wants to kill me? Why're you always putting me down?' I know they want to kill me.

'Why're you always starting a war? A man.'

'My drug supplier?' I need drugs in order to maintain precarious stability.

'A man wants to kill you,' she informed me right after I had orgasmed. Then, I knew.

I didn't bother saying anything. It's a policy of mine: Don't believe in human speech as anything but a stuffer of time. I would, and I would have, run away, but there's no place to which to run, so the only safety is psychosis and drugs.

Without paying any attention to me, as if I was dead, she continued speaking. 'Perception has become a philosophical problem.'

Because we had become too close the fuck could read my mind. But I had an answer. 'It's possible to perceive yourself just as you'ld perceive anything else,' I informed her. 'This is how strippers perceive their bodies.'

'How can you know about normal people?' Someone, probably her, had torn out the sleeves of her jumpsuit to her shoulders. The colours of her eyes matched those of her fingernails and of another part of her body.

'Before I had gonorrhoea I was normal.' I thought. 'But now the memory of normal living is only a dream. My business in life has become infantile neurosis. When I was young, over and over again, I dreamed I was being followed. The people following me were bad. I couldn't run away fast enough to get away from them.'

I didn't bother telling her the particular dreams because she was just a fuck. Instead I watched her personality fragment, over a period of time, calving like an iceberg or space, splinters of identity drifting away, until finally I saw her raw need, obsession which is addiction. I was scared. I wanted to run away.

'How do you know they want to kill me?' I asked.

'A birdie told me.'

I looked down at a head which was bodiless. Through my shock, I saw it was a head. Or, I remembered. Nothing lasts forever.

Sleep or ease is a priority the way love used to be. Before I was psychotic, before I stopped sleeping, my dreams told me someone was trying to kill me. My fuck told me someone was trying to kill me.

When I reached the bar I was accustomed to, the man behind the bar told me nobody was trying to kill me. Nothing bad was going to happen to me as long as I didn't fall asleep.

My boss didn't want to hurt me.

Then the bartender told me that the woman I had been fucking had squelched on me to the boss because, addicted, she needed the money. RAM – whoever that was – would pay her for my death. They were chasing me.

When I fuck women, they always ask me why I don't trust anyone . . .

'Why don't you trust me?' spreading her legs.

Since I'm a gentleman, I don't spit where I should. Even if I don't know who's my boss.

I walked into my apartment. Another cunt was pointing a Luger at me. They were chasing me. I could believe the actuality of hatred now it had become an actuality.

'Who are you? RAM? Are you the ones who've been chasing me? Now I know who you are,' I informed her.

She told me she didn't work for any bosses, she was a free woman, her name was Abhor. Why should I believe what a cunt tells me?

If reality isn't my picture of it, I'm lost.

2. Suicide

My mother's always sick. She doesn't have any time for me. Nursey takes care of me by sticking a pin through my thigh. I cried so after that she didn't have much to do with me. I cried because I loved her because she was the only person, that is, cunt, who loved me.

Then, because mommy still wanted me to be dead because she was, they gave me a new nurse. Since this one was English, she was proper and didn't show (me) any feeling. I decided she was a witch.

As I approached adulthood I learned there are three types of females: dead, dumb, and evil.

My life was a life of separation. I remember. Even when I was growing up life was so boring and unpleasant that living didn't matter to me. Only children who believe in something bother being evil and worshipping Satan. But I was a good child: I did everything exactly that my English nanny ordered me.

Nanny was an alcoholic. As a child I didn't understand this. I couldn't understand why she hated my first nurse. I hated Nanny for hating nursey. I hated Nanny the way children hate: absolutely. As fire burns. Most of my conscious moments were fantasies of burning up parts of Nanny's body.

I knew I shouldn't think like this. I knew my whole mind was twisted and perverted. If becoming an adult equals the process of acquiring self-consciousness, my first recognition of my adult self was my perception of my desire to torture and kill. I hated. So they sent Nanny away; I won the first round; but I still knew (remembered) I wanted to kill.

I have preserved my memory of that naughty period.

Since she's wearing a short T-shirt and ankle socks, the beautiful naked woman looks like a child. A black leather snake which isn't moving lies on her back. She tries to roll either way across the bed, but can't because two extremely wide black leather bands, held by thick steel rings to the bed-posts which are far from each other, encase her pink wrists. My sister was my real mother's and father's daughter. She tortured me by making me look at drawings depicting lobotomies. These scenes caused me horrible nighmares, for I was sensitive.

I questioned to the point of obsession whether other humans are naturally evil, and if so why.

Unable to answer this question, I prayed to God about whom they had told me. God is He Who is unknowable. My sister was so malicious and my nightmares were so violent that I knew any Creator must be a sick pig. I named God 'Sickpig' and 'Turdshit'. Everytime I saw a dog shit on the street, I thought of God. I had no idea what all this meant.

As for cripples beggars malformed bodies lobotomized women and other poor people, everytime I saw one of these living turds on the street I breathed so hard to avoid convulsing I almost convulsed.

The only thing I couldn't tolerate was being told what to do. Since beggars or anyone else who was nothing told me who I was, I couldn't bear any of them. I wanted to kill beggars because I was too scared to kill my real tormentor, my sister.

I shall now by means of my profound rational processes find the explanation for my madness, and human socially unacceptable behaviour.

Once my sister said to people who were walking behind her: 'Look at my little tail.' Another time she told people that she liked the portrait a certain artist friend had made of her because it showed her having a tiny penis.

I felt very happy when my sister's huge hat, while we were both in an auto, flew away.

My sister and I are playing in a room. We are between four and six years old. My sister's hand takes up my cock which is so small it's almost non-existent. She rubs the non-existent.

Then she tells me that my nurse whom I do love because my nurse loves me does this same thing with the cock of the gardener.

My sister was a tomboy and had a very high IQ, higher even than mine. Even though her IQ was high, she couldn't understand how a high IQ and the desire to be loved as a female could exist together in one body. Since her body thus had to be monstrous, she refused to go out of our parents' house. She knew who she was: since she was a freak, she was unlovable. She had to and did pay, rather my parents paid, someone to love her. She loved this paid companion because the paid companion loved her and at the same time she detested the paid companion because, since the paid companion loved her only for economic reasons, she was proved to be unlovable. When my sister suicided at the age of twenty-one I didn't cry.

3. Beyond The Extinction of Human Life

I asked Abhor what she wanted with me. Did she also want to destroy my identity?

'I work for this man. I'm collecting for him.' As if I understood what she meant, blindly, I followed her out of my room. They say love's also blind, but, for me, love has equalled pain.

Her boss's name was Schreber. 'I've never seen you before, have I?' he asked.

'No.'

'I'm going to tell you something about yourself.' Finally perhaps I'd learn something about myself. 'You're masochistic to the point of suicidal and, actually, physically damaged. You believe that, and the neurological and hormonal damage probably is, permanent.'

'Yes.'

He wasn't going to let me interrupt him. 'You were . . . disrupted in your childhood by the usual causes. I'm not the least bit interested in psychological interpretations. They're passé. But there's one thing.'

I interrupted him. 'I don't give a damn. Not only about psychology. About myself.' I continued, 'You're fat and ugly, sir, but I'm dead. Psychology and my psychology's a dead issue.' There were a lot of dead bodies floating around the world. 'All I want to know from you is what you want from me.' Otherwise, I wanted to be alone.

Because, for me, desire and pain're the same.

I didn't want her. I couldn't so I didn't want. Frigidity was a way of life. I didn't know if phenomena such as desires which're fleeting even mattered. Psychology isn't here a dead issue. I decided I would keep her because I had to because she said I had to be hers.

Is reality always this unknown?

My friends informed me that the boss's real name was Schreber. Dr Schreber. He's honest enough, they said, as bosses are honest, to pay me for my work. So I could pay off my last boss so he wouldn't off me. Of course there's no money. Money's flimsy paper people who don't have power carry on them. What they do with money I don't know. I needed drugs.

'Your neurological and hormonal damage is making you degenerate so fast, faster than if you had AIDS,' the fat man informed me in front of the cunt, 'that within a couple of months you're going to be a mongoloid, even stupider than a lobotomy case, due to all the hatred which is festering in you, unless I inject a certain enzyme into your bloodstream and then enable you to receive a full blood transfusion. You will get this enzyme, your saviour, flea, only if you do what I want.'

'What do you want?'

'For you to do exactly what I want until that time.'

The trouble was I had no way of knowing if he meant to keep his part of the deal. I couldn't ask the cunt I thought I loved. Since I was thus dragging my tail through unknowable territory, my memory was useless. My memory was as dead as my desire used to be.

The next day, on a street, a garbage dump in front of the river, my former boss himself cut the throat of the fuck who informed on me in front of me. He slaughtered her because it was a practical way of making room for a fresh employee. Capitalism needs new territory or fresh blood.

I saw: blood sprayed from a jugular.

I needed my drug.

For a long time I had remained apathetic. So sure that my words meant nothing to anyone that I no longer spoke unless circumstances forced me to. So sure that my relations to the world were null that it didn't matter to what I said 'yes'. When I was young frivolity and trivia had been my weapons; now I did whatever I was told because I was no longer me. That is, the I who was acting was theirs, separate from the I who knew and whom I had known. Lots of eyes were watching me.

That is, the I who had SEXUAL DESIRES had nothing to do with the high IQ/understanding. This IQ used to be high but, since now was corrupted blinded covered over, wants seemed more capable and intelligent than I had known. I found myself at that point, that bottom.

I thought all I could know about was human separation; all I couldn't know, naturally, was death. Moreover, since the I who desired and the eye who perceived had nothing to do with each other and at the same time existed in the same body – mine: I was not possible. I, in fact, was more than diseased. But Schreber had given me hope of a possible solution. A hope of eradicating disease. Schreber had the enzyme which could change all my blood.

When all that's known is sick, the unknown has to look better. I, whoever I was, had no choice but to go along with Schreber. I, whoever I was, was going to be a construct.

The sky faded to blood, to the colour of blood. After I left the doctor and returned home, what I called home, which was better than I had ever had, Abhor had gotten there before me and was waiting for me, so to speak. Asleep. Naked. I saw her. A transparent cast ran from her knee to a few millimetres below her crotch, the skin mottled by blue purple and green patches which looked like bruises but weren't. Black spots on the nails, finger and toe, shaded into gold. Eight derms, each a different colour size and form, ran in a neat line down her right wrist and down the vein of the right upper thigh. A transdermal unit, separated from her body, connected to the input trodes under the cast by means of thin red leads. A construct.

In my imagination we were always fucking: the black whip crawls across her back. A red cock rises.

'I don't know who's backing him.' Abhor turned around to face me. She must have woken up. 'All I know is we call him "boss" and he gets his orders. Like you and me.'

'Somebody knows something. Whoever he is, the knower, must be the big boss.'

'Look.' Abhor raised herself up on one arm. She smelled warm, as if from kisses, but to my knowledge no kisses had taken place. 'All I know is that we have to reach this construct. And her name's Kathy.'

'That's a nice name. Who is she?'

'It doesn't mean anything.'

'If it doesn't mean anything, it's dead. The cunt must be dead.' My puns were dead.

'Look. All I know is we have to reach this construct. I don't know anything else.'

'We have the capacities for understanding and, at the same time, we understand nothing,' I replied. I understood we had to find some construct.

She told me again. 'All I know is we're looking for a certain construct. Somewhere. Nothing else matters.' A pulsing red then black cursor crept through the outline of a doorway. With enough endorphin analogue, Abhor could walk on a pair of bloody stumps. 'You don't matter and reality doesn't matter.' The road away from the airport, which became a series of roads, had been dead straight, like neat incisions, into the open body of the city. Poverty was writhing in pink. I had watched, here and there, a machine glide by, bound by fog and grey. Later on there were tenements called 'council housing', walls of mottled aluminium, prison guards' cocks sticking in order to piss through unarranged holes in the brick, more plyboard and corrugated iron walls. The lucky poor had playgrounds. I remembered Abhor was a construct.

Imagination was both a dead business and the only business left to the dead.

In such a world which was non-reality terrorism made a lot of sense.

The modern Terrorists are a new version, a modern version, so to speak, of the hoboes of the 1930s USA. Just as those haters of all work, (work being that situation in which they were being totally controlled; the controllers didn't work), as far as they were able took over their contemporary lines of communication, so these Terrorists, being aware of the huge extent to which the media now divorce the act of terrorism from the original sociopolitical intent, were not so much nihilists as fetishists. I had worked with them before in some way which I couldn't quite remember.

Two days after I had met the doctor, I found myself knocking on the door of a record shop somewhere. Terrorism is always a place to start because one has to start somewhere. A boy, or rather a skull, whose teeth were pointed red, as if skulls eat meat, opened the door which was falling apart so badly it was cracking open. I half crawled through a gap, half walked through the door, into a middle-sized record shop store room. Discs lay shattered on the floor. A celluloid nun moved her eyes horizontally as if a hand was moving her eyeballs. Smiley with one hand bone pointed me to a couch on which a freezer was sitting.

'Among the American international corporations the practice of setting up mixed affiliates is most widespread in chemicals and petrochemicals, rubber and the extractive industries. These ICs combine production on an international scale and organize the vertical and/or horizontal integration of their plants and thus, finally, control the whole product cycle . . .'

'I'm not interested.'

'Du Pont and Union Carbide, Goodyear and Uniroyal, Exxon and Kaiser, for example, organize the supply of semi-finished products from overseas enterprises to others on a wide scale, gain access to sources of raw . . .'

'Shut up,' I said. 'I need to find a code for a certain construct.

I know you're planning to knock over the CIA library and the code is there.'

Smiley smiled at me again. I remembered we had once been lovers; I had forgotten. We still are, I thought, in that his nastiness and inability to do anything but bite in the face of fear – any human presence triggered fear – matches my deeper nastiness. I never actually worked with the Moderns, but then I only work with people out of my need. Things are always the same.

The fact was that the Moderns talked too much. Their talk, or rhetoric, was blab: they didn't care who heard them; they would happily explain anything to the tiny parrots who shitted on the record discs as they flew around. The Moderns had the same relation to their work, terrorism: they didn't give a damn. They just wanted to have fun. Like parrots, they became easily bored.

On this operation the Moderns planned with great glee to reach Washington DC, the location of the library, via chickenwire. The chickenwire was sets of satellite and radio connectives. Like kids gone mad the Terrorists zoomed through the green purple yellow flashlights which are Manhattan, that absence of people, by using epoxy as they touched the midnight glass to control their movements. Then, over black ghettoes.

Except for Manhattan, which had been left to the rich, all of the eastern American urban centres had been left to the packs of wild dogs, wild cats, and blacks who lived in and under the streets. There were no more whites there except for gays.

The library was the American Intelligence's central control network, its memory, what constituted its perception and understanding. (A hypothesis of the political uses of culture.) It was called MAINLINE. The perception based on culture is a drug, a necessity for sociopolitical control.

Being a bit behind their times the Moderns only wanted to destruct. On the other hand my construct (a cunt) and I had to find the code. The Modernists planned to shoot misinformation into MAINLINE's internal video. Due to the misinformation each video screen would strobe for twenty seconds in a frequency that would cause the constructs and other robot viewers to have seizures. Pale green apartments strobed emerald at midnight. Simultaneously the audio portion of MAINLINE's internal video, speeding double, would inform its listeners about the army's use of a certain endomorphin, at this moment being tested, to throw human skeletal growth into one thousand per cent overkill. The red lights in the brothel tenements strobed blood eyes of Haiti.

The Terrorists would be happy when two minutes later their infiltrated message ended with the main system's end in white noise.

The Terrorists were happy.

In the white noise the cops arrived so that they could kill everybody. Round revolving cars emitted sonar waves. Certain sonar vibrations blinded those not in the cars; other levels numbing effectively chopped off limbs; other levels caused blood to spurt out of the mouths nostrils and eyes. The buildings were pink. Preferring mutilation the families who lived in bed-sits ran out into the streets. Outside the black ghettoes, through the waters, sea-cruise missiles with two hundred kt. nuclear warheads swam like dolphins. Carrying at least twelve ALCMs on extended pylons and eight on internal rotary launchers, B-52 bombers rode on cars whose trunks held various nerve gases which seeped out through the city atmosphere at designated intervals. 'Homing-and-kill' vehicles, upon sensing the presence of any living thing with their infra-red sensors, unfurled two-metre-long metal ribs. Metallic weights studded the metal ribs. The insect life moved on. The cops' faces, as they killed off the poor people, as they were supposed to, were masks of human beings. And the faces of the politicians are death. A young boy who lay in the street had hollowed-out eye sockets, skinless arms, and a smile due to the large amounts of acid rain in the air. Red and black deco staircases from the magenta tops of buildings bridged building to building.

Inside the library's research department, the construct cunt inserted a sub-programme into that part of the video network.

The sub-programme altered certain core custodial commands so that she could retrieve the code.

The code said: GET RID OF MEANING. YOUR MIND IS A NIGHTMARE THAT HAS BEEN EATING YOU: NOW EAT YOUR MIND.

The code would lead me to the human construct who would lead me to, or allow me, my drug.

Dead Love

I must have passed out because I had a nightmare: that the world is full of people who no longer feel. They are carrying on their businesses as usual, in fact better than usual, because they no longer feel. In the dream I felt my whole being struck still, as if I had died.

The cunt was hurt. I realized that when I awoke. The terrorists said. Six thousand micrograms of endorphin analogue, however, were coming, down on the pain like a hammer, shattering it. Her back, like a cat's, was arching in convulsions. Pink warm waves were lapping her thighs.

Bodies were piled six deep in the library's halls. The latest body, shot through the neck on Black's road. But he is not dead . . .

I must have passed out because I had a nightmare: To my dead sister, dream somehow of paradise. It's the only thing that can now keep us alive. The sweetness of your mouth. Coming while not being bruised by the hatred of the one who's making you come. You no longer don't have to not exist.

Look, my sister: the eyes are gone. The suns. No one's looking. You can now do whatever you want: Crying out; teasing the thickness of thighs; smouldering by smiling. Since the world has disappeared: there's nothing; no one looks at anyone.

Since the world has disappeared: rather than objects, there exists that smouldering within time where and when subject meets object. This voluptuousness of your thighs. Odours seeping out of cunt juice and semen. Since the only mirrors are distorted; all is secret. Please come back to my arms. Without you I am nothing.

It's winter. Winter is dead time. I don't have any life now that my sister is dead. Raise us from the dead.

Raze.

But no one looks like Abhor. Everyone looks like the female who ratted on me. The boss, the terrorist leader, the terrorists – they all had the face of the female who ratted on me. It was the dead of winter. Or it was the winter of us, dead. The code I had gotten read 'WINTER'. It was the winter of death.

I was safe: outside. 'What does WINTER mean?' I asked the Modern Terrorist leader.

'WINTER's a recognition code for an AI. This particular AI is, that is his money is located in Berne. Money is a kind of citizenship. Americans are world citizens.'

'Does my boss know about WINTER?'

'Does a doctor know about death?' the terrorist replied. 'Let me tell you a story:

'A certain fence was living, well, he was fencing off of the corner of Bowery and Houston Street. Around the corner from the bum bar in which the one-eyed Irish sang,

The Powers whose name and shape no living creature knows
Have pulled . . .

and then cried into whatever whisky he could beg from someone. Life's a waste of booze.'

I thought about dead cunts. 'Life's a waste.'

'Some of the fences sold real clothing such as rubber jackets and army leather. Others, being less conventional, at least in their business, more like the bums who wipe windshields, dealt in prosynthetic limbs and other works of art. Mommy, the off-the-corner man, was an art dealer.

'There was another art dealer who had once been a bum, but now was dealing in the junk for which the rich pay a lot of money. His name was Daddy.

'Daddy came to Mommy to ask for a favour. New York City art dealers have their special codes.

'Daddy said to Mommy: "My newest . . . supplier . . ."

'"Burglar."

'"My newest burglar is a rat who goes by the name of Ratso. Since rats are very intelligent, Ratso has a fondness for art objects. The rat craves art. His latest work-of-art, his newest find, find-and-keep so-to-speak, is a head. Not any head. It's a dead head and death is done up in pearls. Despite the obvious value of this work of art, its humanity, not being a humanist, I advised Ratso to get rid of it. These days times are so hard that heads are worthless.

'"At that moment I remembered I knew a head freak. A head freak who was rich. And liked to spend it.

'"I accepted the rat's human head. Upon minute careful inspection, this head revealed the trademarks of the AI, American Intelligence, who're backing the AMA. Next to the military, the American medical industry take in the largest amounts of legal profit in the western hemisphere. No wonder the head was dead.

'"At the very moment I realized this, a gulag came through my door. A block, a dunderhead, a lump of cement, a lobotomized mongoloid. A man who acted like he had all the muscle in the world because he owned everything in the world. A man who didn't need to walk as if he owned the place because he owned the place. There are people like that. I don't know them. I knew he was a real man because I knew I was staring into the eyes of death.

'"The weight-lifter carefully explained he had come for his head. I explained I don't give head. He explained that he thought I might be able to give it to him.

'"Not having the desire to get closer to death, though I find lack of desire strange and inhuman, I produced my head.

'"'How much does a human head cost? These days?' the owner of the world asked me.

'"I named the price of a masticated piece of bubble-gum. One piece, or stick; not two. I got what I asked for. On credit.

'"Two days later I learned the rat had gotten his price. Death."

'"Extermination's difficult."

'"Death isn't difficult. I don't know why we fight each other since we're all the same. Knowing this, I had nothing left but to understand.

"This' why I've had to come to you, Mommy, even though I'm not used to turning to cunts. Mommy, I'm desperate."

'Out of the goodness of her heart Mommy did a little investigation. It just made her feel good to do good, especially for Daddy. But all she could learn was what she already knew: The AI control information. The AI control the medical mafia. Democracy controls its own death, its medical knowledge and praxis, just as we all control our own deaths,' the terrorist said.

'I know.' My love, the cunt, was dead.

'However,' the terrorist told me, 'there are particulars. Despite the media – not despite the media because the media exists to be wrong – democracy is an old quiet family. They don't move around much. They're stable. They're so stable, they've now got their own genetic set-up.'

'Who? Tell me who. Who controls himself, herself? Who doesn't feel unending pain?'

The terrorist frowned. 'That's not a proper question.'

'What's a proper question? Now?'

'Who can we kill?'

'I don't want to kill anyone because I don't feel anger.' I felt scared.

'Look.' The terrorist said to me with anger so deep that it couldn't be expressed, 'Knowing much information and not feeling anything doesn't get you anywhere.' He pointed his small bone at me. 'The answer to your question is that democracy doesn't get you anywhere.'

The cunt was dead. Afterwards I went down into the tube to wait for her. I had been a travelling man, but now it looked to me like I was to stop travelling. Besides, the tubes didn't go anywhere. No government sinks money into dead tubes. I stood; I cried: I waited. Nothing. I cried; I cried. I would do anything to have her touch me again even though she was partially human and I hated my own wanting.

I looked for her burial place down there. I looked for the

burial place of death. I looked for her whom I wanted. Because I wanted her, she was my demon. Dead and demonic.

Even though I knew she was dead – particles of soil and pieces of garbage and Thames water and whatever else humans are, that is become – I cried for her. I knew she was shit, but I cried because I would do anything to get her back!

('Oh sis,' I cried in silent words which are tears, tears in the fabrics of reality, 'I will become you: I will become as unreal as you.')

Pieces of chopped-up snake tail. Using my tail as bait. Fuck me so I can hate you. Children are born by being shovelled out of wolves' bodies, but who does the shovelling? Are all wolves, therefore, females; are all females, therefore, as vicious as wolves? Tell me, my heart, what reality is.

When I got home, which was like every other home, my love was waiting for me. She wasn't dead, yet. She looked like a piece of red and dead meat. It was St Valentine's Day.

She wasn't dead. 'I'm on your meat line now,' I told her.

'You're what I make you,' Abhor said.

Raze

III In Honour of The Arabs بافتخارِ مردمِ عربی

(*Abhor speaks*)

(آبعهور حرف زیند)

Dead

In agreement with Dr Freud, Dr Schreber defined paranoia as a defence to homosexual love. Dr Schreber was paranoid, schizophrenic, hallucinated, deluded, disassociated, autistic, and ambivalent. In these qualities he resembled the current United States President, Ronald Reagan.

When Dr Schreber was three years old, his mother bathed him only in ice-water according to her husband's instructions. Her husband made various toys for his son including a shoulder-band. The shoulder-band was a figure-eight of metal and leather whose two loops, after curving round the boy's front, met in the middle of his back.

Daddy, please beat me up again.

Another toy, a 'straight-hold', an iron cross-bar fastened to the table, by pressing against the child's collarbones and shoulders, prevented both bad posture and any movement.

He tied belts to his son's bed and his son to the belts.

A child who doesn't lose his reason over certain events has no reason to lose. I'm not hinting at any possible link between the micro-despotism inherent in the American nuclear familial structure and the macro-political despotism of Nazi Germany.

I am giving an accurate picture of God: A despot who needs a constant increase of His Power in order to survive. *God* equals *capitalism*. Thus God allows a smidgin of happiness to humans. His victims. For He needs their love. Humans who do not love (God) suffer.

Who am I?

With such beliefs dominating his consciousness Schreber grew up to become a significant member of the American Medical Association.

Schreber invented 'the head-crusher'. 'The head-crusher' crushes its wearer's teeth into their sockets, then smashes down the surrounding bone until the brains squirt through the fragmented skull. 'The head-crusher' resembled the metal egg-cap the doctor's father used to ensure his son always maintained his proper posture.

Whereas Schreber rarely used his 'crocodile' which ripped off the penis, he often employed his 'scavenger's daughter'. This instrument places the body, any body, in the missionary position. In a short time, the placed human feels violent cramps, first in the abdominal and rectal muscles, then in the pectoral and cervical, and in the arms and legs. After several hours have gone away, unrelenting worsening pains especially in the stomach and asshole render their victim insane.

Who am I? What is the human body?

During the Korean War Schreber delivered discs in his plane. By the end of the war his plane had been gutted, and his arms legs and eyes had been lopped off, gouged out. He was on ice.

The Americans saved him from freezing by sticking in some new plumbing, then explained to him he was unwanted: He was incurable: Practically, he was dead. Dead, the only possible work for him was to be a spy. He spied on spies who spied on spies. He had forgotten what side he was on, if he had ever been on a side. He forgot why, if he was alive, he was alive. He could have been a lobotomy, a terminal, if he hadn't been too low to be anything. But to see. Such was his identity in this America of Peace during the hiatus between wars. But identity had to go public in order to survive; peacetime had to become wartime, for the United States to survive as the United States. If identity equals fame, everyone is a victim.

Who am I?

The doctor, himself, found himself or not-himself lower than any junk victim. He woke up in a hotel room, a needle still sticking out of his arm, blood on the cloth that seemed to be the sheet, blood on the ceiling which otherwise looked like grey morning. The only morning which is now known, public.

In this urban America, for a while, he experienced what we want when we don't love: blank. But he wasn't. Blank. For he was lower than any junk victim. Therefore the chemical research department of the Pentagon began using him as a guinea pig in their tests of a endorfin cure for terminal despair.

The drug was been found to be a success, but too erratic as far as side effects for purposes of political control.

The doctor found himself or not-himself awake in a shabby psychiatric ward.

'I want to get out. Me.'

Some doctor asked, 'Who are you?'

'Who ever I am, I can't be known.'

Who am I not?

The doctor got out. He went to Northern Africa, Algeria, the land of the free. No longer a victim of terminal despair, there, he started working for the AMA.

Me Equals Dead Cunt

1. Algeria

Pounce, my cat, and walk over this craving heart,
For a moment put away your nails;
Cat, I drown myself in your eyes;
Cat: you see flecks of diamond and shale.
When my fingers lose themselves in your head and your elasticity,
When my hands are besotted by pleasure from your electrifying
body,
I see him. His look,

bestial, icy, cuts like a shock
Your stale piss odours his cock

2. Algeria's Cock

'Nothing ever changes.'

What does that mean, I asked Thivai.

'No one ever changes.'

But I did what I wanted to do. My action now followed my desire. I went to Algeria. In Algeria, I watched the sun rise on the landscape of my childhood. The only thing I desire is innocence.

3. The Memory Of Childhood

I remember a hand moving inside my mind, twisting my mind around so that for the first time I could see.

4. Personal History Or Memory

Otherwise I remember only nausea and I remember ad nauseam. Is there any other knowing besides this remembering?

5. Primitive/Before

Climatically Algeria is a sluggish country and cunt. The inhabitants of Algeria do not tolerate strangers. They, or I myself, had sent me to this land of perpetual sun with the code 'WINTER'. When the servants of the hotel told me I had a male visitor, I took out my gun. Not that I cared about my safety. But I have a bad memory of desire.

Then I remembered the scarlet pigeon nibbling at the blood seeping out of my cunt. I remembered truly that at the edges of thinking all which I'm taught to think is only exile. To remember truly, on the other hand, is not to know.

'I remember . . .' I was holding the gun in my hand. 'You want a man.' He, this stranger, was remembering for me.

'Any man?' I asked him.

'The one man you desire.' His English was faulty. 'His address is Küchuk Gülhane Djaddesi 14, for he earns his life by dancing in the bazaar.'

I remember the bazaar of pleasures. I remember pleasure . . .

6 A Memory of Pleasure

'Have you ever seen a horse?'

I looked around me at the bazaar. The bazaar, just as I remembered, was beautiful. As a form of memory, beauty is a representation of what's past, over with, dead; but since now present delight was equal to memory, beauty could not be named. I thought I must be closing in on the man I wanted.

I began to be able to smell, I began to smell.

'Have you ever seen a horse?' a shrivelled cashew nut asked me about my memory. He must have already lived past his death.

'Now that my mind's open, I can't remember anything. Are you trying to sell me me?' Here every man was trying to sell something. To me. Here all the men were trying to sell me.

'I don't have to *try* to sell you,' the old cashew nut instructed me carefully. 'Have you ever seen a horse?'

'Where's a horse?'

'Over here.' The alley was an old place, too old; its walls had been cut from the dripping stone. Liquid is just liquid. Its pavement was uneven.

I looked for a horse. In this turning away from the bazaar, where I no longer knew where I was, or possibly might be: here I no longer had use for memory or was defined by memory. In this alleyway of so many centuries piled on so many centuries, I was time-less, immortal. I, the opposite of time, had become a child, innocent. The only strength is innocence. The old cashew nut could do with me what he liked, in this alley.

His long bone didn't trouble my thigh.

Desperately I tried to remember being a child. Being anyone. As if memory had anything to do with it. As if memory had anything to do with anything. A pink blanket dotted by tiny raised roses. When they took it away from me because, they said, they had to wash it, but they took it away forever; I sobbed. I know I always beg for everything. I remember I present myself as a beggar: A dead image. In *this* alleyway, with *this* old man: I felt nothing. I didn't know, so I didn't regret this architectural degradation, these descents which led nowhere, only to walls of ancient limestone, finally to the endless boredoms. All memories are trivia. The lack of obsessions.

I have discovered something like the key to love. His long bone didn't trouble my thigh.

Then a shaft of white light shone down on the old cashew nut, who was guiding me somewhere; showed me every wrinkle, even the pores, in that endlessly lined flesh, every pre-cancerous mole, every formation which was time. There was no memory here. There was only death.

And as if his spine crumbled, the aged goon sank to the concrete. Bone to bone. The concrete was wet. Someone must have gotten him, something, like something always does. I knew something, finally: time, being all events and phenomena, doesn't crumble anything: time crumbles.

Blood burst out of the old squeek's back. I never before that thought old people have much blood in their bodies. Time in some particular form, a human one, his form, must have crumbled itself. It's difficult for western minds to conceive of unity: they can only conceive death. My guide was gone.

As some sort of gesture I dragged the old croaker, who had croaked, out of the alleyway. Blue of pre-dawn soaked the city and his and my flesh.

I still had to do what the doctor ordered: I still had to find my man. I was trying to be a perceiver, but I had no idea if my unknown man wanted to be perceived. In daylight.

I have read that the common focus of the perceiver and the perceived is the imminent place in that heart. I had to be innocent. My heart had to be waiting, somewhere.

Then I passed through rollercoasters of concrete and other stones which made me remember the Monge section of Paris. Baudelaire, standing upright in his tomb, had sometime before that fallen in love with his girlfriend as soon as he had given her syphilis. A case of heterosexuality. Here, there were no ads.

I saw a square courtyard. Houses rose on four sides. Behind the houses' walls and on their roofs, families and groups of kids were shooting guns at each other. One group or person raced down to the courtyard below, pink and brown, as if on a rollercoaster, racing up. Growing sick of war I walked away from the top-floor window from which we had been shooting, into a hall. Sometime later I would return there. There was nowhere to go.

I was in a second graveyard. The hands of the dead Christians who were standing up in their tombs were rotten.

I saw a torturer. He was spending most of his time sticking electrodes on the genitals of men who protested against the government. He was paid to do what he was told to do because he had a job. I saw I wanted to be beaten up. I didn't understand.

This isn't enough. Nothing is enough, only nothing. I want to get to what I don't know which is discipline. In other words I want to be mad, not senseless, but angry beyond memories and reason. I want to be mad. I went further into the city.

When I was fourteen years old they shut me up in an attic. 1. In the attic, I forced my finger up my cunt so I could pierce my own cherry. 2. I crave someone loving me just as a junky craves junk. Did No. 1 (physical desire) have a relation to No. 2 (mental desire)? This limitless and mad-making craving was a reaction to, an act of anger against, those who had shut me in. I know about moralists.

I am a witch an evil almost inhuman because I am in the act of brewing my own blood. This is why I'm now frigid. I'm not frigid because my mother used my desire to have her love me like a knotted whip over me. I'm playing with *only* my blood and shit and death because mommy ordered me to be only whatever she desired, that is, to be not possible, but it isn't possible to be and be not possible. By playing with my blood and shit and death, I'm controlling my life. Since I'm frigid, you hurt me only when you sexually penetrate me. The iciness of my blood which is my galloping horse proves that memories of past events have and are shaping me. Rather than being autistic dumb feelingless ice, I would like the whole apparatus – family and memory – to go to hell.

I will be mad.

I met a horse, though I never shot horse. I descended through my childhood while I threw it along with everything else away. As I walked past an especially beautiful space, a turn of cracked cement on the corner of the river where, beneath the actual slashes under my feet, a pigeon's body, as if preserved in aspic, lay mashed between chunks of large dead branches and punched-in plastic milk cartons, where empty vodka bottles floated in the river.

There was a huge green ocean. On the ocean were between ten and twenty rowboats. I was in one rowboat with my papers. When I was somewhere else, I saw a huge, partly black, boat at least three to four times the size of any rowboat. The waves which were beginning indicated that monstrous, frightening waves were about to rise. I had to return to my little rowboat to get my papers and wanted to have those wave tops, even though they were dangerous, toss me upwards so that flying I would be beautiful.

I remembered the Thames; there was a flash of a stick in the corner of one eye; tip of syringe needle in the right arm; they left me. I left me. I had just lost my only lover. So to speak. I had no more memories.

The absence of me. Not even the existence of nothingness represented me. When I regained consciousness, unlike the old cashew nut, I lifted up the first public phone receiver I could find.

Somebody answered me. 'Death.'

'That's not my name.' Alive I protested.

'It's your code.' I knew his voice. The curer of death. 'For the living, winter is death.'

Chinese Bosses Never Die

1. A Degenerating Language

I decided I had to find out who I was. When I returned to the hotel at which I was staying, I saw a sign,

روز صَدیوان حاصِران ریستَن اَند.

A sign of nothing. If I had been able to translate it, it still would have told me nothing. Just like my memory of when I was a child, when I killed a soldier fried his flesh and ate it.

I can't distinguish between my memories of dreams, waking actions, and what I've read and been told. For they're all memories. I could say the unknowable in Persian,

ملوان
ناساز مرا دید.

'Who'd you kill this time?' Thivai asked me as soon as I stepped into our hotel room. We broke up every day. But we had to keep working together.

'I don't know who to kill.' I knew who I wanted to kill. 'I don't want to kill. I want to kill myself.' I have wondered about the value of political generalities.

مَلوان
ناساز

'You're always wanting to fuck other men,' Thivai snarled. This is true, but because I'm with Thivai, I repress it into fantasy. 'You're a slag.' Because I repress, this isn't true.

Kill him. Or don't kill him.

I remember: since I wasn't able to hate my mother, especially when she hurt me viciously, I hated everyone who was alive in this world as viciously as possible.

'Love, I want to kill the person I love so that I can be dead.' This seemed to be an apt response to the world.

عَلی خُوسگِل است.

(Ali is pretty.) I want to kill you.

هَرج و مَرج هَمواره بَچّه یک کُشند.

('Anarchy always kills a kid off.') I want to kill.

هَوا خَطَرناك دیوانه عَجیب است.

("Malignant lunatic lust is wonderful.') This is the only thing which makes sense to me now.

I moved away from Thivai's face to my blackened eyes, the reflection of my sunglasses, in the airport hotel window. I looked down at the airport.

The Arabic slogan in red spraypaint on an airport wall read

سَخت کوشید وَلی دِهاتیان جُفتگیری کَرَّند.

(In Paris, old Algerian men at dawn clean the gutters. He tried hard, but the natives fuck like animals.)

I saw a streetcorner beyond the airport building. A human corpse lay on the streetcorner. The cops in an old Buick pulled up. One cop shuffled a cloth over the corpse. The next cop pulled the cloth up. The dead face was coloured brightly. The flesh below the face was cut off so cleanly, he might have been a dead animal.

An army officer and his orderly loved one another. The officer drew up a will. In this will he stated that when he died, his orderly could own his body. He died. In accordance with the will, the orderly ate his dead superior.

I don't think humans fuck therefore lovingly relate to each other in equality, whatever that is or means, but out of needs for power and control. Humans relate to other humans by eating each other. I realized the human part of me always felt pain, therefore was always sick. I wondered if I could escape.

Myself. There are many, perhaps, infinite places in the world. Within my unbearable despair at being human, it seemed to me no human goes anywhere.

د وشَكِ كوچكِ أست.

In ancient Greek mythology a river separated the living from the dead. The only event which any human can know is the one event he or she can't perceive, that he or she must die. Last night I dreamt I was swimming through an ocean. Swimming through an ocean is feeling pleasure. If the only event I can know is death, that is dream or myth, dream and myth must be the only knowing I have. What, then, is this ocean?

Human: I'm a slave or prisoner of my needs. Love is one need. For this reason I wear chains. You could say chains aren't feminist. My boyfriend's a drug addict. His needle is long and thin. After he's inserted and removed it, he puts it and the eye-dropper into a glass of cold water. The blood flowing into the dropper is a river.

In the Voodoo system, the dead help the living. These days the principal economic flow of power takes place through black-market armament and drug exchange. The trading arena, the market, is my blood. My body is open to all people: this is democratic capitalism. Today pleasure lies in the flow of blood. I looked at my boyfriend. He looked at me. 'You look like death,' I said. 'White flesh. We're finished. I can no longer work with you.'

He didn't give a damn. He had never cared about any living thing. 'Abhor, you're dead. Because you're the one who's still looking.'

I repeated his words. 'You're no longer looking. You're not good for anything.'

He didn't bother to show his cock. He showed me the one thing he had. 'I have to go on working because I need my drug.'

I told him he was as good as dead.

'To where can I escape from death,' Thivai asked, 'when

death is in my blood? Can junkies receive total blood transfusions?'

Our code was *death*. I needed new instructions. We, humans, need new blood. I phoned up the doctor of zombies again. I begged him for blood. Blood that wasn't in a dropper. I wanted something new.

The doctor didn't answer.

'Wu Tao-tzu,' I said over the phone,

' نقاش چینی نقاشی جلیل زمین
جلیل. کوهی طلوع کرد مثل اینکه بالای خاک
پرواز میکرد، آنوقت آنجا در هوا ایستاد.
درختها جنگ کردند و پائین به جویهای
برابر منحرفها پیچیدند پس از آنکه این
Wu Tao-tzu نقاشیرا تمام کرده بود،
به کوه، در، در طرف کوه، نشان داد. از
این در گرد و غائب شد. '

'Drugs change you,' the boss replied.

'Death changes you.'

'How does death change you?' the doctor asked. 'How can you care what's going to happen to you after you're dead?'

' "How can I know how I've changed, what change is, if at every moment I am exactly who I am?" I knew I didn't even know what life is.'

'Then what do you want to know exactly?'

I answered him:

' مرد متمول امر داد
که دیگر نقاش جنگلیرا برای او نقاشی

بِکَرد. چرا؟ جَنگی حادثهٔ مجهول شاید
اکنون است. نَقّاش جَنگلی خونینرا نقاشی
کَرد. مَردِ مُتَمَوّل اعتراض کَرد: جَنگلها
خونین نیست. "این کار، فنونِ مُستَطرَفه
حَرام شَدید است." امراضِ مُقاربَتی
شَدیدهاست. نَقّاش مَردرا پُرسید:
جَنگل چه رَنگ است؟ مَردِ مُتَموّل
پاسخ داد: جَنگل سیاه است. مَردُم چشمانرا
نَداشتند. به مَرگ مُوقوف اَم.'

I hung up the phone on my doctor, for I had nothing to say.

2. A Degenerating Heart

Then by myself I decided to go to Switzerland for no reason at all.

Berne is a dead city. Berne is the city, not of Nazis, but of jewellers who deal only in gold and platinum and of clocks. There's no one else in Berne.

Even though Berne was the city of Death, the picture of Death Hollywood had used again and again, I was no longer interested in capitalism. They say that the underneath of Zurich's main street is lined with gold. The people who live in Berne don't bother to hide their gold.

Even though Berne was the Hollywood set for Death, I was going there to learn something for myself by myself. But what was it I had to see? Berne is a city of levels. One level is concrete columned streets. Several levels are thick bricked roofs. Bridges fly from heaviness to heaviness. I remember.

Two bears so moth-eaten they should be dead huddle in an empty stone circle of the bottom level in the centre of the city. Bottom out to dead leaves.

They say, somebody says, that the kids in Berne have nothing better to do than stroll at night through the one empty subway station. Perhaps it isn't poverty but boredom which creates terrorists. Boredom is the lack of dreams. When I entered Berne, dark came down on my eyes. The wings of a bird or a sheet. My spine was a sharp pencil piercing into nothing like herpes gone mad. Nothing was gone.

I had learned something (already) in the dead city: You are wherever you are.

Start again from nowhere: dead heart.

3. Heart Of Hearts

As far as intuition or knowledge went, for there was nowhere to go and no one to be, I read that real human civilization happened in China in about 800 AD. A Chinese prince ordered every painter in his realm to paint portraits of him in his celebration. A certain painter walked into the painting room too late. It was too late for the end of the world. He strolled into that room as if he didn't give even a shit about his emperor or about painting. When he was supposed to bow to the Prince in honour, he crawled on the floor and licked someone's shoes. They tasted good. Masochism is only political rebellion. The Prince ordered him to be given an easel and a brush so he could paint the portrait. The painter looked at his emperor and shat on the ground. If political civilization means society, I wondered how we're all supposed to get along together.

I remembered one final story. I once had a boyfriend. It makes me sad to say this. He told me, 'We should always act however we feel like acting,' and did so and we tore each other apart until we parted. Parting was like dying. I wonder if human civilization is the same thing as alienation and isolation and, if it is, what can knowledge be?

It was as if I knew. I had come to Berne and found out what I wanted to learn. When I came to a corner of the bear park, about two hundred yards from the bears, the doctor was waiting for me.

'You mean as much to me as my own daughter.' I had come to Berne to see my doctor.

'What do you want from me? Now?'

'You know what I want you to do next.' I was listening to the voice outside me like I was listening to the voice inside me. I knew.

'I'm your boss. I tell you what to do. I can make you die.'

In my hearts of hearts or cunt I've always known what men want from me. 'Death,' I whispered.

My father was inside me and my boss was outside me. They answered me. 'Yes.'

I was whispering. 'Death: I don't understand how you can be a doctor. Death: you're a moralist. Death: you know what's good for other people. Death: you're the one who knows what's good for all other people. In the United States you make people as sick as possible so you can amass as much economic profit as possible. Death: you must be in my thoughts. Death: you are my thoughts.'

Death replied: 'You've got inside and outside mixed up. You're all mixed up.'

'Then who am I?' I asked Death. Perhaps I was asking the wrong person.

'Cunt: you are what you get. You've got me.'

'You don't love me.'

'You've got Death.'

But I didn't want to die. I got Death. I lifted up my .357 and shot my boss in the mouth. Full. The boss crumpled, fully.

I'd been right every time I'd seen bloody brains in my vision. I'd been right every time I'd followed my intuited vision. Every thing is just as it is: death is only dead. There's nothing else to be done with bosses. So I had read in a Chinese story. Once upon a time.

Business

More than fifty per cent of Western Europe now has gonorrhoea, syphilis, herpes, or AIDS. One hundred per cent of the members of a certain African tribe by the time they're five years old have herpes.

After I had murdered Dr Schreber, I felt hollow.

There's a joke that a man, I don't know who this man is, steps on to a bus. He sits down on a seat and smells. It stinks. Since he's a polite man, he doesn't want to make a fuss. But he has to smell again. He can't bear this stink. Finally, the stench has become so horrendous that, contrary to his desire never to be noticed, he whispers something to the bus driver. The bus driver, who's Irish, screams out, 'Will whoever's holding a bag of dead fish please leave this bus.'

All of the women on the bus get off the bus.

In the meantime I had left Thivai. Not that that separation mattered. We no longer had a business relation.

If doctors, I reasoned, make their money off sick people, they can't make money out of death. Therefore, Dr Schreber couldn't have been trying to kill me. Someone else must be trying to kill me; someone more powerful must control death. To me it was all Chinese. I once tried to learn Chinese, but it was too difficult.

IV Romanticism

(Thivai speaks)

'I just want to do it,' I said.

'Do what?'

'Find her. I've got to find her.'

'Why?' Findus, who was a bum, didn't understand. Anything. 'Why do you want to find a woman?'

'Because I had Abhor on a string and the string was tied around my little finger. Whenever I twirled her around, my finger moved, so I was never bored. I need to pull strings. But it didn't have shit to do with shit and shit didn't have to do with it,' I explained fully.

'You've lost it, Thivai.' I gathered *it* was *her*. 'You're always losing your women.'

I thought. That just wasn't true. I disagreed with the bum, because I always disagree. 'I didn't lose the first cunt who tried to kill me because she died.' Then I thought about how someone says goodbye to someone:

(My cock got hard. Thinking about it.)

(Whenever I stop thinking, I step out of existing into nothing.)

The girl bears a wide black leather band around her neck. There is only emptiness. Its leather edges are so roughly cut, the band scratches her neck. A second leather band, as wide as the first band and attached to the first band at the part of band in the middle of the back of the neck, reaches down almost to the bottom of her spine. There, two thin black leather bands attached to the bottom of the second leather band encase her wrists. Since she's unable to move, I have to remove her underpants and position her for her and for me. She is my cock and my cock is moving and she will never, because there is no future, be other than me, be not me, be against me. I thought about how to say goodbye to someone. In my world, one doesn't say goodbye to someone.

When I was five years old, I was carving words which I knew were bad into the bark of a monster walnut tree. The knife slipped out of the bark into the flesh of my little finger. Somehow it slipped right through the finger so the finger was dangling from its root, in my mind just like Nagasaki. A year later, I was playing a game with several of the girls in my class. A pair raced from one point of the roof to a rope stretched between two sticks. The rope was as high as the tallest student. The roof was the top floor of a school which used to be a horses' stable. The class creep and I were racing each other. I had to win so badly, I didn't perceive anything besides running, until I turned around, after I had reached the finish line, I didn't yet know who won, and saw her left hand over her left eye. Blood seeped through her fingers. I had taken out her eye. I have never known who won.

'I have to find Abhor,' I told the bum. 'I have to find her because now that she's murdered the doctor, she's my only link to the drug.'

'That's not why I'm poor,' the bum told me.

V Let the Algerians Take Over Paris

(Abhor speaks)

My Mother

I ran away. Not only from Thivai. I would have run somewhere if there had been anywhere to which to run. But there wasn't. I knew, I know there's no home anywhere. Nowhere:

Exile was a permanent condition. A permanent community, in terms of relationships and language.

In terms of identity. But from what was identity exiled?

Perhaps this society is living out its dying in its ruins. But I would have no way of knowing this.

I found myself in a place which I neither knew nor found alien. I found myself living in an old section, a section like every other section of Paris where things seemed to happen, not as in London where nothing ever happens, by chance, as everything happens everywhere.

It's easy to be poor and live in Paris if one has money. I made enough money for my extravagant needs by working as a photographer's model. I took the expensive clothes I bought with the money I earned off my body so that men could photograph me.

One day I found myself, for the purposes of work, in a small brick townhouse's basement, near the Jewish quarter, on a thin winding street. A black man who lifted weights answered the door. His studio was well-equipped. With photography lights and other instruments. Inside he explained to me that he was hiring me to pose for photos on the backs of playing cards. He had to photograph me in the twelve fucking positions which corresponded to the twelve signs of the zodiac. Whatever those were.

'I usually work with my boyfriend.' Not that I had a boyfriend.

'No. Your cunt and my cock.' He turned his cock away from me to lock his front door. 'Take off your clothes.' He reached for his camera.

I took off my clothes and lay on the bed. 'This isn't going to work,' I informed him while he was unzipping his shiny grey pants with one hand and holding the camera with his other, 'I've got gonorrhoea.'

'I'll use a condom.'

I quickly chose a raped body over a mutilated or dead one.

I didn't know what to do about the useless and, more than useless, virulent and destructive disease named heterosexual sexual love. I've never known.

After that, I considered celibacy. My few friends in Paris had stopped fucking, for most sexual activity now caused physical illness and even death. My only straight male friend was celibate. Five years ago he had been sleeping with a lovely social-climbing model who was, unknown to him, sleeping with other men and women. He knew she was publicly humiliating him. His face had been sat on once too often. The pangs of death drove him to abandon the cause of such pain, his sexuality. Being a romantic, Xovirax chose to remain faithful to his strongest orgasm or abandonment of identity.

But in those old days, those days of death, of a political turn to the right-wing when the only saviour seemed to be anything and anyone who was not white . . . It seemed to me that the body, the material, must matter. My body must matter to me. If my body mattered to me, and what else was any text: I could not choose to be celibate.

One part of the Voodoo world is physical. The physical (in reference to a human, the body) an axis, crosses the other axis, mentality (in a human, the mind). A cross; a crossroads; the problem of human identity.

Jesus Christ.

Toussaint L'Ouverture who used Voodoo to defeat Western hegemony said: 'If self-interest alone prevails with nations and their masters, there is another power. Nature speaks in louder tones than philosophy or self-interest.'

These masters, white, had poured burning wax on parts of other bodies, arms and hands and shoulders, emptied boiling cane sugar over heads of their slaves, burned others alive, roasted some on slow fires, filled some other bodies with gunpowder and blown them up by a match, buried others in sand or dirt up to the necks then smeared the heads in honey so that huge flies would devour them, placed some next to nests of red ants and wasps, made others drink their own piss eat their own shit and lick off the saliva of other slaves. The minds of whoever survived lived in and were pain.

Mentality is the mirror of physicality. The body is a mirror of the mind. A mirror image is not exactly the same as what is mirrored.

In my isolation and in my desperation in that dead city chi-chi city city made by and for the bourgeoisie, it seemed to me that my sexuality was a source of pain. That my sexuality was the crossroads not only of my mind and body but of my life and death. My sexuality was ecstasy. It was my desire which, endless, was limited neither by a solely material nor by a solely mental reality. In that city dominated by commodities, more and more unsatiated I cried. I would kill the city of perfection. My tears were the tears of whores. I would have Mary Magdalen tear Virgin Mary's flesh into shreds. My cunt juice and piss, red, would drop out of her eyes. I who am only gentle. I who could not even hurt my mother who hated me. I, little baby: my crying my pissing is my sexuality.

Memories of identity flowed through my head. I got up slowly, my eyes fixed on the muzzle of a black automatic pistol. The barrel seemed to be attached to my throat by a taut string. I couldn't see the string.

I had gotten up. I wasn't alone. I had never been alone.

History shapes all of us; history is the lives and actions of dead people. As soon as I'm dead, I'll be part of this history which shapes. Memory or history runs human blood through the river of time.

He was old, the Parisian, and white. Taller than my skeleton. His facial features looked female. According to my memory.

But my memory's always been poor. It's as if it lies somewhere in the deserts of North Africa, under shifting sands. As if the only map of my mentality is almost formless. The glory in my mind was formless.

When you reside in a city which isn't the city of your childhood, whatever you perceive lacks the resonance of memory. You can see, in the full blaze of day, a black-and-white cat lying motionless and fat against a stone fence. This sight means nothing. Whereas when you perceived such a cat in your home town, you would be seeing dowagers, Abolitionists and freethinkers, talking to each other over lace-clothed tables within seemingly nice houses, you would be seeing the beginning of revolution always made by females. When I saw the gun in the strange city, I saw nothing.

France once owned North Africa. It was and is all a matter of devaluations: the owners of money or of total devaluation are invisible.

'Come visit, child,' the man said. One of his feet was bare; the other was encased in a slipper of black fox fur lying over metallic chain. Thick chair. In French, 'flesh' is 'chair'. The flesh made real. A silk djellaba made him look faintly Arabian, as if he had anything to do with that part of the world, and as if his age was great. He led me, somewhere, a room. 'Come, child.' A bed.

As if in a dream I remembered something: When I was just into the age of fucking, so to speak, puberty, – some say that this is the age of fucking – fucking up and fucking over –, my adopted or fake father came back unexpectedly to his and my mother's apartment. I successfully sneaked my fiancé, with whom I'd just been fucking, out of the apartment by leaving the premises in order to buy my adopted father, who was more than slightly alcoholic, a bottle of Jack Daniels. During my absence, daddy found a tie in the bathtub. After I returned and handed him over his bottle, he told me while he was sobbing that every man wanted to use me. Except for himself. He was the only man who was able to protect me. Crying steadily he reached for my tits. I asked him why he didn't instead fuck my mother. 'We don't do that sort of thing anymore.' Sex must be dirty. He reached for my breasts. I phoned my mother who was in their summer house, explained the situation to her, though I thought she didn't believe me because she hated me, and asked her to call him off. She told me to give the phone receiver to him. He then stopped trying to touch me.

I've always known that story. What I suddenly remembered or knew is that I sexually desired my adopted father.

'Come, child.' None of what I now saw made sense. A lot of noise was coming from out the windows. As I glanced down below I saw objects: nailpolish bottles which seemed silver and pale blue dots or stars, white skulls, coins smaller than the skulls, binoculars, a deck of used Tarot cards. A thin cot covered by a threadbare blanket peeked out of a garage door the colour of dead sand. Strings of brown, red, violet, and black beads were strewn around one bowl filled with white cornflour and one bowl filled by yellow cornflour on the concrete outside the garage. Mirrors of all sizes stood propped against building walls. Packs of Camels and bottles of raw white rum. Objects.

I saw myself in this mirror or seeing. But having no memory, I couldn't recognize myself. 'It woud be customary,' the old goat informed me, 'for me to kill you now.' Suddenly I perceived myself: tense, stinking and dripping out of fear.

'But,' the shrivelled man continued, 'I indulge myself. Who are you?'

Outside the windows Paris was in chaos. Thousands of Algerians were walking freely. Ragged. Dirty. Sticks. Dolls. Voodoo. Blood flowed eyeballs out. Hatred distaste from mistreated on every level desecration of human being botched up face. Blood flowed out of wound cornea resembled mad dog's or AIDS' case fingers extended into ivory carved razor blades. The uses of primitive art. White scholars have written essays. Once again a modern reminds us that the Ancients, the very scientists and philosophers who have transmitted present-day civilization to us, from Herodotus and Diodorus, from Greece to Rome, unanimously recognized that they borrowed that civilization from blacks on the banks of the Nile: on these bones the North Africans' human flesh hung like rags or banners of emotion. Their weapons hung like meteors on a translucent night. Teeth of sages stuck out of lipless lips: within these mystic caves, gums had shrivelled into the labia of those who foretell and even arrange the future. Though the whites had cut out their tongues, though they had neither been allowed nor been able to speak for themselves even as children, though only drool and vomit had ever dropped out of their mouths: from out of these mouths of these old women whose cunts were now caves, the banners of war emerged.

From that room up there, I could hear the old women. My grandmothers.

The French in the past and under the new right-wing regime said that 'doing what was necessity' in order to control the Algerians was 'on the part of their country . . . not a war for riches or local aggrandisement but a war for security . . .'

I turned away from those windows, toward the old man, and told him my name. When I looked around his room, I saw the usual paraphernalia: bottles filled with pills, droppers, jars of white powder, needles. The works. He asked me why I was crying.

'I cry about most things.' I was determined not to give anything away to this ghost, especially my life. In the pallor which was almost black of that room, he looked almost pure white. He was so old. 'How can anyone make you cry?' he asked me as he kept his gun steadily on my eyes. 'If no person is capable of hurting you, how do your tears appear?'

It was as if I had been tied up, but I didn't know by whom. I spat at the old bones.

He didn't bother to wipe off his withered skin; he balanced

the gun on one knee while his other hand fondled a long needle. A vertical wet streak in the corner of his left eye which was wizened made him look as if he had been crying. If he could have. 'I'm busy tonight,' he mentioned my, Abhor, some, name, '. . . with death.'

The needle was fondled again. For some unknown reason, I would have thought of death, if I could have remembered anything. But it was impossible for me to think my own death.

The goat explained that, sick to death of the world of humans, of how humans hurt each other, he was about to suicide. Because he cared for me, just like Hades for Proserpine, he was going to take me with him. He was sick to death even in his heart.

'If history does make us,' I spat at the goat and said, 'if those who are older than us formed us, you're a walking disease.' I wasn't sure he could walk.

He did look at me. I think he saw me for the first time as more than an object of killing in the same manner as a lover suddenly notices that the obsession's a person. Humanness shocks. The old man, who had probably been through all forms of shock, smiling said, 'One must learn how to suicide in this world, for that's all that's left us.

'What do I mean by "us"? We who rule . . . Probably because there's nothing left for 'us' to do. A form of . . . civilized degeneracy. 'We' are . . .

'But: We're still human. *Human* because we keep on battling against all these horrors, the horrors caused and not caused by us. We battle not in order to stay alive, that would be too materialistic, for we are body and spirit, but in order to love each other. My child. I shall never part with you; my own arms shall carry you with me to death.'

I remembered it's now a cliché that the West's going Japanese. 'A double suicide?' There was a useless need to speak. 'You're sick. You're sick because you want to die. Maybe it's necessary to feel pain.' They say that if you feel pain you're not dying. If I could just scream out and feel enough pain, the old bastard couldn't kill me.

'Let me tell you how we're going to die.' the old man said. 'Who are you?'

There were loud sounds down in the street. Even a speech. 'Bravo, our masters. Yet another effort, Frenchmen, if you would become republicans. If you do this, we shall yell:' yelled the Algerians, 'bravo, our masters!'

'Let this be your cry: MASTER. MASTER MISTERY MEESTER WANNA COCK SUCK. With this cry – MASTER – let your places of business – our bodies and minds – resound. With this cry – MASTER – reap your profits in us, out of us. With this cry, by means of your press, press and oppress us. Oh. For then, pressed down by your irons, we shall become harder and stronger than iron. We who are darker than iron. By means of this cry – MASTER – your media have pressed their way into our middles. Doctors, by means of your media, you have successfully operated in us and turned us into stars. Now we shall burn you away.

'Bravo, masters, on your success! Like Prometheus, you have created fire or us.'

One voice cried out:

'Bravo, my master. Look at me. Take a good look at me. I am old. I am poor; my health is at best delicate. Where do I live? My flesh is shrivelling but not so much as the shrivelled hearts of those who do not care for me: My arms like scarecrows scare others away. Couldn't you give a nice old bum like me just a pence? What? This amount of money's an insult! Who do you think I am?' Baron Samedi asked.

'Look. Look at this helpless old man. Give out of the goodness of your hearts. Give alms to one dying Algerian. Just as you raised tons of money to give to the starving Ethiopian children who were starving because you had decimated their lands, now out of the wisdom of your white hearts give to Papa Death.'

The Algerians who were so thin they were skeletons were screeching. 'Gone are the glorious days of sailing. No longer do you love to build ships out of our flesh and sail around our hearts. No longer do you construct huge masted boats out of our spines. Gone are the glorious days of sailing when white men, by marketing slaves, ruled the entire earth. No longer do you mine in our depths cut open: for now we've been cut open so long so deeply, we're stripped. Clean. Dead. We are your death. May this be the slogan on your toilets or for your cities. No longer will you work in our muscles and our nerves creating herpes and AIDS, by doing so controlling all union, one and forever: being indivisible and narcissistic to the point of fascism, you have now closed down shop. Sick of democracy which has failed you, you've split. Shits. Forever.'

Papa Death wailed on a street corner: 'Stupid and isolated and alienated, alienated from your government, isolated from knowledge, I'm always on holiday! Death is on holiday! This nothing society this nothingness, being every possibility, heralds total carnival!' The blacks threw over a few lampposts. 'Tell me, then, masters, more about your RIGHTS OF MAN and your CONSTITUTION. Tell me what my freedom is.'

A black boy cut his right arm with a razor blade: 'Since I'm now making blood come out of my own arm, I can't be nothing.' The boy stared at his flowing blood.

'I'm hungry,' Baron Samedi answered, 'so I'm no longer named "Death": I'm "Hunger" and "Desire". For when the blood flows, the heart is alive. Rejoicing in living the heart, screeches "Bravo!" Bravo, our masters, for this life!'

Finally I could hear. I heard what the old man with a gun had been telling me. He thought he controlled everything, even Death. Perhaps that was true. I wondered if he had been the one who controlled Dr Schreber. I asked him if he would tell me before I died who gave the doctor his orders.

'Someone,' he replied.

'Someone,' I replied 'whose dreams have grown like obsessions.'

'A rich man.' He added, 'Once I knew a rich man . . .'

'Once I knew a human.'

'. . . The rich man brought me something. Something . . .' He trailed off. 'I once knew a rich man . . .' Down below on the street a man wearing a wig of brown hair which was so straight it stuck straight out of every angle of his head grabbed on old Beebe gun and held it upwards. 'Here is your liberty!'

'The rich person I knew, he was actually the head of a conglomerate, a very large one, despite every material luxury which exists, hated being rich. Either out of this guilt, or, knowing this person this is probably the truth, simply due to intelligence, this person understood that the rich are creepy. If you give a cat two separate and opposite commands, the cat becomes unable to move. In the same way, my rich . . .' the old man hesitated for a moment out of forgotten emotion, '. . . lover, because he was unutterably intelligent, became allergic to himself to the point of autism. Autism within and without himself.' The old man closed his eyes. 'I think that the people who control this world are autistic.' He did not know whether he was speaking about himself. He had forgotten who he was. He shuddered, as if into consciousness, again. 'I think most people in this society now are autistic. Look around you.' I looked around me. I didn't see anyone but a gun. 'Maybe most people're trying to imitate their controllers.' This time the old man sunk into his total insensibility.

Like a cigarette ash or a cut-off limb, his pistol fell to the carpet. It was too thick for there to be a sound. Sound might be frozen. Soundlessly in this soundless world I crossed the old man's room back to his chair. When I looked back, I wondered if he was the rich boss about whom he'd been talking.

There are different forms of suicide. Autism is a suicide in life. The rich who have suicided in life are taking us, the whole human world, as if they love us, into death. It seemed to me that any form of human suicide was neither a necessary nor an unnecessary act, but an act of unbearable anger, an act of murder in which the murderer self-destroys and desires to destroy the whole world.

I looked at the fart who had held a gun to me. No suicide is guiltless.

Something came trickling out of the shadows, on a level with my left shoulder. It paused, swayed its spherical body from side to side on high-perched legs. I screamed. Left the rich man to his nightmares. Went down back into the street.

Ugly

In the face of suicide, in the face of those living corpses who are trying to drag us into their own suicides, in the faces of those old men, there seem to be two strategies:

One is a pure act of will. To bang one's head against a wall, preferably a red brick wall, until either the red brick wall or the world, which seems unbearable and inescapable, breaks open. The Algerians in Paris had banged their heads against walls for years, on the street. Finally their heads opened into blood.

The second strategy wasn't exactly one of will. The heads, being broken, gave up. Gave up in the face of the unopposable suicide of the owning class. Gave up in the face of the nothingness of the owning class. Because, for the Algerians, the world of humans was creepy disgusting horrible nauseous shit-filled exacerbating revolting, humans not revolting, green smelling of dead rats which were decaying and, in endless decay, covered in, like a royal blanket of flowers, purple herpes pustules which had rivetted and cracked into fissures either to the body's blood or to the earth's blood, pale green and pale pink liquid minerals in the bottoms of one-thousand-feet diameter strip mines in Arizona. Blood of the earth leaks into death. A chicken whose head had been cut off ran around like a chicken without a head. Because the head of a person who'd just been guillotined, lying on the earth, for five minutes remembered what had just happened to its head and body. Because in almost every nation political torture was a common practice so there was nowhere to which to run. Because most of the nations' governments are right-wing and the right-wing owns values and meanings: The Algerians, in their carnivals, embraced nonsense, such as Voodoo, and noise.

The Caribbean English slave-owners in the nineteenth century had injected a chemical similar to formic acid, taken from two members of the stinging nettle family, into the already broken skins of their recalcitrant slaves. Ants crawl ceaselessly under the top layer of skin. And forced their unwilling servants to eat Jamaican 'dumbcane' whose leaves, as if they were actually tiny slivers of glass, irritating the larynx and causing local swelling, made breathing difficult and speaking impossible. *Unwilling to speak* means *unable to speak*.

When Mackandal had been a child, a cane mill shaft, running over his right arm, had crushed his arm to its shoulder. With every force he had the tiny child pulled the mangled fragments out of the machine. Delirious he remembered something – Africa – many kinds of animals easily running, loping, over rolling hills – him running alongside of and as fast as these animals who accepted him as their friend, without effort. He remembered all that he couldn't name. From then on, the child did not name. Not until. He wanted to unite his people and drive out the white Parisian owners. Once he knew unity, he would begin to name. Until then, his words were the words of hate. Mackandal was an orator, in the opinion even of Mitterand, equal in his eloquence to the French politicians and intellectuals, and different only in superior vigour. Though one-armed from the childhood accident, he was fearless and had a fortitude which he had and could preserve in the midst of the cruellest tortures.

'In the beginning of the world,' Mackandal once explained, 'there was a living person. Because a person has to be living before he or she can be a corpse. The white people believe that death is prior to life.

'In the beginning, in his or her beginning, this living person is both physical and mental, body and spirit. The body must touch or cross the spirit to be alive. Touching they mirror each other. A living person, then, is a pair of twins.

'In the beginning, the twins are children. Children are the first ones. I'm a child,' Mackandal explained himself. His brown hair was sticking so straight out of each angle of his head that it seemed to be a wig.

'After a while, my children,' Mackandal also wore a top hat and was as thin as anyone's shadow, 'it was no longer the beginning. The two children had aged and died. There existed two corpses.

'After another while, the people who came after and after remembered the first children. Those first two beings were now two loa.

'I, then, or you, or he or she or even it, is five: body, spirit, living, dead, and memory or god. The whites make death because they separate death and life.' Obviously this black, like horses dogs cats and some wild animals, judged a human not by the skin's colours but by how she or he behaved.

From 1981 to 1985, for five years, Mackandal built up his organization. But revolutions usually begin by terrorism. His followers poisoned both whites and their own disobedient members. But this wasn't enough terror to start a revolution in such a bourgeois city.

Most of Mackandal's followers were Algerians, and even other black Africans, who hadn't been content only to hover in the shadows corners alleyways of the city like tamed animals who had once been animals of prey, who were not content only to be alive by dying, slowly. Being godless this *trash* had only itself to turn to. Being ambitious vengeful burning with pride fierce as any blood-stained beast these remnants of oral history sought more than their own survivals. They sought revenge for the past and paradise for the future. They lived in camps in the squalor of the northernmost sections of Paris or in the crime-infested eastern areas. If you could call it *living*.

The Parisian and the French government desired simply to exterminate the Algerian trash, the terrorists, the gypsies. The urban sections inhabited by Algerians were literally areas of plague to the Parisians who knew how to speak properly. The French authorities murdered pregnant women. They made every Algerian they could locate carry a computerized identity card. As a result, one rebellion, for instance, that took place over a vast city block, part of which was a deserted parking lot, in the south, lasted a hundred years until every Parisian deserted the zone altogether.

As a result of this *urban* rather than *political* situation, by 1985 city ordinances prohibited all blacks from going anywhere at night unless accompanied by a white and carrying a special governmental ordinance. Even in broad daylight three or more blacks who talked together or even stood together without at least an equal number of whites were considered to be a terrorist cadre and subject to penal disciplines up to death. Night searches in the slums, the gypsy camps, would have been frequent if the flics, as bourgeois as all other Parisians, hadn't preferred the warmth of their own Parisian couscous to a possible knife in the groin. Whenever a flic caught an Algerian with a weapon, such as a pencil, the flic was rewarded and the Algerian punished in some manner that was always very public. But there were too many Algerians, blacks, in the slums, the shadows, the alleyways, the deserted Metro stations: by 1985 an official police report states that 'security was now nonexistent' for whites in Paris. It was unwise for whites to act.

Not only did Mackandal's direct followers steal on Metro lines, from the apartments not only of the rich, not . . . Mackandal himself walked through the city of the whites as freely as he pleased. Whoever was of the disenfranchised and unsatisfied the poor those so wallowing in misery they were almost mindless, what the white call 'zombie', followed him and did not know why. Not knowing was their only possible way. Just how many of the urban semi-inhabitants – *semi* – because only partly alive – chose to follow this desperate man and this desperate path cannot be known. We have wallowed in non-knowledge for not long enough.

Since it is easy enough to kill, terrorism, unlike conventional rebellion, cannot be stopped. Mackandal grew sick of thievery, pillaging, arson. When a person arises from that poverty which is death and can begin and begins to dream, these dreams echo the only world that has been known or death. Soon such dreams of negation are not enough. Mackandal no longer was interested in petty violence:

he dreamed of paradise, a land without whites. He determined to get rid of every white.

The Algerian women who had been forcibly sterilized by the French. The street-cleaners. Etc. Everywhere, in the shadows where they couldn't be seen because they were too low and black, Mackandal's followers learned the fastest ways to poison whites. Mackandal especially concentrated on those who laboured as servants: he taught them about herbs, the puffer fish and the scaly toad. From old women who lived alone in basements and in the outskirts of the city under used-up and left-over McDonald's stands, Mackandal himself learned how to regulate the human body with natural chemicals. A person who eats even a small amount of the tetrodotoxin of the puffer fish or fugu feels pale, dizzy, and nauseous. Insects seem to be crawling just beneath the skin. The body seems to float. Drool drops out of the mouth while sweat runs out of the pores – the body is deserting the body – the head is aching and almost no temperature exists. Material is cold. All is ice. Nausea; vomiting; diarrhoea; the eyes are fixed; it is almost not possible to breathe; muscles twitch then stop, paralyzed. Unable to move you. Eyes are glass you. The soul lies in the eyes. The mental faculties remain acute until shortly before death; sometimes death does not occur. Many many herbs. In time, like ink on a blotter, poison seeped into the lives of the whites. Poison entered the apartments of the bourgeoisie. There is a way to stop guns and bombs. There's no way to stop poison which runs like water. The whites had industrialized polluted the city for purposes of their economic profit to such an extent that even clean water was scarce. They had to have servants just to get them water and these servants, taught by Mackandal, put poison in the water.

One day Mackandal arranged for the poisoning of every upper-middle and upper-class apartment in Paris. The old man didn't need to suicide. While, due to their beloved, almost worshipped, victuals, the white Parisians writhed around, bands of Algerians and other blacks appeared out of their shadows and alleyways.

In the meantime, Spanish sailors, longtime anarchists, had

flowed in from the ports near Paris, via the Seine, in orgies of general hooliganism and destruction. Pale blue and pink condom boxes cluttered up the brown river. Diseased and non-diseased sperm flowed down the Champs-Elysées. Empty needles lay under bushes north of the Ted Lapidus on the rue du Four. Drunk with animal blood and whatever else they had been pouring into their mouths, these sailors, black white and other, who couldn't speak a word of French, began breaking into shops, taking whatever merchandise they could stuff into their mouths pockets pants and assholes. As soon as they realized this merchandise meant nothing to them, (except for the contents of the pharmecutical cabinets), they trashed the stores. Soon the hardy men, though inured to longer days of boredom, grew tired of this game.

They joined the Algerians, their brothers, who were breaking into flats of the rich. The whites were already trembling from fear, nausea, and diarrhoea. A few of them managed, hands raised over heads, to shove themselves against wall-papered walls. The blacks no longer backed off.

The few sailors who had been doomed to remain on their ships, at the western edge of the city on the filthy river, from the far distance saw this city: Algerians, blacks swarming everywhere; dogs nudging over garbage cans with their cold black noses. The flames of cigars and lit candles overflowing the churches falling on this mass of garbage ignited it, starting thousands of tiny fires which finally had to grow. The whole city was in flames. In the middle, a very tall very thin black man stood. Finally the winds, instead of fanning fires, swirled the dead ashes which used to be a city.

A group of white soldiers in the American Embassy, off the corner of the Louvre, when the looting had started, had held three innocent Algerian boys and one girl who had entered the Embassy out of curiosity up to one wall with machine guns. The soldiers acted exactly as they had been trained. First they asked the blacks the name of their leader. There was no reply.

'If you don't tell us what we want to know, we're going to kill one of you.'

The Algerian boys were between the ages of twelve and

eighteen and the girl was six. They looked at each other. None of them said a word.

Doing his duty, a soldier, a lieutenant, twisted one of the Algerian boy's arms behind his back until the cracking of a bone could be heard. 'Watch,' the American lieutenant told the other three Algerians. The lieutenant's other hand, grabbing the boy's chin, yanked it up and back while his knee kept the lower spine straight. When the boy's growing black eyes fell straight into the lieutenant's face, the lieutenant's face registered no emotion. He simply increased the pressure of his double pull until the young neck cracked. The boy still wasn't dead. Blood fell out of the left side of his mouth.

Finally the youth said more than blood to the American. 'Kill me.' The American had already killed him.

When another soldier started playing with one of the youngest boy's balls, the girl tried to protect her friend by biting at the soldier's hands. The soldier kicked her head. She lay lifeless on the expensive marble floor.

'Who's your leader? Do you want all of you to die?' the soldier who had the authority asked the two boys.

'Don't tell them anything. Never tell Americans anything cause all they know how to do is kill,' the oldest boy instructed the youngest.

From the floor the girl watched another death.

All the soldiers turned to the remaining boy. The girl watched them turn to the remaining boy. She watched them emotionlessly, sexuallessly, without caring, torture him to the point they realized they could not get information out of him then murder him. She perceived these men were not humans.

One man grabbed her by her hair. 'Slut.' The word surprised her. She wasn't sure what they were talking about.

'Do you see what's happened to your little friends? Don't you want to grow up?'

'Yes,' she said. They were adults.

'Do you know how much pain your friends felt?'

All she knew was that the world, totality was terror. She screamed out Mackandal's name, all the other names of leaders which she could remember, and then they killed her.

Such betrayals or rather such hideous perceptions of the totality of terror, of the fact that there is nothing else in this world but terror, happened so often that finally the whites who were left had Mackandal in their grasp.

They didn't bother to speak to the Algerian leader. They hit him over the head, handcuffed him to a steel post inside some room in the same embassy, which by now was almost deserted. The lieutenant who had killed the first boy took out his cigarette lighter. He was going to burn Mackandal to death in reprisal for the lack of respect the Algerians had shown to the Americans. With this, the whites seemed to have regained the city.

As the first flame lit up the bottoms of his pants and socks, being more inflammable than his shoes, Mackandal whose guiding spirit, surprisingly, was Erzulie, the spirit of love, that is not of fertility but of that which longs beyond reality infinitely, of all unrealizable desire, screamed so awfully the soldiers who were burning him thought they were in the presence of a victim of madness. His body began to shake, not in spasms, but regularly, not as if from flames, but as if possessed. He tried to tear his wrists from the handcuffs. A small section of a corner of that room had been decimated by a bomb. With a single almost invisible spasm the black leader in flames succeeded in wrenching himself out of his handcuffs. Before the dumbed Americans could react, still burning he was half-way across the room and through the hole.

It was not known what happened to Mackandal. Poisonings of whites continued: finally the Algerians won Paris. Except that more than a third of the city was now ash.

I had escaped from the rich old man, from his seemingly causeless desire to murder me, to this. I wondered whether I wanted to return to the old man. They always say that money equals safety, though I'm not sure who 'they' are or about whose safety they're speaking.

It used to be that men wandered over the earth in order to perceive new phenomena and to understand. I was a wanderer like them, only I was wandering through nothing. Once I had

had enough of working for bosses. Now I had had enough of nothing.

Daddy

By the time I saw Thivai in that city of ash, you might say that I had had enough of something. You might say that I fell into his arms.

'Get the fuck away from me,' I said cautiously. Cautiously, except my hands were grabbing for their life, if not for mine, on to every part of his flesh they could reach. The way someone tests a dead fish to find out whether it's fresh. He was fresh. Food poisoning's unpleasant, to say the least. Deadly. But I've never been sure what parts of my body have to do with what parts of my body, including my mind heart and cunt. Being trained to be polite, I didn't say anything to Thivai.

He was fresh. I didn't say anything to Thivai about anything that had to do with anything. 'I was up in some old croak's room. I don't know how I got there. The same way I get anywhere,' I explained fully. 'The geezer held a gun to my head. I had no idea who he was. He was a guy. But he wasn't planning to murder me, he explained to me.' I was trying to calm Thivai down. He becomes very nervous about things. 'The poor old man was planning to suicide. That's what he said to me. He wanted me to help him by letting him take me along with him. He even held my hand.'

Thivai, who was holding my hand, blushed. The city all around him was ash. 'Thivai, I don't trust men. I don't trust old men. When the drool told me he was the only man who could protect me because he was the only man who truly loved me, due to his age: I didn't believe him. I foundered in disbelief. I guess he was foundering more . . .'

'I always wanted you,' Thivai said. 'I guess I don't talk that much: I guess you never knew.'

'He didn't kill me, Thivai.'

'You murdered Schreber.' We looked at Paris which was now a third world. 'What are we going to do now we don't have a boss?' He thought. 'What are we going to do now there are no more bosses?'

'I didn't even know who that old man was. I don't know now. I have to know. I think he owned something . . .'

'I've got you again. Now, I'm your owner. I'd do anything for you.'

'You've got me, Thivai. Did I ever tell you about my father? I had two fathers: a real one and a false one.' I was getting my mother and father mixed up. It didn't matter. 'I never met the real one. The false one tried to rape me. I wouldn't let him. I realize now I desired him. I never met the real one. Now you know.'

'Know?' He looked at the black city. Black except for the white ash.

'That old man was my real father.' As soon as I had said this, I knew it was true.

'Dead men have bosses.' A tall thin man stood behind us. Hair so stiff it had to be false sprang in strings straight up out from a black top hat. 'This city is death, . . .'

'It was almost my death,' I interrupted this ghoul.

'. . . but death and life are fucking each other,' he continued speaking.

'They must be using contraceptives these days.' Maybe someone should have been using contraceptives as far as I was concerned.

'Maybe you should get out of here,' the ghoul suggested.

I realized not only didn't I give a damn about my real father: I didn't care what his name was. Half of Thivai's face was bright red.

'Trouble here, mon. Any boat go. You smell that . . .'

A door, padded with dark grey ultra suede, slid smoothly back into its housing. The ghoul was right that in this Paris death and life were fucking. Just like my father gave birth to me and wanted to kill me. In Paris, death smelled like life and vice-versa, especially in human beings.

'. . . bridge.' The black man said, pointing a skeleton finger down a streetless, almost-crumbled-into-air alleyway. 'Be there.'

I saw crude wooden handles that drifted at either end of the boat, like worn sections of a broom handle.

'Bridge is escape pod, lifeboat. Bridge of life to death. Vice-versa.'

The Algerians had taken over Paris so they would own something. Maybe, soon, the whole world. 'The old man: there's something else about him. My father's no longer important cause interpersonal power in this world means corporate power. The multinationals along with their computers have changed and are changing reality. Viewed as organisms, they've attained immortality via bio-chips. Etc. Who needs slaves anymore? So killing someone, anyone, like Reagan or the top IBM executive board members, whoever they are, can't accomplish anything,' I blabbed, and I wondered what would accomplish anything, and I wondered if there was only despair and nihilism, and then I remembered.

A boat was floating under the bridge. The body of an old man lay in the boat. I looked and saw this boat.

'Old man,' the black skeleton said. 'He an important man. Whole stretches are being ripped to steel and concrete. Now he dead man.'

In the boat my father I had never known was dead.

Dead: Carved Into Roses

The long-postponed realization of my dream conceived in the confines of the cursed, obliterated city: hitching myself to the yoke, joining the horde of Dervish camp followers and ex-whores trailing along in the wake of the North African, mainly Moroccan, infantrywomen and soldiers of the Legion, throwing away my useless high-heel shoes, sinking my bare feet into the delicate ripples of the sands of what once must have been a city, Paris; lifted lifted, thick sand dunes, walking on and on, losing myself in the desert.

As if dreams were coming true, my dream finally: passing by the Restaurant de l'Union, the mataam el-Jurria, the derb Sebbahi; with footsteps as supple and stealthy as those of a lover whom you believe you trust and who's actually secretly poisoning you, for what reason?, as if you are still nineteen years old and horny as hell, as if. This is your fortune, girl: A refuge has lent itself to a thousand and one love duels. Each love was a tale because a tail. Strong bodies have excited and refused you. This will happen again. Everything will happen again.

Within some drowsy Portuguese city whose streets and intersections are deserted in the full heat of the sun, you will meet a sailor. His dong itself will be a rebel against its tremendous nodding weight.

As far as sailing goes . . .

As for the victims of the negligence boredom and addictions of the owners, the French and the English owners, who've come down in this world; as for those former owners . . .

All humans and animals now sail over the same seas . . .

You're here now. At last. I've been waiting for you for what seems like a really long time. For a second. For a minute. For an hour. For a day. For a month. For a year. I knew you were going to come back to me. To the exact spot where we first met. In a river. In my cunt. I'm sopping wet. Let's fuck on top of this fountain. Splashing the waters of hydro-chloric acid into my nostrils. Daddy. Pull off my fingernails. My back has been carved into roses. You scream that it's not only by you. As if you're alive or as if I'm not dreaming. As if I really possessed you and you really possessed me, we tore off each other's head and ate out the contents, then pecked out the remaining eyes, pulled out the sharks' teeth and sucked opium out of the gums, my vagina was bleeding. And I said to my father, the sailor, 'Let's not be possessed.'

But like the rain, blood will always continue. Finally it didn't matter, in that driving rain, that everyone was staring at us. Finally it didn't matter that my squawks and our screeches of blood made the lunatics high up behind their asylum-barred windows mad. I alive and you dead together'll warm the bones of tombs. We together set splinters under their, the owners', fingernails, then light them up. We together made their dead bodies shrouded in soil into our beds. Only because they're dead, they envied our love which has been agony. We'll make the whole graveyard our playground because we're playing with ourselves. Then there'll be nowhere left to set on fire.

Soon there was nowhere left to set on fire. We wanted to travel, like sailors, but we had one living body and one dead body. The graveyard perished when you were buried in it. End. But what did I have left? Is a former victim an owner or no thing? From death, the place of your death you said that I, your daughter, would be nothing. But now my mind and the inside tips of my fingers and my lips and my mouth are blood.

Here I am, daddy my love, waiting for you to come.

When I woke up out of this insane dream, I realized that daddy's dead body, daddy was lying in some lousy Algerian hospital. Or that some dead old man's body was lying in some hospital for the dead. Stinking flies were probably eating it up.

'Why'd he kill himself?' Thivai asked. Thivai looked dead himself.

'Why's anyone kill herself?' Free of my dream, I shrugged. 'I don't know.'

'If anyone knows, you know.'

I examined my own blood: 'He had been trying to kill himself for a long time. It had taken him a long time. Because he was a tedious old fuck. Christ.'

Since he was now a tedious dead fuck, the new Algerian doctors were keeping him in a repulsive hospital in order to conduct experiments. Thivai and I knew that if they kept him in that hospital long enough, he'd die.

I had to get daddy out of the hospital.

Biker mags had informed me that prison and medical prisoners can escape their prisons only by faking death. In a manner such as this: Prison authorities usually bury the prisoners who they've tormented to death in mine shafts. In order to make sure each corpse is a corpse, they beat in each corpse's skull. But usually instead of beating in the corpses, they fuck the corpses and leave. It's no good beating about the bush. Most of the prisoners, after they've been beaten and tormented, prefer giving head to being dead. The now-homosexual prisoner, who's still alive, escapes.

If daddy became dead, I wouldn't be able to give him head anymore. I had to rescue him out of the evil hospital by making him go through his own death. I told Thivai all this.

'All I wanna know is who's gonna do the rescuing,' was what Thivai replied. He was cynical right down to the junk in his bones.

'Whoever gives the best head.'

Thivai, attractive like a junky, got the medical student who was in charge of wheeling corpses, for purposes of hospital household decoration, to fall in love with him. The young boy wheeled a corpse straight out of a window. The corpse was daddy. Night. Daddy fell right into my arms.

I was crying. In the nightmare of my mind, I desperately clung to that body as if it was alive. Like a shipwrecked sailor, I desperately clung to life. Thivai was no better, junked to the gills. But still human, not fish enough to swim through the depths of dreams. Sailors have huge dicks. Sailors have no hair and big arms.

But reality is something else. Reality is enough to make you crazy. For the loss of my dear love, I scream.

His rotting body lay on the concrete. Cut away. Slouching over bent almost double over a stinking hole enduring this brutal mistreatment stench flies blind you brush them away with useless arms. There was nothing left to do. So Thivai and I went and got tattooed. Carved into roses.

Alone

THEDEEP

I Child Sex

(Thivai speaks)

In front of their parents' former homes two teenage hoods held on to each other with affection. Then they let go.

The door to a squat opened. Dawn flowed in along the carpet and the tiles of its entrance. A naked boy and a naked girl lay on the floor. The sun of blood and egg-yoke fascinated their almost dead eyes into waking.

For a few hours, a young woman who had been a maid had been sleeping in a large straw chair. A ray of sun, like a pigeon, walked up and down the tiles, then climbed up the hairy leg. She awoke, half stood up, stumbled to the kitchen sink, tucked the rags which were partly covering her thighs into another rag which served as a belt, took hold of what used to be a dishrag and scrubbed her face and cunt lips with icewater. The cold made her shake while the water streamed down her fat thighs. Under the rags, her two pillars of fat chafed each other into a heat which resembled the sun's.

In the evenings, the revolutionary Algerian soldiers drank themselves almost to death in the brothels. The houses stood on the boulevard in front of the sea. There, teenage hoods searched for soldiers. When they found one, awed they beat the mother-fucker up. At least they tried. The ones who couldn't beat up soldiers, most of them, ran after the few girls they saw, though they didn't care about girls. Whenever they got hold of a bunch of girls, they tied them up with ropes and gagged them. Then they rubbed them in dirt.

Certain of the guys were able to rape a girl without having to kneel or fall on the ground. They could standing up rape a girl, feet planted firmly on the street and their hands on their hips as if they were sailors. The other hoods admired them.

These boys weren't nice. They beat up those younger than themselves. They had killed one or two. They knocked about those who were still babies and then slapped at their tiny cocks. They cut off young girls' hair with switchblades. They ripped up their delicate blouses, and tore the heels off their shoes, and cut through the tight blue-jeans to the flesh.

It was after the revolution.

Six jeeps of The New Revolutionary Arab Police

(اثامی انقلابی عربی)

braked in front of a group of young children. The cops butted at them with the ends of their pistols. The kids surrounded the slow, heavy police and forced them on to the tops of their own jeeps. Then the black-and-blue-and-bloody children crammed themselves between the jeeps. They had nothing else to do, so they returned to their former nurses who would still wash their knees cut their hair mend their socks right through this never-ending night.

Half-naked and Mercurochrome-dotted on his chest, a child sat on his bed.

Somewhere else, St Bubu, wearing only a white cotton slip, slept on his back. His knees were tucked into his stomach.

Audry who was Abhor's sister was sleeping right next to the boy. Her right hand was lying on his thigh. It slipped under the slip. Then it fell on his ass. Though he was still asleep, St Bubu opened one eye and rolled over Aud.

Audry woke up and consciously stuck her hand under his slip. She wangled it between their bodies, heavy and hot from sleep, until St Bubu caught the hand as if it was a wiggling fish. His weight alone spread apart the young girl's thighs. To do this, his hands held on to her white bra.

One hand rubbed one cup. It pulled it slightly down. The hand discovered a small breast. Touched it. Held the animal. It awoke it.

The young girl's cunt juices had already run down his right knee.

With his teeth, St Bubu unhooked her training bra. Two were adult teeth. The bra, slipping beneath one tit, tickled his tummy. When she felt the results of this tickling, the young girl's face turned as white as the corneas of her eyes: she understood. 'Don,' she said. 'I forgot about him.' She went white enough to not exist. 'Don't mention him again. That . . . Then was the time of true morality and affection. Before the war. Now morality and affection are dead. Now I no longer see now I no longer cry now I no longer love. Anyone. Even you. I won't cry or smile again because I'm concrete.'

The boy kissed this war-time face, this sun of blood, this milk, these tingling ants. His lips aspired to this transparency. His right hand tugged at, then pulled away the slip which had slipped between his and the young girl's sexes.

The young girl pulled him down to her foot; the boy pulled himself up until his hands took hold of the head, shook it; the blue hair rolled, and rolled over the pillow. In the next apartment, some girls were talking with their former maids. One of the ex-maids bit a thread she was holding between her teeth to break it. The coldness of the thimble she was balancing between her teeth made her lips tremble. St Bubu licked the hairs, on the right and on the left, of Aud's cheeks. Hairs stuck to his lips.

'Bub . . . sometimes I think about my mommy. She's the only one who could make me warm.

'That memory's almost gone . . . Maybe that memory's false . . . That memory's almost gone . . .'

'Don. He's my brother. He shouts his head off in front of the sea. He's uppitty. He's foul-mouthed. He even made up a dictionary for the foul-mouthed. On the beach he and I used to coat our bodies in sand. For a while we lived in a tiny cabin which we had found. We didn't have to eat and we didn't have to sleep. We loved each other. Since we loved each other, we weren't going to die.

'All other children and the soldiers left us alone.

'Our clothes were seaweed and tatters of blue-jeans, slips, shells, bras, and condoms. We were naked kids.

'As for daddy, daddy's dead now. He's probably in Hell, the old shit. At last at least he's got a real home; as for me with the war I went from place to place. In each place I met some boy and he did whatever he wanted to me; I survived by not caring about myself. Hookers understand me. And I understand them. I haven't been a prostitute, understand, but there's one thing life's taught me:' Abhor's younger sister explained. 'I can always find a home in a whore-house. I can stay alive as long as I don't care about anything or anyone: what other people say about me. How many hands touch my body. The physical pain I feel. What happens to me.

'With you, Bubu, I've allowed myself to feel something. But that's wrong,' the young girl said.

'Being a whore means you separate sex and feeling. Sex is an activity as meaningless as is money. I'd be a great whore, I'd even make a fortune,' she cried out, 'if my cunt didn't get so sore! Physically. I can hardly bear to fuck: if I fuck more than once in a row, my cunt bruises and then I get an infection. If I was a whore, I'd die.'

St Bubu didn't reply.

'My brother, Don, used to try to pull my hair out. Then he'd push me with his knee. He believed his knee was a gun. The top of my body would fall forward. The gun would slide into my legs. As if I was now his prisoner, he coldly informed me that if I didn't do exactly as he said I'd be shot. I took my clothes off. But I wasn't able to entice this real commander away from his commands with just my body because he didn't care about sensuality. Both of us were unable to touch a person physically. In order to touch he had to command. He commanded me; he commanded positions; he invented a world. When I became too tired to play anymore, to obey him: he put his arms around me and stuck his nostrils into my armpits. Then he rubbed his sweat-soaked nose into my cheeks. I pinched the tip of his cock in my teeth. I laughed when he cried out from the pain.

'As my brother and I form one person, now like mine his

heart is gone because it's been cut out. Like me, Don obsessively stares at his dead heart. We're gonna be free, Bubu, when we shit on it, on ourselves.'

The children such as St Bubu and Audry, and a sailor and a gypsy, in this time after the war all lived in the section of Paris of the rats.

Throughout the night, after the revolution, all I wanted to do was get my rocks off. With whomever I could find.

There were only prostitutes; the women had all become prostitutes. I didn't understand why.

But I found, for I'm consistently losing myself, myself seated in the middle of the fur of white wolves. We, a young girl and I, nibbled cherries which reminded us of our blood. Red dripped on to white. The fruit at least was fresh. A mutant who was singing a rock-n-roll memory began to cry. There was a past, somewhere. I took my weapon, rose up, and walked to the front of the squat.

Outside, next to the purple steps, roses stood in the witch-like winds.

I went back in to get something to eat. While I was choking on some nuts, the girl sat on my shoulders so that her cunt juice ran down my neck. The skin at the back of my neck and my eyes felt allergic. My eyes were burning as they should be.

I took hold of her thighs. I ran my hands around them. I put my mouth on them. I bent her forward so I could run my hands up and into the ass. Red head backwards, she kissed me on the lips. I had her ass.

Dinosaur, who was a stuffed animal, was sitting next to us. Dinosaur was female therefore a prostitute. I could see her cunt. Cherries were sitting on top of her thighs. One of her gigantic paws as if she was a wild cat grazed my knee in affection. The buzzing of a mad bee caught prisoner in the bathroom resounded from tile floor to tile floor. When I managed to get my head up, the red-head rubbed her thighs into the back of my neck.

There was a gun-shot. In one leap I managed to grab the PM and jump on to the front steps. Still, my nostrils opened as wide as possible, moonlight resting on my face and hands, I looked out over the sea, to the port. The girl knocked on the window glass: 'You have to eat, Thivai. You can't remain on guard all night. Abhor'll return. C'mon. What do you want to eat? There're dead hamburgers there's whipped cream.'

When I opened the door, wind blew through the room. The whore was hugging her stuffed animal to her tits. '. . . that mouth you've got down there below . . .' I stuck my hand into the hole between her wet thighs. For a second I reached the clit . . . though she was a whore, she was too sensitive to be touched . . . I reached for her stuffed animal's clit . . . that little nothing of a tongue . . .

I, shivering in anticipation, walked back into the cold. Car lights flashed blue along the bay. There was nowhere, for me, to go. From the squat.

I walked back inside. Inside the whore. I pushed her under me. I threw myself down on her. She sang out like a blues singer . . . I didn't know why. Dinosaur poured about a cup of her whipped cream down her open mouth. I stuck my tongue between the cliffs of the lips into foaming cream. I became a ship, sailing. I tried to suck it up.

Dinosaur tugged at my army belt. Excited beyond belief by her touch, I threw myself on the animal. The young girl, excited beyond control, threw herself on me. I reached over for her and she, whore-like, rejected me. Her hand rose out of the fur and slapped my red cock.

'Don't touch me but whip my cunt,' the young whore said to me.

'I'm not a brute:' I told her. 'It's wrong for any human to hurt or kill another human. Even to reject to the point of banishment another human. Corporate executives commit atrocities. Must we act like them, sexually, in order to fight them successfully? No.' I was answering myself. 'Acting like shits will only make us become shit. Greedy and maniacal. Of course we have to use force to fight for our freedom. For forceless humans are dead. We should use force to fight representations which are idols, idolized images; we must use force to annihilate erase eradicate terminate destroy slaughter slay nullify neutralize break down get rid of obliterate move out destruct end all the representations which exist for purposes other than enjoyment. In such a war, a war against idolatry, ridicule'll be our best tool. Remember, whore: Julien's sarcasms did more damage than Nero's tortures.'

'Decomposing flesh moves me the most:' the young whore said. 'Give me hell.'

I laughed at myself and gave her what she wanted. I pierced myself through her belly-button. I thrust and pushed her own blood up her womb. As her red head rose out of the white fur, her mouth opened: monstrous scarlet. Tiny white shells appeared in that monster sea. 'My little dead shark. Better than dead fish.' I whispered to her while I fucked her in her asshole.

Stray sprays of my sperm streamed down the stuffed animal's left leg. Our fucking had made her less fearful for the moment. She actually touched my arm and left her paw there. Then this paw pulled my arm to her monstrous body, lifted it and placed it on her swollen belly. Then she stuck the hand in and squeezed it between her two hot hide thighs. I thought that my hand was going to break.

I had already stopped fucking the whore. I was rolled to, almost over, the dinosaur by the dinosaur. My soft gluey cock pulsed against her thigh which was made out of sackcloth. She looked at me. She licked my eyelids which looked pale to her. I turned away from the monster, back to the whore.

I took her in my arms. I adored her. I separated her arms into my cross. I placed my cross down on the white. Her red cunt was the center of the cross. I fucked her, not it.

I raised myself up into the night. I buttoned up my canvas pants, I rebuckled my belt, I reached for a glass of red wine which was on a nearby table, bolted down the wine, took my gun, a soldier.

Outside the squat, the winds were now cold. They froze my still-wet legs right through my pants. My throat tightened and tightened. I was standing on the steps. Below them, the bees and quail who weren't asleep yet were playing in a small garden. Holding on to this railing with one hand – the other one was keeping my stomach together – I breathed. The sea breathed. I vomited. I groaned. The liquid part of the vomit dribbled off me then rolled over the black roses, weighed on them, bent them to the ground. Then the vomit rolled down their purple stalks.

'. . . after my escape . . .' I thought.

I ran down to a beach where the tide was rising. In a wall of seaweed I fell asleep. The sea-gulls rode on top of the waves. White-capped surf ran up to my feet which were sleeping. Another whore ran along the red and black cliff; gusts of wind turned parts of her skirt upward into a broken umbrella; a scarf like the wind whipped around her bare teats.

She ran down to the still-warm water. She climbed over the green seaweed which was hiding me. She, the princess, stumbled. Without waking up I grabbed her neck and drew her, which wasn't too hard for me for she was very light, into my stomach. She was curious about me; she examined my pants; inside my pants' pockets. She pulled out some crumbled bills and half a movie ticket. My cock was as hard as a nearby rock. While I felt my cock's hardness, she was counting the money. She slipped all of it into the elastic of her underpants. Her breasts were almost all chest. The girl took my right hand and yanked; she tried to drag me out of the seaweed on to some clear sand.

'C'mon. I'm gonna earn my money however I have to do it. I'm no whore.'

Later, away from the beach:

Her room. My sperm even splattered her torn curtains. A shitload had come out of me. I rubbed my raw cock in a rag of sheet.

'Don't get it dirty, baby. You're not gonna make it like yourself, are you? Did you off your mother like they said on the radio?'

'Sure,' I answered the whore. 'And my sister too. I tossed both of their bodies into the sea.'

'Your attitude's bullshit.' She paused. 'Why d'you really kill them?'

'Because my father had asked me to. She was fucking every gook and wop she could lay her hands on. She had always had weird tastes. But she wouldn't touch my father. Every fuckin' night, she'd lay on her side of the bed. She was a bitch. In the morning, every fuckin' single morning, she'd go out, find a new sailor and make it with him. So I made lunch, one day, then I took the knife, pushed open the door of the room I knew she had been fucking in . . . she was sleeping on a wet bed . . . the sailor must have come . . . come and gone . . . no more comings and goings for dad and me . . . my mother's legs were so far apart, they must have disgusted each other . . . knowingly . . . I could have shoved an unpeeled pineapple up between the two of them. I lay one hand on those sheets which were still wet and focussed on mother's throat I pierced it. I thrust through there. Her blood ran along my arms. Outside the room my brother, Xaintrilles, screamed. He had a nightmare. I smeared her blood over my face like a tattoo. On my beach, my father was waiting for me. I ran to him.

'My father and I were running away through rabbit hutches. Then we came to fields of sugar-beets. What had been red had become purple: the blood on my clothes had become the colour of murderous royalty, of the President of Austria. Until the night, my father and I hid ourselves in sugar-beets. We ate mulberries which leaked blood all over us. My father started crying until I beat him up with my fists.

'Finally: there was night. We made it to the second beach. I buried dad in burning sand in order to keep him warm. My father fell asleep, his hand in mine.

'Gulls rode on top of the waves. They played, advanced and withdrew, until daybreak. With daybreak they disappeared. The pain I felt didn't let me sleep: over and over again I rubbed my bloody hand against the white sands.'

Now the whore's rose was opening. As the tip of my third finger grazed and grazed and grazed the top of each petal, each petal curled backwards, as if against itself, like a wave, according to its own nature. Her petals turned back and back: the middle, which was becoming her, opened towards the world. Her physical centre was too sensitive to be touched. It revealed itself to every part that was outside it. Was raw, was pollen, was touching everything and then wanting to touch nothing.

I had found the whore.

'Dad sat up, as soon as he woke up, right beside me.' I continued while I was lightly touching the young girl. 'He was still crying and trembling and snot was running down his chin. His face was a piece of drool. Bits of sand were caught in this drool.

'"I've got some money." He apologized for himself.

'The sand as if it was a prehistoric dinosaur ate up dad's tears. I wasn't going to take anymore. I leapt up, grabbed hold of him, hit him in the face. Fuck you, father! My right knee butted into his groin. He tried to protect his face with his hands, but he was no good. And he didn't have any hands left to protect his cock. I punched him a few times then picked up a small rock and threw it at his forehead. Blood spurted out of his bone. I proceeded to beat him up until he was wrapped around himself like a baby, weak. I beat him up I beat him up. I leaned over the burning sand and vomited.

'His feet stomped on my back. He kicked me over. He stomped on my stomach.

'In the middle of the morning, the cops got us. Dad went back to his baby act, but the cops didn't fall for it: one of them beat him up with an Arab bludgeon. Then all of us, me and dad and cops, walked along, and down a water-sluice gate. At one point I clambered up the gate. A bullet burst my left wrist into slivers of paper. I fell into the canal right on my head. My head bounced up and down. A pig threw himself on me, down there, and dragged me up to the ground. Two cops snapped handcuffs around my good and my non-existent wrists and around my ankles. They had me good.

'My fingernails were dried blood. The back of my neck was a fire. At the end of the world there was a police truck. It had rolled up the road made out of huge roots which had been flattened by storm after storm. The cops threw my father and me into this truck.

'Before I even had time to stand up on the truck's metal floor, it was moving and a pig was standing on my back. He took out a lash and unravelled the flesh of my back. A rat leapt up. A cop who looked like a boy threw the rat a bit of red meat. It had probably been a prisoner. The rat nibbled the meat delicately, then pounced on it like it wanted to fuck it. Then the rat pirate-like sank its red prey into a hole in the truck.

'I fell asleep. Sleep, as is death, was a relief.

'It was morning. Any morning. Swift winds were rocking a flowering branch. The emitted perfumes were winds. My shoulders were shivering, slightly, under their white shirt. My throat was bare. The head was close-shaven. The honey in the middle of my ears was sparkling like the first lights of dawn. *Alive* I looked at the sky. I saw every thing there: Circles. Seals. Car-signs. Ships.

'My lips quivered, then froze as if they were no longer usable. My throat had already dried into pain. My knees buckled. I was forced to fall down on the cell's mattress.

'"Do you want to blow this hole?"

'I kissed the convict's shaven head. I didn't say anything.

'Until it was night. When it was night I was able to think to myself:

'Yes!

'My father was shaking in a pile of his own shit. I said, "There's him."

'"His little boy isn't going to stop taking care of him?"

'I nodded yes.

'Three days from then, at dawn, we made the jump. We hid in garbage in a garbage truck; then ran to a town. Father, you stopped in front of the bakery. Your feet were bleeding. Drool was dropping out of your mouth. A man walked by you, he touched your shoulders; the other con and I, behind you, hid ourselves in a sewer hole; the guy put his shaven head against yours and led you into the fabulous bakery. The bakery of all sweetness. The bakery of all stories. The bakery of the Arabs. In the bakery, you ate a pale pink and pale green cake while the guy was as all over you as he could get. I saw all of this. Back in the street, he got to you: between your thighs, gently. You in the meantime were more interested in the shithole in which we were hiding: the rat hole, the home of all rats, our home. But, daddy, you couldn't stop eating your cake. Father. Sugar sparkled on the tips of your ears. Then the guy took hold of you by your shoulders, again, and bore you behind the shithole in which we were temporarily living. He shoved you against a red wall; his hands touched every part of you. I saw. You only moved your knees: you were weak-kneed. White cream was sitting on your lips. The guy squeezed himself as close as he could to you. He thrusts his hand into your boxer shorts and under your cock. I didn't see: I knew. He made a small cry. He zipped his pants. When you lifted up your arms to push yourself away from him and the red wall and escape, he stayed right behind you, your new shadow. Finally the ex-con who'd engineered our prison break, now covered in shit, walked up to the guy: "You're going to give us your money, aren't you?"

'The guy could have been mute.

'"If not, I'll scream out loud that you just sodomized this old man and his helpless boy."

'The guy made an attempt to raise his arm to hit Custer, the ex-con. Custer spat on his feet: "All of your money, owner of the world, of misery."

'Since Custer wasn't used to waiting for anyone, even the Queen of Sheba, he dug his hands into the queen's nice pockets and turned them inside out as far as they would go. As gently as if he was turning the guy inside out. Instead, he laced the guy up with shoestrings and a piece of rope which he had found in the gutter. In front of us coins were sitting on the concrete, as if they were dogshit.

'I picked up a passport. Custer got a Casio and a scarf. There was no real money, just coins. There was only fake money. "Now you spit on 'im," Custer directed me.

'I didn't get a chance in that Hell: dad, you walked right up to the owner. He went red, then white, while you spat systematically and slowly on his dark coat, his white shirt, his dark belt, his dark pants, and the bulge under his pants. Your drool rolled down his face and coat into his socks and shoes. You aren't Jesus Christ on the ocean, daddy: you're the Creator of the ocean which houses all the pollution in this world. Custer dragged you away from your delight, sat you down on a curb streaked with dog shit, and walked back to the guy and punched him as hard as he could in the stomach with his left. The rapist collapsed into shit which wasn't his.

'We scrammed. Dad was laughing his head off so hard his head was almost dead. I ran in and out of the stores, using up every coin I had picked out of the street shit. Breads cheeses wines smoked fish fruits cookies like coke cans weighed down my bruised arms.

'And we passed through Ecbatane. We walked to the north of Bezar. And then through Ouranopolis. We came to Myacin where people make fires in clay quarries. These were their homes. They were the bums of this world.

'We saw ex-cons, like us, slouching against the windows of abandoned, broken vans. Fleas were visibly nesting in their shit-stained hairs. Young girls, their daughters probably, were hugging them. Custer ran over to a small fire and threw his arms around some old hag who was squatting down either shitting or because her legs didn't work anymore. She, or someone, had tied a filthy red scarf around her forehead, hippy-style.

'The ex-con said to the old dish who was a bit cracked, "I've bought you an almond cookie. All the way from jail. It's so old now, it's probably cracked."

'The dish just grabbed hold of his hairy arm, all the way past the elbow. Custer, the muscle-man, turned to me. Father was occupied with a blonde stud, playing knucklebones under a huge deserted van. Custer looked at me and motioned to the van.

'Inside two boys were sprawled, asleep, on a heap of glitter and blue chiffon. Wearing lace cut-off slips nippleless bras girls with fingers encircled by ring after ring stroked the boys' limbs. A boy who was lying on his tummy curled his left knee into his belly. I saw, between his newly spread ass-cheeks, shit-crusts. One girl thrust her hand in and kept it there. Custer plopped himself down on the mattress. Another girl snaked her arms round my neck so I was strung up, my memory of a childhood game, against the van's metal door; she dragged me down to the mattress.

'"Don't worry so much, Thivai. Just you stop worrying

'bout a thing. These kids never wash themselves and they don't wipe after they shit."

'While my ice saliva mingled with her saliva perfumed by sugar and incense and rose water in the bowl of my mouth, I felt her rags slap then glued against the skin of my thighs. I felt like vomiting. I tore these rags of dried vomit off my skin. I separated the bare thighs; I put them between my knees; I opened my mouth as widely as I could so the gypsy could inject all her vomitaceous poison into me. Without that I felt I would die.

'I needed her in order to live.

'That night, in the winds swollen by dead meat, I tossed against Custer. We were both sailing on a pirate ship. The young girls were sleeping off sexual desire in another caravan which stood under a chestnut tree. Over branches buttressed by this caravan's roof, within leaves rustling with drops of rain seeds and bird shit: flies tossed, rubbed their faces, buzzed. Female ears, weighted down to the van floor by silver and copper rings, peeked out of their satin sheets and listened, in sleep, to the insects' buzzings crossing the wood laths.

'Outside the camp all was frost. We left the camp. Men were following us. Their lips were blue oysters.

'Fingers of ice stroked the butcher shop. Inside, chestnuts smoked. Father held my left hand and Custer, my right.

'"Goodbye, Thivai. We're going to separate. Cause of the cops. You and your dad: get out of here. I'll go it alone. If you want to see me again, ever: come back here, to the camp. They'll know where to find me. Nowhere.'

'My throat dried into nothing. I died: now I knew I was forever nothing. Not a man, but a whore. Custer removed himself from the picture. Father, like usual, was crying.

'"We'll go back to the whores in Paris," I told him.

'I dragged myself on. Just as if I was lifting weights. The rest of my life was going to be a drag . . .

'. . . I found myself in a lit street. I finally saw a whore whom I approached. If there is any variability to reality – functions which cannot be both exactly and simultaneously measured – reality must simultaneously be ordered and chaotic or simultaneously knowable and unknowable by humans. As soon as I began speaking to the whore, a man pulled me away from her so unexpectedly my foot slipped into the gutter: the bloody mud splashed my toes.

'"Wait next to that cinema over there. I'll be along in about an hour. I've got to finish up now for the evening." The whore patted the skirt-part above one of her thighs.

'I looked at the girl; eyes filled with water looked back at me. A cigarette was trembling its ash. A city was death for some people. I walked away.

'While the cockroaches who had become Kamakaze pilots in their frenzy for Jap fashions, humanoid, were banging themselves to smithereens against blue windows in the buildings under the covered arches made out of dead people's bodies, the intelligentsia of the city's rats were throwing over the tops of garbage cans for nuclear waste. The blackened animals, in front of my eyes, dragged their bones into the whores or holes of the city. One rat looked at me. I saw honey hanging, like an earring made out of drool, from her ear. Her neck was a Rembrandt made out of filth. Blood the same colour as the nailpolish of the hooker I was about to meet painted her teeth and claws. Her nose had the same red, but crusts of white and brown came out of her eyes. Her mouth was a bruise. The bruise, I knew, was going to be me. It was definitively proven that in the urban environment the species of rat has more chance of survival than that of human.

'Wind was sliding along the concrete made out of dead rats and then climbing up my thighs into the sulphur pit surrounding my cock, then up along my ribs whose flesh had otherwise been untouched except for tattoos of pirates standing in their realms of sunken mains and snakes who physically resembled the coasts of those sun-blazed lands, then up to the shoulders. Wind pushed a bit of newspaper on my knee. I crushed it into nothing. Saliva and blood striped my hands. My cock had shrivelled into a bit of newspaper. I threw another bit of newspaper against the wall of a brewery. The wall was graffitied. One of the graffittis was a red circle around a red cross, the anarchist 'A' for those who are beyond death, those who live in the world of Multi-Nationals. Next to the cross were these words, 'LONG LIVE DEATH'.

'I had to return to my place of safety, the only world in which I could be accepted, the brothel. The cops were after me. The black whore walked up to me and grabbed my hand without saying anything.

'Afterwards, in her room, she said, "Tonight you'll be able to sleep."

'The room must have once been part of a girls' school because the bed was narrow and nailed to the wall. The only other furniture was a desk and a sink and bidet. Her skin was the colour of a bruised rose.

'She returned to silence. I touched the flesh. My fingers needed something intangible. Flesh. Behind the door was laughter, the creakings of schoolgirl mattresses, kisses, smacks, sighs, garglings, a cry. The black girl shut the door. I sat down on the edge of the bed.

'Her sheets were rags. Rags sat on rags. Tiny ivory earrings and specks of white powder sat in the middle of the piles of rags. The black dragged me up and against the porcelain sink. She stuck a sponge on my face. Then she actually scrubbed me behind the ears. Though I was too tired to laugh anymore, I laughed myself silly. The black whore held out the red sponge to me, "It's for you, now." She threw the red sponge at me. "C'mon. You're gonna get every piece of dirt offa' that body."

'I plunged the red sponge into the water that was boiling on top of the stove and placed it on my cock. I laughed. The whore's arms were now loads of white rags. "Just rest yourself. I'm gonna get you clean sheets."

'Water was steaming up and streaming down my stomach and legs on to the floor which had become a pond. I carefully placed the red sponge which was now slightly cold on my stomach; the sponge fell down to the floor; the whore returned with her clean rags, put them down on the bed, picked the red sponge off the floor and stuck it into my nose. I squeezed the red sponge over her clothed shoulders. She sat down on the bidet, looked right at the sponge and laughed: "It's for you. You're gonna get every piece of dirt offa' that body."

'I threw the red sponge at her while I carefully explained: "You're dirtier than me: you're black but I'm white."

'"Then screw you blue. Boy. Hurry up 'n wash yourself, boy: It's carnival time! From now on we celebrate! Thea's gonna give us all the cooky and nooky we can eat!"

'She threw the red sponge at me; I threw the sponge off me; I danced around the black; I sank back on her bed. "I want to go. I can't go. Not to carnival. I've been through hell. I killed my mother."

'"It's your decision, mon."

'"You go by yourself. You'll have a great time. Bring me back some cooky?"

'"I'll bring you back fresh whipped cream. I'll pour it right into your scarlet mouth. Now you get into the clean sheets I brought you and don't you think about nothing. You think 'bout nothin' and all good's gonna happen to you. You just get your wet sponge outta my bed right now."

'She left. The door banged shut. The whores, now washed, perfumed, free of men, walked down the stairs. They squawked like the parrots of New Orleans.

'I threw the wet sponge out of her bed.

'I'm a woman and you're a boy. I'm making demands on you that you change yourself. Demands that you don't want to do. And there's no reason you should. Also: you're stifling me: I haven't been happy in your company for a long time. We love each other. We just need to separate ourselves from each other so that each of us can be who we are. So we'll stop making these impossible demands of each other: These winds within my mind woke me up. The light was upset. As I woke up I couldn't distinguish between right and left. I realized my whole spine, the area of my middle right side toward my back, my bladder, deep within my groin, and the tip of my cock were blazing. I thought I must be sick. I must be unable to cope with something. The ceiling, and then the whole sky were sitting on my chest. They were crushing me down. Then everything became one knife. You once wanted to knife me.

The knife came down from the ceiling into my belly and slashed around. The knife cut my throat as if my throat was a pig's bladder which was full of blood. I was a placenta which had been cut open. Yours. Then you, mommy, cut the red cord which united you to me. After you alienated or murdered me, you kissed my mouth and told me you loved me. I awoke: anger made my heart awake. I murdered you: I cut through the red blood that united your mouth and mine: I cut out all emotion which is hatred. I woke up in the only democracy of freedom. I woke up in a black whore's bed. Whatever memory there is of you in me, or of me: get the fuck out of here, mommy! Get out of here before the rats of the city get your body! Rats live in shit and the sewer pits here and they piss on human eyes and their blood hungry teeth kiss red lips. So get out of here, mommy. Rats own the city of piss. Do you know what a rat does to a human? It gets in somewhere, it gets in somebody, it stretches the ass-cheeks so far apart it can get in there and slit. That's the nature of the rat-human relationship. Get out of here, mommy! Get out of here before the rats eat out your heart and tongue!

'But you didn't get out. So now there's no more you. So now there's no more mommy. Men killed you off. Since I'm a man, I killed you off. I killed you.

'No, I couldn't have. You're here, aren't you?

'"Yes," a whore answered. "You're not sleeping."

'I came out of my dream. "No, I'm not sleeping. Come over here, child."

'I'm Antigone. I'm gonna start school next year. If there's a school left in Paris now.'

'"Me: I'm Thivai. I don't have the faintest idea what I'm gonna do. I know what I did:" I told the child who I was. Hopefully. "I killed my mom. Then I became a mercenary. I palled around with Abhor."

'"You smell great. But your forehead's burning up. You sick or somethin'? Maybe that's why mother said you have to stay here 'till she gets back."

'The black girl left the room. It was full morning. I packed my bags. A boy who was chunky rather than fat walked into the room. For some reason when I saw him my heart beat faster. I picked up the plastic bag full of my rags. I couldn't stop looking at him. He sat on the edge of the mattress. I put the grey plastic down so I could turn on the hot water. I took hold of his filthy head and held it under the water. I scrubbed his cheeks and skin with a stone. He acted like he was mute. He touched my eyelids. He touched my shoulders. I took off my clothes. My fingers trembled as they were holding the bottom of my undershirt. All my clothes were wet. I lay down on the mattress and spread my knees apart. The boy took off his clothes except for his once-white undershirt and lay down next to me. He took my hand and held it. I rubbed my body against his body, lifted his almost white undershirt. When I reached his nipples, as if I had been travelling and had finally found home, I kissed them. I reached his cock, which had been buried beneath his balls, which was palpitating. He rolled on my body; his chest hairs stung like coals; my dirty fingernails found bits of soot within his cock hairs; my tongue licked the dirt between his eyelids and eyes.

'I washed him. I dirtied him. I washed him I dirtied him. I washed him I dirtied him. I spit on him I licked him so hard that he fell. On to my plastic rag bag.

'Rising on clenched fists, the young boy said, "Listen. In my womb revolution still thrills. She comes, spurts on my eyelids, gets them all dirty. Now that it's full noon, she's coming in all the mouths in Paris. Whoever will lick and suck this first milk is blessed beyond human." The boy got up. He dressed. He put his makeup on in front of a broken mirror which was already splattered by rouge.

'He left the room.'

Thivai stopped speaking to the whore.

At noon a bunch of kids left their squats. They marched to one of the formerly rich sections of town. They broke into a few abandoned apartment buildings. They busted up whatever furniture and decorator objects they could find. They burned books. When this trash left the buildings, there was a lot of trash left, for the only things they kept were kitchen knives and bathroom razors. They slipped and dug the metal into their own flesh to destroy their own flesh. There was a lot of trash.

'Antigone,' one boy asked a girl who was blacker and younger than him, 'are you a slave?'

The girl touched the ring through her lower lip. 'Do you see this ring through me? Do you know there's one down below? In what society do you think we're living?'

'Me –' the boy, Don, answered, 'I'm free. We've had a revolution. We're the real children of the revolution. I go wherever I want in this city. Now. I might be a physical mess, filthy, crazy cause I'm wrapped up in my own thoughts which still are mirrors of their desires to enslave me: but now I see this. Me. My eyes are naked now.'

'By the end of this winter, I'll be free,' Antigone answered the boy. Now that they were almost vinegared her lips tasted of orange blossoms. The boy took hold of her hair filled with lice, then filled her mouth with sperm. Dawn had burned the sperm into light while his Dr Martin's were burning her toes and his teeth black fingernails and badges were scratching the top layer of skin off her nipples. While the insect riffraff of the war was roaming under the first layer of this skin. Whose freedom is dirt? Antigone thought to herself while she was sucking his cock. Her mouth left the cock once it was clean. She didn't cry though she wanted to. She leaned herself against the boy's shoulder so the boy, drunk as a skunk from booze and coming, fell into the mud in the gutter and vomited into the black . . .

In the livingroom of their squat two twins slept, entwined on a couch.

Audry, Abhor's sister, threw her hands up at the black sky as if to catch something; she cried out that this dawn was tormenting her cheeks.

A mosquito was rocking itself to sleep on a pile of green seaweed. Audry touched St Bubu's temples, 'Since dawn, Bubu, there's been a baby moving inside me. She's the last-born of this old world. Rats made her.'

II The Beginning of Criminality/ The Beginning of Morning

(*Abhor speaks*)

I lie vulnerable to the genesis of this dawn.

Yes. The Algerian revolution had succeeded. Whatever political success is worth.

I didn't know where Thivai was. Where in hell Thivai was. In the post-apocalyptic mess. Fuck him, he was only a man. Men, especially straight men, aren't worth anything. Anymore. A bit like success. Maybe, before the revolution, men had been too successful. Anyway, most humans are now women. In this city, women are just what they always were, prostitutes: They live together and they do whatever they want to do.

I felt like a mutant in such a social, socialized city, but I've always felt as if I don't belong. In this city, I didn't belong absolutely because I'd never tricked, for sexuality was too devastating to me, and because I'm used to having Thivai around so that I can hate his guts.

Since I understand why there are only women in this world and I don't understand at all, I feel strange to myself: I don't know whether or not I know and can know.

But I made an important decision. I decided if urban areas are now composed of yuppies and mutants, I'm a mutant.

Since I was a mutant from outer space who was living in exile in Paris, Paris looked as if it was made up of glass. Glass cuts through the flesh. Paris was a bloody city. Rectangular blocks of mirrored glass intersected tall buildings of black glass about a quarter way down their lengths. Some of the mirrored glass then sloped either to rectangular patches of fake green grass or to red concrete fountains. These Parks For The New Bourgeois Workers seemingly intangibly, seamlessly metamorphosed into the largest bank in the world. Under the bank, there was a building of opaque grey glass which was nameless. 'Nameless' meant 'useful'; there was no end to the depth of the building.

Someone may wonder whether in a post-industrial world a revolution can change a city's architecture. Or anything.

The streets were now the property of cars. The cars were now the property of those who had real (government) jobs. No prostitute had a car. This is why there were almost only women in the visible world. The men who worked in the corporations spent so much time in the corporations or driving to and from the corporations inside mirrored styrofoam cars, they were no longer visible. They were dead.

The urban areas of the Western world were now composed of dead and mutants. I was confused to the point of psychosis because I wasn't sure what I was.

Thivai was gone. I wondered what it was to have a friend. A friend who didn't go away. It seemed to me that human identity had to begin with and in friendship.

Since, not even clearly, I wasn't anyone, I was catatonic. Since it didn't matter what I did, it didn't matter to either the dead or to anyone alien, I decided I had to get my hair cut off. That would be the next step to getting a limb cut off. Only a criminal could get a limb cut off. Before the Algerian revolution, there had been only women's haircutters and men's haircutters in Paris. No women's haircutter would do anything to a woman's hair besides trimming, perming, styling, teasing, then holding it in place with silicone. I realized that the Algerian revolution had changed nothing. There is always a reason for nihilism.

My main problem was now that I still didn't know enough French to talk whatever haircutter I might happen to find into cutting my hair. Off. Off. Off. Off. Most haircutters still had morals. Revolutionaries are always puritanical. My ignorance of morals gave me something to do. I did what I always do. Just as a bee goes to honey and then with the honey back to the Queen Bee who's going to off him, I half ran half wandered to the slummiest part of town. Where the sailors were. I know one thing for sure: in this world, right-wing or left, there are always slums. Only with the right-wing all places besides the homes of the upper middle-class are slums. Me, I went north.

There were neither gardens nor planes about to take off nor buildings. There was nothing. Just like my heart. Thivai was gone. I found a haircutter who was willing to cut off my hair. The front of her shop, SHOT, was three grey Venetian blinds. A pair of scissors hanging from a string in front of the blinds indicated the purpose of SHOT. The blinds concealed an operating room. Just as outside the scissors hung from the blinds, inside a pair of grey handcuffs hung from a string from the ceiling. Under no circumstances were the customers allowed to touch their own hair. On one of the white walls there was a black-and-white photograph of a woman in a black corset blindfolded and handcuffed in leather restraints.

I felt so comfortable, when I was inside this operating room, I began to dream. The haircutter, one of the few women who wasn't a prostitute (due to her profession), was stocky. Her hair was dead, white. I was dreaming. When she asked me what I wanted to look like, I replied, 'Yours.' The truth always surprises me.

She didn't ask me again what, who, I wanted until she had shaved off my hair.

She sliced off most of my black hairs with razors without cutting through my flesh once, then carved lines into the fur which remained. 'Do you want to see yourself in a mirror?'

'No.' I've never been able to or interested in recognizing myself.

I still sat in that leather chair. Her wide hands were holding my head between them. Then she asked me if I wanted anything. *What* is always equal to *who*.

'Then go.'

Because I'm stupid, it's taken me half a lifetime – stealing from a government, an evil one, as governments go, killing a boss, as bosses go, a revolution, blood upon blood on every level of human existence, as blood flows – for me to learn that I have to say what I want to get what I want. Who. Perhaps if human desire is said out loud, the urban planes, the prisons, the architectural mirrors will take off, as airplanes do. The black planes will take off into the night air and the night winds, sliding past and behind each other, zooming, turning and turning in the redness of the winds, living, never to return. Red fingernails will scrape the sky of living flesh. If I could have spoken at that minute to the haircutter, perhaps I could have been free!

The word *free* means nothing to me. I left. Walking past a pile of rubble was being in a panic. Because rubble was the memory of Thivai. I remembered being panicked all the time Thivai was my partner.

I remember. He might have or might not have been my boyfriend. He cared about me and he didn't care about me. Since I gave and he took, everything was about him. Since everything was about him, everything he thought about me was true of him. Since I remember I was nothing, my memory is nothing.

To remember is to beat war.

Since we were mercenaries, and thus lived in a world which was adversarial, and partners: our partnership was adversarial. The particulars of this partnership, a partnership of life and death, were that at every possible moment we undermined, subverted, and feared one another. Because we were partners, we didn't attack each other directly. Because we had no other partners besides each other, there was no escape for either of us from the reality of each of our attacks.

Perhaps I was remembering heterosexuality. Whatever remembering is worth.

I no longer remembered. Without my memory I realized

reality was gone. There was no one. I panicked. There was no feeling. I didn't have to cry because, inside, my stomach and intestines were crying themselves into shreds as my blood, crying, dripped through its arteries and veins into the places to which it wasn't supposed to go. My body bloated with winds. The winds were as red as my fingernails. Material tears, the tears of the body, neither bring relief nor can ever be entirely healed.

Of course time cures everything. Human. It does because that time which will come, the future, is never present. Since everything will happen in the future: the present, me, was null.

I was the only end which could be present. If I was an end to the present, and I was: in the future there will be no end to human tears.

Since I saw no temporal possibility to other than the present, I saw no possibilities. Thivai was gone. I panicked.

Sailors appeared everywhere on the street. They jostled against each other. Even in the black of light, in the heat which remained from the now – absent sun, their tattoos gleamed.

I've always wanted to be a sailor.

The demand for an adequate mode of expression is senseless. Then why is there this searching for an adequate mode of expression? Was I searching for a social and political paradise? Since all acts, including expressive acts, are inter-dependent, paradise cannot be an absolute. Theory doesn't work.

Throughout history most normal people have thought that sailors are immoral and should be burned. Despite the Algerian revolution, this is still true. There have also and are now a few people, human fringes, scraps of dog food hidden in cracks under shoes, who say that sailors' hairs are silver and that sailors have huge dicks. Female. For today some sailors are female.

Those who despise and spit at sailors agree that sailors have dicks. They say that sailors have huge dicks because sailors're trying to take over their moral societies. Sailors leave anarchy in their drunken wakes. A sailor's left hand lies in his pocket because it is a knife. The knife of the hand will slice off the knife of the law.

I say that a sailor is someone who came out of poverty which was hateful. Because a sailor has spat on and shits on poverty, the sailor knows that the worst poverty is that of the heart. All good sailors espouse and live in the material simplicity which denies the poverty of the heart. Reagan's heart is empty. A sailor is a human who has traded poverty for the riches of imaginative reality.

Such an act constitutes destruction of society thus is criminal. Criminal, continuously fleeing, homeless, despising property, unstable like the weather, the sailor will wreck any earthbound life. He or she who has been killed, kills. Don't trust them. A sailor has a lover in every port and doesn't know how to love. Heart upon heart sits tattooed on every sailor's ass.

Though the sailor longs for a home, her or his real love is change. Stability in change, change in stability occurs only imaginarily. No roses grow on sailors' graves.

This long night made fears rise: longings, lusts, remembrances. The night brought emotions which were ferocious as the winds. I watched the sky and the winds fuck. I needed to fuck and be fucked. I watched the sailors wandering in and out of the shadows of low buildings and alleys, directly searching for and finding what I was too shy to find for myself. Because I, Abhor, couldn't act for myself, I watched them having sex.

The town was fog and granite which had decimated into pale pink. The sort of thing my mother used to make me wear. The sailors were places to which, as yet, I hadn't dared to venture. They were those humans whom no other human would dare to touch.

Just outside this port, the ship VENGEANCE sat on slate. Slate was a long piece of shit. The part of the land right next to the dead ocean belonged to the Customs' office, no man's land. Dead land. It was there that most naval crime took place.

Right beyond the barrier, a multitude-of-times-beaten-up old hag, by now a crag, who used to be a smack-head until her flesh had petrified, just like some old sailor to whom junk is the sea, had set up her shop. A shack. She told the fortunes of those whose only fortune was living death in a city where there was no future. For these services, the riffraff gave her their criminal money. She told these death tunes with cards which were so filthy none of the pictures enscribed on them were visible. Thus, The Crag, as she was called, always gave the same fortune: You will fall in Love. Beware a dark stranger. You will become deathly sick in a foreign land. On the same side of every card was the picture of a young naked girl whose breasts were gargantuan and whose nipples were blood.

Since I knew I didn't have a fortune, I walked into her shop to get my fortune told. I usually wear men's clothes. Why, I don't know. I'm not a Freudian. At that moment, I was wearing the accoutrements of a naval lieutenant. I had traded in a moth-eaten dead animal coat for these clothes in a second-hand punk store in Copenhagen. The Danes love animals. Punk died eleven years ago. As soon as the crone got a glimpse of me, she placed her cards under her feet on the cement and kicked them three times. There are different ways of shuffling cards. I'm no moralist. And she must have been a lazy old bitch. Then she spat on them. If there had been more, or any, light than the one dim lightbulb which was on, the spit would have been green. There was so much spit, it was drool. Sort of like language. 'The lieutenant's situation,' she gurgled up, 'is that he's a goodtime Charlie whose only thoughts are for booze and friends. Sure he can get it up for young girls, whom in his mind he covers with the tenderest of kisses before pulling the sheets up to their cheeks. After all is over. Always over too soon or too late. The lieutenant will always be lonely. So lonely that the lieutenant will feel that loneliness is equivalent to him.'

Obviously, she had me wrong.

'Ask a question,' The Crag regurgitated.

Was it possible that someday – someday – I would hold naked in my arms, and continue to hold and continue to hold, pressed close to my body, a woman on whose femininity and masculine strength I could lean, trusting, whose mettle and daring would place her so high in my esteem that I would long to throw myself at her feet and do as she wished? I dared hardly believe what I was asking. I dared hardly believe myself.

'The lieutenant is trying to repress his sexual desires. His foul cock. The lieutenant is struggling not to fall overboard, but he must fall overboard if he's to experience anything besides loneliness. The lieutenant must fall overboard if he's going to experience pleasure or pain. Pleasure and pain are always fucking.' The tenderness of these words overwhelmed me, for I knew I no longer wanted any men. 'You know your own rotten situation:' the rotten gypsy said. 'Your situation is that at this moment you're rotten with desires to fuck. How much money are ya gonna give me now, sailor? As far as sailors go, and they go far, you're rotten.'

'Tell me some more.'

Then, the rot-toothed-and-mouthed gypsy with a tube of crimson lipstick drew a crown on the cement. She drew a naked dame to the left of this crown. The dame's breasts were so large, she was almost sitting on them. 'This' what you want.' The rotted crag giggled. 'You're gonna be insanely jealous of this one cause she's got big bazooms.'

I wanted to say I didn't have a lover. I wanted to say that the lonely never know jealousy, only despair. For any motion which a lonely person – a sailor – makes toward another person, being denied, is thrown back on the sailor like wet cloth. The sea was cold.

In order to survive a sailor's muscles must be huge. Maybe I had known jealousy, I had known love in the past, but it was past. *Past* is *dead*. Thivai wasn't a cause for jealousy: he was dead. I yelled, 'Fuckin' bitch.'

The bitches weren't fucking.

'Fuckin' bitch. Death is floating down the Seine. Where's this future which you're telling me? Where's this fortune which you're telling me?'

'I'm telling you your past.' She drew a card through whose dirt a sailor was lying on his back on a tomb. He appeared to be smiling. 'You've been smart about your life, lieutenant. Maybe too smart. Maybe that's how you got to be where you are. In order to survive, simply because life isn't survivable, or knowable or humanly controllable for that matter, but what matter: you've had to pit your will against all desire, your own and others. Your will is strong and your sexuality's repressed.

'But what of the dreams which the ocean brings? Have you forgotten, lieutenant? What is the imagination of the fish? Have you forgotten, lieutenant? In order to survive haven't you thrown away the best part of yourself? This is your past: no roses will grow on a sailor's grave.'

When I placed my hand on her rotted calf so that I could win her sympathy, feeling didn't touch her face. She wasn't going to want to fuck with me. She told me that when she had been a child, her father had raped her. She had guiltlessly induced the rape – seduced him – the father. 'The hell with the past. Ask me about the present.'

Outside her, the night was red and purple blood. All the sailors were looking to fuck each other.

I removed my hand to nowhere. 'Should I go back to the haircutter's shop?'

'Your heart is broken.'

'That's nothing new.'

'Your heart is broken. At the present you don't love anybody. No one loves you. Without relationships, a man's lost at sea. So lost, waves leap like living walls, he can no longer see through. Look out the door.' Outside the night was red and purple blood. All the sailors were looking to fuck each other.

'What else do you want to know?'

I was scared of the shadows of this town, of the shadows of sailors' fingernails, of the shadows of ants, of the shadows of the knives of control. I wanted her to tell me reality; I wanted her to tell me what to do. I must have been two people. I must have been thousands of people. I desired exactly that which I couldn't accept. 'Gypsy, I want to know the source of dreams.'

Finally the old crone and I were going somewhere. Like sailors who were having dreams. Somewhere was nowhere.

'As soon as you step out of here, everything in your life will be exactly as it was. You will spend all your time sleeping. When you sleep, you will dream you have a lover. She will be about to come. Always about to come. Your body straining to come into her will waken you. In comparison with this woman whom you just were forced to leave, all other people will be remote to you, unreal. For your lips will still be warm with her lips. For your hips will still be aching with her heaviness. If she happens to resemble one or several women in your waking life, you will search for her through your waking hours. Sailors set out on perilous journeys just so that they can see in actuality cities they have only imagined. People generally believe they can see and have in actuality what has charmed them only in their fantasies. This memory of love will dissolve until you have forgotten there is love. After dissolution, the people among whom you've searched, the sailors, will be the only people you know.'

I told The Crag I didn't know any sailors. 'Who are they?'

'Sex's going to get you into trouble.'

'What kind of trouble, ma'am?'

'I've had enough trouble with you. Get out of here.'

The town was fog and granite which had decimated into pale grey. About forty years ago, the port had received tourist and the more expensive part of a vast international shipping trade. Even Hollywood movie stars had walked out of the pale green and pale pink deco hotels to a beach, which had subsequently mutilated into garbage, whose whiteness would rival their own superstardom. At night there were no colours. Today, only a few old white people whose memories are Stephen King novels sat in wheelchairs on the steps of the remains of the Grand Hotels. At night, the old white people disappeared. Below the ruins of art, members of the navy and Merchant Marines idled in the alleyways. Gypsies and tattoo artists hid behind wood slats and sheets of aluminium. These scum at the edge of criminality were all Cuban: almost every toilet, shack, and bar was filled with useless fetishes: candles and dolls, pictures of the Holy Virgin Mary as a mermaid always unable to fuck the lonely sailor. Christ's wounds, the colour of shit, flowed into the earth. The night was Christ's brown wounds.

A pair of Cuban twins dominated the sailor section of Paris.

Though only one of them was a sailor, they dressed exactly alike. Huge calf muscles burst through slightly flared pants legs, for they were among the few sailors who were male. The older one by exactly three minutes, Agone, as a child, in the way that kids want to be ballerinas or cops, had hoped to become a criminal. The older he became, the more he hoped to become exactly what he couldn't be. For he, like his twin, was a true artist: together they had frescoed the insides of all the cheap Cuban cafes. Their frescoes revealed pimps with wide-brimmed white hats sitting on black cars, waiting for the rich white men whose puffy chin skin hung down like sausages who were dealing smack to the teenage prostitute whose facial pockmarks foretold, to the Chicanos and Cubans, the end of this white world. Their frescoes were the memories of Chicano America.

Since Agone couldn't be anymore criminal than this, he ran away to sea.

Though the revolution in Paris had eradicated most of the middle class, the middle-class cops were left. These cops, dumb as they come, (a human has to pass a test of dumbness in order to become a cop), still considered the pornographers, the massage parlour workers, the streetwalkers, and the homosexuals who openly committed 'crimes of sex' in the urban shadows of corners their main, often only, enemies. Whereas, the closeted homosexuals were the cops' heroes. In fact, half of the cops, the ones who saw anti-pornography legislation as the centre of their existences, were closeted gays. Beneath this concrete of repression, the sailors and cops loved one another.

As soon as Agone became a sailor, he cut himself off from his younger brother. This brother worked for the flics, designing guns for them. He finally adopted the belief that his older brother was a pervert and a criminal. Thus, when Agone believed that the cops had his number, he wasn't being totally paranoid.

Agone wore the same thing every day: slightly flared pants, the huge black sailors' shoes that cushion the tenderest of feet, and a black wool sweater. He didn't care what he wore, for clothes could never make him criminal enough. Since society hates and casts out its lonely, therefore its sexual perverts, Agone would never find criminality which could be equal to his loneliness.

The first time I saw him was in a bar near the haircutter's shop. I don't remember why I started following Agone. Maybe it was because he knew his own power. He would stand stock still and let the rest of the mutant humans, of that reality turn around him. There was a smile deep inside him. In me there was the memory of my dream.

It was, perhaps strangely, perhaps not strangely, in this place, which was really too sleazy to be a bar, that I began to find my dream's face. Fake glass chandeliers were hanging from a ceiling some of whose parts were hanging lower than the red lights. The lizard was shedding its skin. Yards of red velvet and dried urine sheltered dry rot and cockroaches, both living and dead. Perhaps there are Martians. The 'bar' was a mixture of falsity and death, a mirror of the pre-revolutionary wealth. It was now a sailors' bar.

One of the sailors, having turned up the colour, was buttoning up her thick wool coat. One of the sailors had a huge sapphire and crimson panther tattooed over her left buttock. Agone was comfortable only here. Why? How did he know he was a monster? As he told me later, as a child he had been a victim of incest. 'Like most women.' As with most of his statements, I didn't know whether I should believe this.

I wanted his comfortableness with himself and the world, his swagger, his ability to be in the world, his hands-in-the-pocket; I wanted him to show me how to go somewhere. Somewhere I knew and didn't know. He was my thread and my Ariadne who would take me to the criminal.

I used to think I was a lost being. That I didn't fantasize. That I had no sexual desire. Real sexuality or identity. Lost in a maze that, perhaps, was politically controlled. Just Agone's physical presence somehow mirrored, presented to me a sexuality which was mine and which I had never known. Due to Agone, I was no longer nothing. I was now on my way to being somebody. A criminal.

Holding on to Agone's hand, I entered the world of muddy rivers, the Amazon, whose jungles were so entangled that the wings of vultures, being almost useless, grew monstrous. Entered the endless areas of the heart. I became afraid, for the moment, not that I had found a self I had once rejected, but that the serenity which had descended upon me would, as it was appearing, prove to be false. For this reason I needed Agone although he would remain a stranger.

In the bar, I thought to myself about that woman about whom I had dreamed: What do I want of her? I should adore if – no, I don't want anything that stupid, that fearful! – I really should adore if she was feminine and a motorcycle rider. Tough as any weathered rider! Then I'd be able to ask her what to do!

The sailor walked out of the bar into the street. By the time I had realized this and left the pub, he had disappeared. Two gulls were fucking. The lower gull stood on one of the few aluminium roofs which was still intact. She spread out wings tipped in the sky as if she was flying. The other gull stuck claws into the fur below the back of her neck and climbed on to that back. A haystack in the burning sun. He maintained his balance with difficulty. He moved his tail from side to side and his cock inside metronomically. Their feathers rustled. Their movements lasted for twenty minutes. He straightened his spine, spread his wings out, and screamed. The bottom gull hadn't moved once. He fell off her. Her smile left and she looked confused.

Still in my men's clothes, I wondered whether any human sexuality remained. Certainly there's human sexual desire, for it's desire that sends a human off to sea.

The vestibule of the largest brothel in this part of the port was empty. Its Madame entered the room, alone, and took a shot of Remy. She was about forty years old and in better shape than most twenty-year-olds, being a body-builder. In the last five years she had placed in seven amateur contests. Her brown and red hair curled around her jugular. She no longer got periods.

She was thinking about that. It must be due either to

weight-lifting or to middle-age. Perhaps, she would never bleed again. So much for blood. Perhaps periods were the same thing as sexual love. Her hand touched her cunt lips through the material of her boxer shorts.

Mathilde want to shave off her cunt hair again, Madame thought. (Mathilde was Madame's lover.) Shit. I hope she uses an electric shaver. Depilatories are worse than hydrochloric acid. Hand razors pull out the hair with its flesh. She's going to hurt herself again. Why do women have to be so self-destructive? Cunts . . .

She'd better tell her immediately not to shave too closely and to stay away from the vulva.

Just as the Madame, too caught in her own thoughts, was thinking she'd better go to her friend immediately, Agone knocked on the inner door.

'Boss?'

He walked into the room without caring about the boss' answer. She didn't glance at the perfectly shaped buttocks of the sailor.

'Mommy Death,' Agone was thinking to himself. 'Mommy Death, you died before I had a chance to believe that reality was anything but inimical to my wishes. My wishes to love you. Mommy Death, don't be scared.' He must have been thinking of someone else, for the Madame wasn't frightened of anyone. 'In no way am I cured. Maybe I can't be cured now that I'm a sailor. I'm a wall whose surrounding territories are homeless and who's impervious to the weather. And what there is of me that's still human – desiring – slips like a shadow in an alleyway at night along the looming piss-stained wall.

'Finally they're going to take me away cause I'm not human.' This is what the sailor thought. 'They tried to throw their nets over me when I was a kid. I escaped them: their rules. I don't sink like a dead fish. Then they came to take me away with hypocritical social smiles which uncovered the crimson teeth of shark. When they finally caught me, they lay me out on an operating table otherwise full of cucumber sandwiches and tea cakes.'

'How soon'll it be here?' the boss asked.

'They stuffed my ears full of wax so I couldn't hear the lies in their words.'

'I want the drugs. How long'll it take to deliver?'

Agone woke up to his situation. He had to do what he was told so that he could get money. He hated this. Her. Himself. Anger like wax flowed through his stomach and sealed it up. His being was rigid. 'Drugs?'

'No. I want a condom so we can fuck.'

'I have to get them out.' Agone almost said 'Sir'.

Madame wouldn't deign to look at her servant and the sailor was too stiff with anger to see anything. To each other they were speaking words from two different worlds. The Madame had had enough. 'Forget it.' She turned the muscles of her back.

'Don't go back on me,' the sailor pleaded. 'I'll get it out somehow.'

He imagined himself drawn and quartered. Bound he could no longer hear the roses screaming, nor the plops of the eyes which were being plucked out of the drug dealers who'd been caught. Eyes were being plucked out and dropped. Because society had dropped them out.

Agone thought: survival's not possible. It's impossible to survive when survival's not possible. I'd have to be drunk. I've got to get money so I can survive. I've got to get the drugs across Customs. To do that, I can't see what I'm seeing. I can't feel what I'm feeling. I can't see the prison bars. I can't feel these prison bars. I can't hear the old woman scream as her daughter puts a cigarette out in her eye.

I must not hear what's left of my living body slip like a shadow at night along the looming piss-stained wall that separates the international and French sections.

Agone felt so faint that he'd do whatever the Boss told him.

As soon as he left the brothel, he regained his strength. He'd been vomiting himself out for the sake of money. 'I'm strong enough to vomit,' Agone thought to himself and thus was able to draw all his selves into one unit. 'Mommy Death, don't be scared. Your son is the bearer of drugs, Hermes and Baron

Samedi.' This criminality, being not the criminality of the businessman or of society, but that of the disenfranchised, reminded him that he was absolutely alone. The Customs wall was impenetrable. He was human and absolutely alone.

He walked along the concrete street for several minutes, then turned right up another concrete street. All the streets were the same. What was the nature of bosses? As street drifted into street under his feet, one unpleasant thought drifted into new unpleasantness. The nature of bosses is to get whatever and whoever they want however they have to. One would expect the disenfranchised to revolt against the rich and the bosses. Those who don't have should know they don't have, that there are those who do, and that those who have are controlling them. Sure. No man wants to be a worm. Have a boss. But it was precisely the wretched masses in Germany, Agone thought, who helped put Fascism into power. And it was that class in the United States who are moving from middle-class splendour down to lower-class or, rather, no-class stagnation who put Reagan, for instance, in power and gave way fully to the Multi-Nationals.

The Boss is going to double-cross, Agone reasoned. He thought about a case he had known. In the late 1960s, the United States again, doesn't the United States ever go away? dumb hippies would cross the Mexican border in order to play with the cool Mexicans and score. They'd find weed practically growing wild. Mexicans were always happy to sell them some. Then the Mexicans would phone Customs. When the stupid American was back at his own border, Customs would confiscate the drug, throw the child into jail. The Mexicans would get their grass back plus make the money the American parents had to pay in order to get their brat out of jail. There was a moral. Agone shook his head. Never have a baby. The Mexican dealer would make the drug-deal money and the payoff Customs gave him for squealing.

Dealers and cops always work together because they're bosses. Drugs are bad for you, the sailor contrived to reason, only cause there are bosses.

He looked down, found a butt in the gutter, rescued the

baby, scraped a dot of dogshit off it, and lit it. But what about me?

If I smuggle the O through Customs for the Boss, how's she going to screw me? Agone contrived to reason. If she rats to the pigs, she loses her drug. Though she's a whore, she ain't dumb. She wouldn't just give away a drug to a dumb cop. Furthermore she wouldn't squeal on me cause she herself is on the wrong side of the law, naturally, and therefore she's naturally and automatically guilty of every crime. Since she's in danger, she has to toady up to the cops. She probably fucks them, the whore, fucks them for free: It's her whore-like nature. The sailor's left hand rubbed the hair which wasn't on his head. If my boss is working with the cops, which she must be – her lover's a cop – she'll turn me in just so she can maintain her status in the world. That's how this world is. So that's how bosses are . . .

The sailor's left hand rubbed the hair which wasn't on his head. Maybe O's evil cause look where O's going to get me. As for bosses . . . I have to consider this business of bosses further. Madame's boss is the cops. Madame's dominated by them. The dominated classes' ideological structures, obviously, determine whether or not they'll continue to be dominated. After all, she could always say 'No'. The whore. Now: just as the dominated classes' ideological structures determine their future political, economic, and moral situations: my own view of my position to my boss determines my relation to my boss. These thoughts in the sailor went round and round like hamsters strung out on dex. The boss is my boss cause I do what she tells me. Since what she's telling to do is criminal, I'm . . . fucked.

His thoughts, being thoughts, went round even faster. Now, I understand. By smuggling the O, I'm walking right into a nest of drugged-out wasps. Right into prison. No matter. For the moment, we're helpless, we sailors, to blow up our bosses.

The sailor's left hand rubbed the hair which wasn't on his head. The fog around the head was as thick as ever. He would again give into weakness, his evil; he would do as the Boss ordered; he would smuggle in the O. The world was reduced to evil, to just tactics, to how.

There are no more decisions, Agone thought, for in this unending growth of multinational capitalism, nothing ever changes.

The fog was as thick as left-over sperm which has turned grey.

Now the sailor thought this: Night's the time to do it. It's tomorrow night that I'm going to do it. There'll probably be fog. Certain of it. I'll be able to edge through the fog like a bunch of criminals till I reach the wall. That wall looms: easy enough to find. Not easy to escape. Not easy to get through. I'll slip against it till I reach that sewer pipe. I'll know it when I smell it. This fog right now's so thick. It's solid. I can't do it alone. There has to be another sailor. She'll have already thrown a string tied around a rock over the wall. You can always smell shit. This fog's so thick, even the people who're being murdered scream in safety. I'll substitute the stuff and the stone. Then tug. Fog hides everything, like sperm.

At that moment I was thinking this: Still wearing lieutenant's drag. I must have looked like a boy to him. It's not that I don't enjoy fucking men. It's just that every time a guy's screwed me more than twice, he's thought he could tell me what to do. Since I had to fight the fucker for my own power, my life: I either gave up the fuck or gave up myself. Usually myself cause I like fucking so much. Fucked up. I don't want to be fucked up, no more, thank you, sir.

Now let's look at this more carefully. Don't want to be simplistic. Why, I don't know. If you ask me: throw it all away. But now that I'm a lieutenant in the British navy, I must be rational. Any slut, I mean *man*, used to be able to persuade me to fuck him just by fucking me. I wasn't into compliments. I wasn't into being feminine. Physical pleasure was . . . pleasure. It was such pleasure that I just gave myself to him, whoever, so that he could really do it to me. Fucked and fucked and fucked. 'Do anything to me, baby. You're all that I want.'

He did everything to me to such an extent, I no longer was. In order to live again, I had to stop fucking the fucker.

No wonder heterosexuality a bit resembles rape.

What the hell's happening to me now? Me, Abhor. Do I hate fucking? Where's physical pleasure in my life? Physical pleasure can only be pleasurable if it is pleasurable, not the cause of suffering and fighting all the time. I'm beginning to believe that physical pleasure can be pleasurable now.

A man's power resides in his prick. That's what they, whoever they is, say. How the fuck should I know? I ain't a man. Though I'm a good fake lieutenant, it's not good enough to have a fake dick. I don't have one. Does this mean I've got no strength? If it's true that a man's prick is his strength, what and where is my power? Since I don't have one thing, a dick, I've got nothing, so my pleasure isn't any one thing, it's just pleasure. Therefore, pleasure must be pleasurable. Well, maybe I've found out something, and maybe I haven't.

When I met the matelot again, I realized I had met change in myself. Since it was change, I had no way of being conscious of what was happening to me. Since I without doubt knew I had to remain with this guy and since I didn't know why – he wasn't and he wasn't going to be my lover – he frightened me. Fear has never been anything but incentive to a sailor to follow the far seas.

The town was covered in fog thicker than dead sperm.

'Are you sure you should be so far away from your ship?'

He looked down at me. 'Are you scared of something, punk? You're too young to be scared of nothin'.' I must have looked like a young boy to him.

'I'm not scared for myself. You're going to get into trouble.' I paused. 'You're going to get into trouble some day. There are diseases.'

'I'm too old and I've almost died too many times,' the young man shoved his hands into his groin in reaction to his own words, 'to care about dying. What's the danger in this dead town?'

I didn't know what I wanted to tell him. Not to leave me alone. Until. Perhaps until death. Please don't leave me alone.

'I can't tell you anything. But there are men around here. They don't mean well – they mean shit. This town has been . . . , it's a town of the dead. Like London. England.' I looked over my left or dead or red shoulder at the wharf buildings in the Customs area. The buildings looked like giant rats gnawing on humans' red digestive systems. The grey rats were larger than the buildings. Less formed.

'A lot of men want me. I've got you,' the sailor replied.

I wondered if the sailor knew what he had gotten. When I had been a kid, I had one, or one recurrent type of, dream. I was going somewhere. The place to where I was going was unknown. It was the unknown.

To get there, first I crossed an uncrossable sea. The sea was the river several hundred yards below the concrete park wall in front of my rapist father's house. A narrow dirt path one day appeared on the surface of the river of garbage. I easily walked across.

I reached either an island or a peninsula. There, there was a merry-go-round which was multi-coloured. I kept walking straight through the carnival still on a narrow dirt road. I travelled through cities, or a city, through lands, or a land. I definitely walked over a long and high steel-girded bridge. After that, the path kept simultaneously turning right and narrowing, the land might have been turning and narrowing, turning in on itself, a snake whose head is looking for its tail, turning in on myself. The centre of me was monstrous and unknowable. The monster took me in his arms.

I wasn't sure he knew what he was getting: I was the wrong sex. But I would do anything so that he wouldn't leave me. I had to find out.

'You don't fit into my world.' The sailor was rejecting me and telling me I couldn't be a sailor like him. I could only be no one because I had no sexuality. But the tar started mumbling to himself, 'Oh, stay around. Young enough for a night. What do I care about that – trivia – anymore? There's work to do. I have to get the boss her O. Maybe I shouldn't. Hot water. My thoughts're burning. If I don't do it, I'll have nothing. I'll be

. . . nothing. Either criminal or zero,' he kept babbling to himself uselessly.

At this point we were walking down a street narrow enough to be an alley whose horizontal limits were bars lit by pink and orange neon lights. One of us was a real sailor and one of us was fake. Here and there, a few punks, leftover, indefinable as to sexual gender, sat on stone steps which led either to one of the bars or to nothing.

At 4:00 in the morning between a hundred and two hundred kids vulnerable in black leather sat or lay on this street. There were no more cars because there were no more businessmen. The world was still. The children talked to each other calmly, drank from bottles of vodka and whiskey. They seemed to have no sexual desire. Now and then, in the black, a tan switchblade flashed. The switchblade was useless.

There was one Denny's which was still open. Hot dogs which were probably the dicks of dead dogs were slotted out on thick white paper. Paper was the most edible substance there. The children who desired to eat, eating wasn't necessary to them, covered the paper with thick mustard the colour of shit. The mustard sat in large red plastic bowls. It was all as colourful as the human digestive system.

Beyond the Denny's there was a store which was so narrow and signless, it was invisible. The sailor walked into this store.

As he entered the shop, he felt himself to be in a 'mysterious region', a place more precious than any he had ever visited. Here must be his sexual desire. White papers of all sizes covered the clean white walls. Female pirates, snakes winding around razor-sharp white swords, sapphire cats larger than a human head whose fingernails were black or blackened roses, anchors stuck into the tails of larget scarlet and magenta fish whose eyes held the maps of treasures seized through murder, and other oddities of the rainbow covered the white pieces of paper. The walls were worlds. In the back, a clean white operating bench ran from wall to wall. The man who was facing us, resting his right elbow on the operating table, was both shrunken and lively. Not a shrunken head, yet.

The sailor held his eyes on the old-seeming man and the old-seeming man kept his eyes in his secret space.

Cruel Romans had used tattoos to mark and identify mercenaries, slaves, criminals, and heretics.

For the first time, the sailor felt he had sailed home.

Among the early Christians, tattoos, stigmata indicating exile, which at first had been forced on their flesh, finally actually served to enforce their group solidarity. The Christians began voluntarily to acquire these indications of tribal identity. Tattooing continued to have ambiguous social value; today a tattoo is considered both a defamatory brand and a symbol of a tribe or of a dream.

In 1769, when Captain James Cook 'discovered' Tahiti, he thought he had sailed to paradise. In Tahitian, writing is 'ta-tau'; the Tahitians write directly on human flesh.

'I . . .' the sailor ventured.

The old-seeming man next to the operating table moved as much as his eyes moved.

'I . . .' the sailor tried again.

'Do you want something?' I realized that tattoos were completely covering the artist's body. In the grey dark, they looked like wrinkles. His left hand was holding a cigar. He stubbed it out in an ashtray made out of his hand.

'You tell fortunes, don't you? One of my mates said you did.'

'You must have lost your way, sailor. It's dark around here. It's only dark around here.'

'One of my mates said you tell men's fortunes.'

'I make fortunes here. I don't need to tell or be told anything. For me the only telling's making.'

'What do you make?'

'You need to make a decision. Ever seen a cat who's been given two contradictory orders? The cat handles the contradiction by becoming catatonic. Maybe there's something you don't understand. Some catatonia. I can give you what you want if you want me to.'

'I have to smuggle something,' Agone answered.

It was as if I was watching two ships pass in the night. The night of fogged-away ports. Ships look for ways out of the wet and cold. Ships blow their horns to find out if anyone else's around. Look for an end to wandering, for earth, end, death. The lost children in the city wanted to die.

I would have closed my eyes, too tightly to ever open them again, a long time ago, but I'm too proud to ask even death for help. Like a tiny boat which is afloat, I float along with things. Out of the shadow to the left of the door, I watched the two men.

'No man can make fortune. Tell me my fortune, pops.'

'Where do you want it?' The filthy man reached across to the end of the operating table for an even filthier pack of playing cards. The dirt of each of these cards, just as it hit and infiltrated the air, was enough to make any just-made tattoo fester and blow up like a Watergate blow-fish. On the tops of the cards, in the dirt, pirates either slaughtered, buggered, or shared treasure with one another. The deck was just an ordinary set of playing cards. The older man handed them to Agone. 'Go on. Arrange them yourself.'

'What do you mean? It's women who're so rich they can do whatever they like who spend their time arranging cards. I'm not a dead fish.'

'Mess them up. You know how to mess things up. As if they're a cunt. They're filthy enough.' The older man could sort of remember something. But he couldn't remember what. Not that anything had ever mattered to him. 'Part of you goes for cunts and part of you hates them. Make them yours or else, they'll make you. Filthy things.'

Instead of vomiting the sailor shoved a few times at the rotten pile. For a moment, he saw the world of the rich burning up in electric flames, a skeleton leading an androgynous boy or girl across a country which, whatever it had been, was now a desert. He wondered whether deserts have Immigrations and Customs. The older man's words were racing on his breaking nerves like trains whose computers had broken down. 'Make it yours, boy.'

The sailor stopped trying to move the cards and looked up at the older man.

'Your fortune is what you see. You're a sex maniac and you want a man to fuck you.'

Fog, a cat, slid in through the unopened door.

'That's no fucking fortune.' The sailor placed his third finger on the forehead between the older man's eyes. 'Tell me about smuggling in the O.'

'A sailor has only one fortune.'

'This fortune stuff is bullshit.'

Their voices were increasing in volume.

'No roses grow on a sailor's grave.'

Agone took away his finger and raised his head. 'What do you think I am? Dumb? I've always known that.' A sailor's eyes are the ocean. The bodies of unknown and unremembered sailors. Suddenly he understood the older man: There was something else besides death. For death was all that was known. 'Give me a tattoo.'

'Where d'you want it?' The filthy man reached across the operating table for Agone's arm.

Agone had half-opened his mouth, as if he was a fish. Gasping for something. He stayed open. At once a rush of wind from the cracks in the door, the exact cylindrical size and shape of a well-used penis, filled the mouth. There was no reply.

'Pull down your pants.'

Agone didn't do it.

'What is it?' The tattoo artist had no intention of putting up with shit. Babies are shit.

'Come outside with me for a second.' The sailor pointed with his shaved head which looked like a cock toward the door. 'I want to tell you something.'

'Right you are.' The tattooer decided to go along with the young man. For the moment. He walked into the pinkish night which was as cold as a dead person.

When they were out. 'Where're we going?'

Agone turned around to his mentor. 'Here's good enough.'

'What d'you want from me?'

'Haven't you guessed by now?'

'I never thought reality had anything to do with my

suppositions.' As the older man reached up to scratch the dead skin of his chin, Agone's fist hit the skin first. Happy to be scrapping – he wasn't doing anything serious since he was only using his bare hands – the sailor felt that joy free of fear which birds must feel when they sing. Birds of prey sing since they live at night and need to see each other, like ships whose sails are tipped with ruby ebony and ivory, draped over masts in the wet dripping scrappy enough to be the seaweed that traces paths through oceans upon oceans. Oceans, like winds, are the world. Since Agone felt lost, he felt happy. Perhaps for the first time in his life. He hit the tattooer again.

The tattooer parried this second blow, then replied with a straight left to the jaw.

They kept on fighting. As they were fighting, Agone remembered a boy he had once left. The boy had been about thirteen years younger than him. Thirteen. Thirteen. The boy's curling dirty blond head, Agone actually knew the boy's hair was straight, lay in the middle of a black pillow. Agone recognized that his own emotion was something like this: 'My baby's with me again. I'm happy.' Happiness like a radio or a more destructive beam radiated through his body. Deeper, or at another level, in the tar's heart was the memory that this boy had envied him and tried to hurt him deeply. He realized that his love for the boy was both real and self-destructive. Now he further remembered that the boy had been unstable and, simultaneously, narcissistic enough to deny his instability. Such a bind is always a source of danger, for it acts as a reifier. Narcissism, if unhalted, acts like a whirlpool which drags all lovers into its depths of death. Oceans, like winds, are the world. The whirlpool's surface had been beautiful, calm, and serene, the icy glacialness of a mirror which is all surface and whose surface is winter. Agone hit the tattooer again. Agone thought: I am not serene.

When the tattooer realized that the young man was serious, he drew a knife. He had a knife because he had been using it to experiment with a new way of tattooing.

That part of our being (mentality, feeling, physicality)

which is free of all control let's call our 'unconscious'. Since it's free of control, it's our only defence against institutionalized meaning, institutionalized language, control, fixation, judgement, prison.

Ten years ago it seemed possible to destroy language through language: to destroy language which normalizes and controls by cutting that language. Nonsense would attack the empire-making (empirical) empire of language, the prisons of meaning.

But this nonsense, since it depended on sense, simply pointed back to the normalizing institutions.

What is the language of the 'unconscious'? (If this ideal unconscious or freedom doesn't exist: pretend it does, use fiction, for the sake of survival, all of our survival.) Its primary language must be taboo, all that is forbidden. Thus, an attack on the institutions of prison via language would demand the use of a language or languages which aren't acceptable, which are forbidden. Language, on one level, constitutes a set of codes and social and historical agreements. Nonsense doesn't per se break down the codes; speaking precisely that which the codes forbid breaks the codes.

This new way of tattooing consisted of raising defined parts of the flesh up with a knife. The tattooer then draws a string through the raised points of flesh. Various coloration methods can be used on the living points.

Agone couldn't see his own death. He was still too young. Yet he sensed it was there, his main interest in living. It was his, the only point, object and subject, purpose and being. It wasn't so much the hidden knife. It was that the knife was the tattooer's being, as if he was holding it fully in his right hand. By recognizing it, Agone was agreeing to allow the unallowable.

Though the tattooer had turned top, by an almost futile, silly act, he wasn't sure of himself. Such is the case with most men. He wasn't sure if he should exert this power which was deeply arbitrary, based on a tiny, almost absurd instrument. Held by flesh which was always quavering, the tan knife quavered. The older man found himself forced to decide when and where there was no possible decision. 'I don't understand what it is you want, sailor.'

Pathos made the sea beautiful.

Agone had always been unsure if he wanted sex. Caught between the rock of a false self-sufficiency and the rock of a need to go beyond his identity, he instinctively recognized his mirror: his friend: the tattooer. The knife had become their point of looking at each other.

The longer he held the knife, the more the tattooer grew ashamed of his inability to be who he was, to act decisively with a knife on another person's skin. As Agone perceived the tattooer's self-dismay, he recognized his own fear and insufficiency. For the first time in his life, he began to feel something sexual.

The tattooer shut his knife and extended an arm. He quickly reached for the sailor and drew him to him. 'You're OK.'

Agone gave up.

As fog disappeared into fog, they disappeared into the fog, walking side by side, though not hand in hand, like two brothers who know each other so well they no longer see each other, disappearance into disappearance. They felt isolated from the other humans. Humans are packs of wild dogs. When they speak, their teeth are new razor blades. Their institutions are crimson chain saws. The sailor's and the tattooer's low voices were almost confidential. As one red architectural corner jutted out into a gutter, the voices of two females cried out like babies. The two brothers turned left, down the alleyway of neon. The air was still black, but the neon lights had almost turned black . . .

Agone was frightened. Though he was always frightened, now he was more than usual. Sneaking O through Customs would be easier than this. Since he couldn't allow fear, much less deal with it, he took his fear as if it was a cancer and transferred it, mysteriously, into the tattooer's body. Thus, he and the tattooer became brothers. 'You want to do it to me, don't you?'

By now they were in the shop. I was watching the shadows of my own desire.

'You came to me.'

'Has anyone done it to you?'

'Yes.'

'Does it hurt?'

'The tattooing has two parts. In the first part, I'll draw the design. The ink'll be black. That's traditional. In the second part, I'll colour in whatever areas you want coloured. The first tattoos that were made were only red and black because red . . .'

'Does it hurt?'

'It'll hurt or it won't hurt. That's not the point.'

'I don't know,' Agone said, but he knew that since he wanted this (him), he didn't care how much it was going to hurt.

'C'mon, take off your clothes. I'll have to clean you.' The tattooer said. The sailor always kept himself immaculately clean, but not enough for the knife. 'The reason you're doing this has nothing to do with pain. It's about your own beauty.'

Though nothing outside had changed, Agone felt that all of his perceptions were now abstract. Pure. As the other man and he backed away from each other, as if they were engaged in a ritual, they drew closer to each other. The expectation of the pain this other man would be giving him, a gift, made Agone able to rely on the other man. The complicity of friendship is pain.

He was amazed how indirect his human soul was: how there were goals of desire, objects of desire, resting places, beds, and he never sailed to these places directly. There were no straight routes, except by chance. Rather, the soul travelled in such turns and windings, snails, that a world was found, defined. The soul created out of its own desires. But, suddenly, in his swerves and curves, he found himself stopped. Unable to go further. Unless someone took him by one of his hands.

'My little pal.' The tattooer's calloused hand which had been resting on Agone's shoulder as Agone had been pulling off his sweater slid down the sailor's hard back muscles until it reached the curve of his ass. Agone moved his ass muscles, almost involuntarily. Feeling this the older man squeezed so deliberately that lust suddenly appeared brutal. Lust appeared without emotion. Just as brutally he slipped his free hand down into Agone's trousers. He touched the navel. 'Maybe we can be friends.'

The word *forever* is equivalent to *death*.

Winds rode on the swords of the red fingernails of prostitutes. The winds were streams of carrot juice in what remained of the blackness of the bourgeoisie. Behind the winds, there was nothing.

'We'll see each other again.'

'No:' Agone breathed. 'Keep on going. We'll keep on going . . .' At that moment he was utterly alone.

The tattooer saw he had found what he had been looking for. He was reaching further into Agone's pants.

'. . . forever.'

'Give me your hand.' The tattooer unbuttoned his loose pants stained by human blood and put Agone's hand on his prick.

For the first time Agone's legs were unsteady. For the first time he had to hold on while the seas started to rise. He knew, from experience, though he didn't know from where the experience had come, that he was about to no longer know where he was. That it was about to be a matter of his life and death. Both life and death were suddenly dear.

The cocks now stood up. For the first time Agone was both holding on and being held to: he lay, rocking, his mouth in the tattooer's ear, the tattooer lay his mouth on the other grey cheek. Carrot juice flowed out between legs.

'I've never done it before. I'm scared,' Agone said. He was rising fast.

'Hold on. Hold on to me.' The tattooer squeezed his limb harder and harder until he was forced, as if by the seas, to ask to be sucked.

The tattooer, bending down, opened his lips over the boy's tip. His lips were waves which had parted to let the kid walk safely through the monstrous ocean. The father parted himself, all of His world, all of being, to let the child walk in safety.

The as-yet-hairless child ran his hands through his father's hair as if the hairs were nets which had caught the fish of dreams.

The dreams of criminals became alive.

The sailor was surprised as soon as the needle touched his back. There was pain; the pain was sharp and particular; the pain was so particular that he was able to isolate it. He turned his mind from the actuality of this pain away to dream, which was easy, for the actuality of pain doesn't reach very far. A dream whose beginning was a calloused, obviously large hand resting on his naked back.

The first tattoo lines were black. The tattooer was drawing the outlines of a sailing ship. Reminiscence of that dream-time when humans were free. Historically, criminality is the only freedom humans have had. Like the edges of a dream during the waking state, tattooing showed the sailor that dreams are made actual through pain. Humans make themselves and 're made through pain plus dreams.

The first sail of the rising was rose. A perfect bright, red rose. There was nothing else.

As his flesh grew used to the touch of the needle, Agone, who was usually reserved, began to blab to the tattooer. Under the influence of the needle and of beauty, he started to approach his own vulnerability by iterating his successes – how many women he had fucked in Copenhagen and Sweden, how many ports held his fucks. On the whole he was lying about holes. For the sailor was now frightened that 'he' was lost. The ocean rose above his head. His skin was a wreck; he was wrecked.

As the skin that had been torn up and the nearby skin became sore, for the tattooer was now honing in on the details of his drawing, Agone for the first time found himself forced to pay attention to the pain. His pain. He was feeling himself wrecked.

The tattooer began to fill in the outskirts of the drawing on the flesh that was the most sensitive.

The far seas contained paradises. There, people lived harmoniously with themselves and their environment. Their writing was tattooing or marking directly on their own flesh.

At the far edges of the ship's sails, the roses' petals turned into snakes. Medusa's hairs writhed through holes in the skulls of innocent humans and ate out their brains. These were the realms of danger.

Finally Agone's flesh accepted the needle. Now and then, there were quick sharp stabs of pain when the needle hit a nerve or moved near enough to the bone to vibrate it or reached flesh which was not used to being touched. Agone noted each stab of pain clearly since he no longer felt any fear.

The tattoo outline was huge roses surrounding a larger old-fashioned sailing ship. Below the ocean was a water dragon, a carp who had made it through the gate, who rose in folds and loomed over the ship.

The tattooer filled small paper cups with red, brown, blue, black, and green inks. Agone, free of pain, breathed freely. His tattooed skin ached less sharply but more generally than when the needles had been in it.

The colours began.

The first colour was red. The first colour was blood. The ship's sails were crimson. Blood makes the body move. Blood made the ship's body move. Blood changed the inhuman winds into human breath. Agone sang with the pain. The crimson streams of the winds were the roses surrounding the ship.

The second colour was brown. Brown is the colour of excreted blood or shit. The ship was flying on its human-made wings in harmony with the elements: blue sea, blue sky. The earth, home, nations are the sailor's enemy, end to his journey, his death. The brown of the ship's body reminds the sailor that his journey must end in death.

Blood and death.

The third colour was blue. The same substance was below and above the ship. It was inhuman. It was inimical to and separate from humans. Its colour was blue and its shape was that of a dragon. In the seventh century, a young warrior was carrying a jewel to her government on a ship. This jewel controlled the tides. The Dragon desired to steal the jewel. Just as he was about to grab her, to touch living human flesh, she slit open the skin between her left-side ribs and inserted the jewel into her hole. Since dragons will not touch dead flesh, her dead body was able to float until it and the jewel reached her land. The dragon's eyes are black.

Red plus black were the dream, living. As blue plus red become green, the dragon looked down at the ship over blood-red petals which had sprouted leaves. Their stems had thorns that caused pain. The inscription of this dream on to flesh was painful.

The tattoo is primal parent to the visual arts. Beginning as abstract maps of spiritual visions, records of the 'other' world, tattoos were originally icons of power and mystery designating realms beyond normal land-dwellers' experience.

The extra-ordinary qualities of the tattoo's magic-religious origin remain constant even today, transferring to the bearer some sense of existing outside the conventions of normal society.

In decadent phases, the tattoo became associated with the criminal – literally the outlaw – and the power of the tattoo became intertwined with the power of those who chose to live beyond the norms of society.

In the same manner, normal society had ruled that he shouldn't touch another man, but he was, that he shouldn't love another man, but he was, that he shouldn't come simultaneously with another man, but –

The realm of the outlaw has become redefined: today, the wild places which excite the most profound thinkers are conceptual. Flesh unto flesh.

Male hand on male hand. Stomach on stomach. Male feet on male feet. Mouth on mouth. Cock on cock. Agone pulled away from the tattooer before either of them came because he didn't want to reach any port.

No roses grow on a sailor's grave.

As the two men moved away from each other, I went outside into morning's beginning.

III On Becoming Algerian

(Thivai speaks)

The Violence of Those Who Are Alone In Jail/ The Violence Of Roses

Hot female flesh on hot female flesh. And it doesn't go anywhere: flesh. Flesh. For the cunt opens and closes, a perpetual motion machine, a scientific wonder, perpetually coming, opening and closing on itself to ectasy or to nausea – does it, you, ever tire? Roses die faster. Roses die faster than you, you whores in my heart.

All the women in Paris were now whores.

A man cannot fuck a whore because fucking must be a two-way matter. Roses open and close only on themselves. Cunts open and close whether or not they're opening and closing on anything. It's almost as if a cunt doesn't need food in order to move, to feel. It, she doesn't need any sustenance because it's, she's a red dead cunt.

I should know. I once had a girlfriend. Now she's gone.

After she had left, I had lived in Madame's brothel. Because it was easy for me to love hookers. It was easy because no hooker wanted anything from me or noticed me. Because the only thing a hooker wants is money. After the Algerian revolution, money wasn't anything.

I existed when I shot up. The sperm or me was evanescent, floating. Sparks of stars exploded in black sky. Went back to nothingness.

Just as material is always attracted to a vacuum, some CIA flew to Paris and took over Madame's whorehouse for their own purposes.

During World War II, Drs Sigmund Ruff and Sigmund Rascher, two Bobbsey twins, worked for Dr Hubertus Strughold. Drs Ruff's and Rascher's job involved injecting the Dachau inmates with gasoline, crushing them to death in high-altitude pressure chambers, shooting them so that certain possible blood coagulents could be tested on their bullet wounds, forcing prisoners to stand naked in sub-freezing temperatures and immersing them in tubs of ice water to find out how long it takes a human being to freeze to death. For instance. These experiments were part of 'aviation medicine'. Planes fly through the stars of sperm.

After Hitler lost to the Americans, Dr Strughold, who now lives in Texas, USA, started to work for the Americans. NASA has hailed Mr Strughold as 'the father of space medicine'.

One of the surprising results of the World War II experiments was that the Nuremberg Tribunal ruled that scientific testing, which includes drug testing, cannot be done on subjects who haven't consciously agreed to be tested in the specific ways.

Dr Strughold hired Dr Sidney Gottlieb to conduct the MK-ULTRA programme for the American CIA. Subjects whom the CIA questioned, unfortunately for the CIA, remembered the questions, that they had blabbed, and whom they should tell that they had blabbed. The CIA had to destroy this human memory. Murder, in many cases, was an impractical solution because it tended to be public. The same with lobotomy; especially because an increasingly conservative American government wanted to close down all loony bins and schools and the American public, who ordinarily worshipped their government as movies stars or gods, were unwilling to have lobotomies and other strangers walking down their streets. MK-ULTRA was designed to find safe ways to cause total human amnesia.

As this programme developed, the CIA became generally

interested in the uses of mind chemicals or drugs. Partly due to the fact that most of the CIA agents were now stoned on acid. It was those days in American civilization. The Americans probably hadn't heard that the Algerians had taken over Paris.

بستوئیم خدای تعالی را برای جهل
مردم امریکائی

Praise Allah for the Americans' ignorance.

The CIA agents (and the American 'Born-agains' or most of the American populace who devotedly followed the CIA) hadn't even heard of Algeria; they knew that the Russians were poisoning the American water system with acid. Just as Rasputin daily ate strychnine in order to avoid strychnine poisoning, so the CIA agents imbibed acid to make sure they won't be the ones the Reds murdered. This was the birth of the MK-ULTRA programme.

During World War II, there was another man – there aren't many of them around – George Black, who ran a training school for spies. This school was supposed to be for American spies, but spies have a way of spying on their own. After something permanent happened to Hitler, Black worked for the Narcotics Bureau. He busted hippies for acid and other chemicals.

By this time, since the CIA had tested chemicals on themselves to such an extent that they were now either lobotomy cases or insane, they needed new experimentees. Since the experimentees couldn't know that they were such – victims – they had to be part of socially despised closed groups: prisoners, homosexuals, etc. The CIA needed socially despised closed groups. The birth of OMC.

Gottlieb asked Black to head Operation Midnight Climax. Operation Midnight Climax's purpose was to test drugs on Johns.

By this time, things had changed in the United States. Things. There were now those humans who had things and those humans who didn't. Those who didn't have things knew nothing of education, lived in the streets, concrete lumps of the lumpenproletariat, and ate shit for food. They were just too low to be drug test-worthy. Lobotomies can't be given lobotomies. Such is the effect of radical poverty. Whereas those who had, having imbibed drugs for years, especially dex and downs in the case of the female, coke for the male of the species, were too drugged-out to drug-test. Just as the USA now desperately needed new economic markets for its coke (the mild variety) and McDonald's, so the American CIA needed new drug-test victims.

By this time, things had changed in the United States. One of the CIA agents who had drugged himself up with speed rather than hallucinogens noted that the Algerians had taken over Paris. He informed Gottlieb of the fact. Gottlieb decided that Paris was the perfect drug-testing ground.

It used to be hard to get drugs in Paris. The pre-revolutionary city had too much food and other luxuries. So the few whites who remained in Paris didn't know about drugs. As for the blacks, the CIA didn't consider them intelligent enough to know about anything. As for the Eiffel Tower, it was dead.

The CIA bought Madame's brothel for Operation Midnight Climax. Their deal with Madame was that nothing would change when the Americans took over. ('We're not ideological.' – Kissinger) The girls would do what girls always do: bring home the bacon to the pimp. Only now their new super-pimps, American, generous to a fault, would give each girl 1100 new francs a night for this drug-testable bacon. Then, a little something would get slipped into the living bacon's drink, just like the Russians were slipping drugs into the American water. After all, for years, the Americans had been leading horses to water.

Behind newly installed two-way mirrors, Black Man, Madame's new head, took scientific notes on how each John reacted to each drug. If a John flipped out permanently or disappeared permanently, there was nothing in a name. It was the time of AIDS. One never knew what disease a cunt had.

Especially a black cunt. This was a perfect set-up for the white Americans.

I saw my friends in that brothel destroyed by madness starving hysterical naked dragging themselves through the whitey's streets at dawn looking for an angry fix I saw myself fucked-up nothing purposeless collaborating over and over again with those I hated old collaborating with my own death – all of us collaborating with Death –

One day this kid whose hair was kinked like a lamb's strutted into the brothel. He and Mathilde, a thin transsexual, were arm-in-arm, young lovers. He was on his last day of leave and so had fallen in love with a whore.

War is engraved in the human flesh; human flesh enscribed around human flesh.

The lamb was eager to blow his top. And did. Because Mathilde did what she had been told to do, slipped

It's you who, though I cry I plea I excuse,
won't let me kiss your foot even once.
Make me walk through fire or water.
You're the Sultan of Reality

BZ (quinuclidinyl benzilate) into the kid's JD. The kid had always been fond of JD because his dad, now dead, had drunk it. After all, it was truly his last night on shore, or earth,

who gives the orders.

When M left the room, the tar blew his top and bottom. A CIA skunk entered the room, gave the kid a local anaesthetic, as if anyone needed it, and instructed him, as if they were back in an American school which some child hadn't yet burned to the ground, to describe everything the kid saw. Inured to hard conditions the sailor started to describe the fake red velvet walls while the CIA skunk removed chunks of his cerebral cortex. (This is true. Oh, Sultan of Reality.) After the American doctor put away his scalpel, he gave the kid another dose of BZ. For the CIA wanted to know whether super-acid (BZ) affects a damaged brain in the same ways as a normal one.

Behind two-way mirrors, Black Man sipped vodka martinis and watched this scene. He needed his martinis. In order to do this kind of work. One night while drinking martinis and watching through two-way mirrors a lobotomy take place on a John, Black accidently turned left and saw his own reflection in a one-way mirror. His right hand lifted his smaller pistol and shot at the mirror or himself. It could be, in that brothel of lobotomies, that he no longer knew who he was.

It could be that the CIA has never known.

I was watching when the sailor's cerebral cortex was chopped. I knew death when I saw death. I knew, in the brothel of lobotomies, I was a dead man seeing my skeleton in a mirror, the land of the CIA, or a dream character who knew that he lived only in the darkest region, of himself, a land or face which he didn't recognize when he was awake.

That lobotomy was both a lobotomy and a sign: my pleasure (my imagination, dreaming, desiring) was being cut off from actual life.

At that moment Black saw me watching him.

A half-hour later two muscle-bound men took me away from the brothel. My hands and feet were chained. Though I don't think they took me away from Paris, the ride in the armoured police-car – were the new flics now working with the CIA? – was long, rough. I barely sat on bare remnants of a seat. Perhaps bare remnants of a society. My bones had turned cold.

This haunting memory of Paris is of a city completely empty. Industry had left after the disappearance of the Rockefellers and their banks. The Rockefellers' industrial buildings still remained. Forty-storey glass sheets. Windows smacked open. Two or three white punks lived on the top floors. Thirty-storey deserted hotels totally empty of all but the winds. The clean white art complex, in which the Picasso Museum, Beauborg, and parks stood, in the northern centre of the city, was now void of humans. But not of bands of wild dogs and cats. Cats ran through the rare yellow snows. Just outside, on all sides, of the huge clean complex, miles and miles of small boarded-up buildings between large now-torn advertisements for Tampax and Sani-flex, a type of cleanser, an occasional mini-market, which was a focus for left-over thefts, and the most important boxing ring in France were the new city.

The true city of dreams. Paris, a city in which a person could do anything. Be a pirate. Have the tips of the ears tattooed. As long as he did it himself. I knew that from now on I would have to learn to do everything for myself.

Two guards or dogs started playing cards. Two pairs . . . straight flush . . . We picked up three other convicts. The dogs stopped their card-game long enough to attach us in pairs in chains. I have always wanted a lover. Wanted so badly, now, that I would desire to be chained to her. That's what love is to me.

I don't know where we stopped, were stopped. I guess it's not possible to know a prison from its outside. I wouldn't know. I guess it was somewhere. In Paris. After all, I had to keep on knowing in order to stay alive.

Finally I was lost. My total being could have been a total scream. My total being could have somersaulted in and into that panic which is nihilism. But an act of will kept the fiction of 'me' going.

The dogs led my lover and I by our chains through the hall of a building, as if we were descending, through rivers of piss, into a narrow cell, a coffin. Now I knew where I was.

I know this prison is at the bottom of a valley, in an infernal pit out of which the fountain of light of evil gushes, but there was nothing to stop me from thinking that this prison was on a mountain-top: There, in that place, everything led me to think that my isolation was the *isolation of air*. Could I be anyone if I was totally isolated?

I had been thrown by the CIA into the isolation of air.

Who descended into nihilism, who descended deeper than nihilism into the grey of yuppy life (the worship of commodities, the belief that there is nothing left but commodities, who turn to the surfaces of class race money for reality, who despise taboo).

Thrown Into Nothing

It wasn't just my isolation. It was the evil. Prisoners are evil. I should know. They like evil. You know why? Cause prison is a being, a social being, who is against human life. So anyone who is in prison is evil.

The fact is that all prisoners should be killed by the state and, since they haven't been, they're in actuality beyond death.

Thus, prisoners are sacred. Their lives are imaginary, *imaginary* as in 'imaginary number', not rationally possible.

Between one-third and two-thirds of all prison inmates wear tattoos. Being tattooed shows a tendency for violence, property crime, and self-destruction or self-mutilation. There is a 'strong relationship between tattooing and the commission of violent, assaultive acts. This propensity toward violence in general may well be signalled by the violence these men have done to themselves in the form of tattooing.' – some doctor.

In prison, my imagination soared. I told myself stories. Like this one.

....

یک

One

باری

Once upon a time,

باری مُردِ فَقیر هَست.

Once upon a time there was a poor man.

مردِ فقیر مردِ ثروتمند، ما لکِ جهان
را دید.

The poor man saw a rich man who owned everything.

چشمانِ تو ببس،

Close your eyes,

چشمانِ مَن.

My eyes.

مردِ فقیر پس الله را ستود. "شما،
الله، مردمِ ثروتمند و فقیر را
کردی."

Then, the poor man praised God. 'You, God, made both rich and poor people.'

پس پسرِ زیبا و جوانِ مردِ بدگِل
و پیرِ فقیر را نزدیک شد.

At that moment, a beautiful young boy approached the hideous and old (poor) man.

با مَن بیامَد.

'Come with me.'

مرد بدگل و پیر فقیر امد.

The hideous and old poor man came.

با او.

With him.

به مردم ثروتمند.

To the rich people.

انجا مردم ثروتمند بودند.

There, there were rich people.

مردم ثروتمند در یک منزل
قشنگ زندگی کشتند. بوان خوب
بودند. قشنگ بو دادند. خوراک و
گردنان مردم ثروتمند را
خوسنود کردند.

Rich people kill in a beautiful house. The smells are good. The rich people smelled good. Food and necks delighted the rich people.

مرد بدگل و پیر فقیر تعظیم را به
مردم ثروتمند پس کرد. مرد بدگل
و پیر فقیر نام خودش را پس

پا شید. "گناهبد، فقر. "رئیس،
مردم، ثروتمند، پس گفت،
"نامم گناهبد است. گناهبد،
ناوی."

Then the hideous old poor man bowed to the rich. Then the hideous old poor man said his name, 'Sinbad of Weariness.' Then the chief rich person said, 'My name is Sinbad. Sinbad the Sailor.'

گناهبد، ناوی پس حرف زد:

Then Sinbad the Sailor said:

"اینجا حکایتهای سفرهای من اند،

'Here are stories of my travels,

"سفرها از فقر به نشاط، سفرها از
مجهول به تعجب، سفرها از تعجب به
تعجب، سفرها از بیماری به جنس.

'of travelling from poverty to sensual pleasure, from unknown to wonder, from wonder to wonder, from sickness to sex.

'Why do I tell stories?

'Let me tell you why,'

گناهبد، ناوی حرف زد.

Sinbad the Sailor said.

'Shah Zamam, the King of Samarcand, and King Shahryar were brothers. When they realized that all women are sex maniacs, they decided they had to control women. This was the beginning of patriarchy. In order to control women, Zamam murdered his wife and her lover who was black and his cook. Sexuality and negritude are allied. King Shahryar murdered his wife and all her friends, then fucked and murdered one woman every day for three years. Finally, one woman, Shahra'zad, wanted to end patriarchy. Finally, one woman, Shahra'zad, wanted to fuck this king more than life. He fucked her. In her prison of herself, or the world, she began her marvellous exploit, a tale which lasted one thousand and one nights, which staved off death, which staved off patriarchy, a tale of

سفرها

travelling

فقر

poverty

نشاط

sensual pleasure

مجهول

the unknown

تعجب

wonder

بیماری

disease

جنس.”

sex.'

گناهبد ناوی حکایتش را گفت:

Sinbad the Sailor tells his story:

My lousy stinking home city.

When I was fifteen, already I was in jail. Children whose faces and souls were charming swarmed in the jail. Every day, for a few hours, the children were cabin-boys. Cabin-boys of a sailing ship.

For the sadness of being locked up in prison is the sadness of a sailor who finds himself alone on the ocean.

For a few hours, every day, I became a cabin-boy. The ship I was on was rigged and masted, sails and winds, actual winds, amid roses which had cracked and let loose the perfumes of human bodies. Under the orders of my jailers, huge rugged men, who were often mean to me, I learned how to handle a boat even in the most dangerous seas.

One of these jailers – topmen watches first mates frigates – was especially hard on me. I've never had much to do with love: I received too many wounds too early. Maybe. Anyway. Only gratitude made and makes my heart turn to sexual desire.

This jailer was above me. Since he was above me and he had been good to me, all I wanted was to crawl into his arms and stay there.

While he was walking ahead of me in the corridor, one day, I ran up to him from behind and grabbed him by the shoulder. As if I was going to kiss him from behind. I often kiss the backs of the necks of friends. The huge man ran. Perhaps he had been frightened. I ran after him; I again grabbed his burly shoulders, then the olive cloth of his uniform, through the olive cloth flesh and bone, quickly drew a razor I had been secreting across his throat. Why did I do this? Blood spurted out across my hand which was holding the guard's shoulder. Why did I do this? Part of me was aghast at what I was doing and part of me was reacting to love. Not to ownership, but to love.

The other guards handcuffed and gagged me. They couldn't off me because I was still a juvenile.

They threw me into solitary for three months until another, younger guard confessed that the guard I had murdered had been homosexual.

They, some people, say that a child who's in prison either makes himself or dies. What is true is that the child erects himself stone after stone without any tools. They, some people, ask if there are such things as human feelings. I can tell you what human feelings are.

It was in solitary that I began to try to understand why I had murdered. Had I slaughtered, as the sociologists say, because of poor economic and social conditions?

I thought about my parents. I didn't usually think about them. My father, I remembered, came from Alpha-Centauri. His head, the case with most Centaurians, had been green and flea— or dried-drool —shaped. Unlike him, my mother, a moon-child, was just a good-for-nothing. She was beautiful by night-time or lightless standards. Like the moon which hides behind the sun, mommy kept her brains hidden.

I came out of the cross-racial union. Multi-racial marriages usually lead to disaster. Murder is a disaster for someone. It is true that our racist, sexist, classist mores have to change or we will all kill all of us.

Mommy, when she was thinking, must have been racist, because as soon as I popped out of her cunt with a great deal of pain to someone, even before that, she tried to pretend that I didn't exist. Pretending that she was stupid had made her good at pretending generally.

When I turned eight years old, she told me that my real father wasn't Alpha-Centaurian, but robotic. Thus, I became a sailor. This information which I believed, whether rightly or wrongly I have no way of knowing, didn't bother me because I hated the colour green.

Daddy, whom I now called 'Robot' just to make him angry, later on asked me if I knew who I was. Human or alien or mechanism.

Daddy (Robot): You obviously don't have a clue who you are, dumb-dumb. Dumb fuckin' cluck. Do you, cluck cluck, have any idea who I am?

? (me): You're my friend. Aren't you, dad?

Daddy (Robot): I'm not your friend because I'm your father. You must learn to use language correctly. Does it say in the dictionary that a 'father' is a 'fiend'?

(I didn't reply.)

Now, *son*, who am I?

? (me): You're Mr Tagglepuss and whatever I am, I'm not human. Whatever HUMAN is, it's not human. We live in New York City between people who own most of the money in this world and people who own so little they're not human. If I'm not human, dad, am I able to fuck?

Daddy (Robot): That's right, son. You're too fucked to fuck. That's what being inhuman means. Now: do you think you're able to walk? A man has to walk in order to fuck. Do you know why, son? Do you know why? Because THAT'S WHO A MAN IS. A man is someone who goes after everyone and everything he wants. Men do not need permission. This is why a man has to be able to walk. Now: can you walk even though you're not human?

?(me) (At ten years old I take my first baby steps and fall flat on my face): Yes! Yes! I'm walking! (My left elbow, on the ground, is jabbing into my belly-button. Mommy rushes up with her camera to take a picture of this first anti-yuppyism or descent into disintegration.) Yes! Yes!

Flat on my face, like a snake or a lovebird, I crawled. You might say that I crawled from there to there, from parents to jail.

After a while, they let me out of solitary.

گُناهبَدِ باوی اِدامه داد:

Sinbad the Sailor continued saying:

When I had served my full term, they let me out of prison. I found myself in a world which stunk.

(The stink: My father died fifty-five years old of five heart attacks. Then my mother blew two million dollars and either suicided or was murdered. Then her mother died from grief. My lover left me. I was broke. Alive, I had seen only death. This city, New York City, was the city of death.)

Since ANY PLACE BUT HERE is the motto of all sailors, I decided I was a sailor. Since no reality seemed preferable to anything, to reality: I wanted to sail away.

I sailed away to England. From England, away to Holland, Sweden, Denmark, Austria, around to France. On each trip I made lots of money. Not yet strangeness.

From France, I sailed away, south, to an island which turned out to be a whale. I had sailed away to strangeness. This whale was so gigantic, it was unable to move. Trees and shrubbery shot out of the dirt on its flesh.

All of us left ship to explore the island. If the whale moved, we would drown.

The whale began to shake. At that very moment I understood that my capacities for understanding are so puny that reality (for me) is Chance. Due to this ignorance, my will is useless. For me, strangeness was and is everywhere.

I floundered in the inhuman sea. No friends anywhere to be seen. I saw three wooden planks attached to each other. I clung to these things while death ate at my heart.

مرگ دلم را جوید.

Death eats my heart.

تبعیدی هستم.

I'm an exile.

Sinbad the Sailor gagged.

The waves led me to a second island. This island was hilly. When I awoke, I met a horse. The horse was white, as white as the hair of an old junky woman. When I tried to mount the bitch,

سگِ مؤنث

bitch,

she tried to trample me down.

I ran away as fast as I could from this bitch who was epileptic. Foaming in the mouth like all bitches, not sailors. As I was running away, as a dreamer runs through deeper and deeper sand dunes from his murderer, an old bastard rose out of the sands and asked me why I was running away.

'Lord,' he asked, 'from what are you running and running? What has your life been: what disasters are so hideous in your life that you're trying to run in to strangeness?

I replied, 'I'm a stranger or Jewish. My home is only strange. I didn't have a real father or mother. Now I have no one. In my unending despair, I fantasized that I just drowned in a strange ocean. Allah! May the ocean of human pain overwhelm me so that I can't feel anymore!

'I mustn't think that.

'Not knowing how to escape, I'm looking for escape. I'm a sailor. I set sail a long time ago.

'ANYWHERE OUT OF THIS REALITY, PLEASE FUCK. ALLAH'S NAME IS FUCK.'

I continued, 'Now I'm here. Wherever in hell this is. My life is strange.'

'What are you running from? Why do you run from strangeness into strangeness, like a lovebird hopping from branch to branch? How can you run from yourself, sailor, if you're strange? Maybe you're actually a smelly cunt, sailor. Can a cunt run from itself?'

The old man gave me his hand. Since I'm a baby, I'll take any hand I can get even if it isn't a cock.

The old man took me to his underground lair of criminals.

I asked if he was a criminal.

'I steal horses.'

'Are you a cowboy?' I had heard that there are cowboys in Argentina. There's torture in Argentina.

'Horses are beasts. Beauty or bestiality was born in the sea. Horses are born in the sea.'

Suddenly I understood everything.

'At night, by the light of torches, pillage is made. Bombs explode the central electrical units; fires spread to the few carpets and curtains which are left. We pillage the few left churches with theft. Rebels we relight the gas lamps; the gas explodes in their faces. They're strangers. Strange females run pell-mell through the pews to hide in the tabernacle, the holiest of holies.

'By the light of the full sexual moon when all cunts are pounding, I take an Arabian mare who's in full heat and lead her to the icy waters. Horses rise out their waters in order to fuck her. I bind and imprison as many of them as I can.

'This is how we make our living. Some of our couples have bound themselves to the church. Others, to the pianos of orgies. Groups of kids, crouching among the church's sacred objects, eat their victims. We're criminals. Already the living are exhausted. Already the living are exhausted by death.'

While he was talking the old bastard dragged me to his chief.

'New-borns, abandoned in half-existing houses in the lowest part of the city, left to rot by their mothers who had been mounted like mares only more violently during the most recent pillage, new-borns died while the rats watched them die. Rats, cockroaches, and fleas: the survivors of this world. One child was rolling a victim over broken slabs of concrete, a hoop, a hula-hoop of flesh; another kid shitting next to a vase the Church had been fond of displaying farted. Lightly. A guy was hugging a wood statue of the Virgin then he pierced the Statue's cunt, if the Virgin had a cunt, with his knife he threw himself on Her his teeth biting Her cheeks and bruised lips, he asked Her to fuck him.

'با مَن جِنس بِکُن.'

'Fuck me.'

'با مَن جِنس بِکُن.'"

"Fuck me."'

The criminals treated me more gently than humans have ever done. But I was homesick. Since I no longer knew what home was, I was even more homesick. A sailor knows that loneliness is worse than impossibility, that loneliness is worse than death.

گُناهبَدِ ناوی گُفت.

Sinbad the Sailor said.

When I said I wanted to return home, they didn't judge me. They just said they would help me return to my home.

But I no longer knew where home was. Perhaps the ocean. The ocean of wonder.

They didn't know where home was either. Skulls never say anything.

When a sailor is out at sea, what can a sailor follow? A sailor follows his heart, for his heart is shining in the sky. Stars are the knives of infinity. Into my total despair into the blackness that my eyes saw outside them and the miasma in my head that just wanted to die, I looked. I looked into the blackness which is reality. Into the hell of intertwining snakes of desire and void of me.

I had to follow my heart. In my past, I've never been able to find a heart, just sexual desire.

IS THERE ANY INTEGRITY ANYMORE?

One of the criminals who was a leper told me he had seen a face. When he saw the face, he knew it was the face of love. I've never seen the face of love. Maybe I'm out of it. Born in exile even from criminals. Born in exile from humans. Jews wander from lack to lack.

The street musicians are drumming out their anger while the rats who're attracted by human sperm and bruised rotting human flesh, the rot that comes from malnutrition, by left-over wine, by the bits of the city stuck by dried blood to whores' rags – blood's the only glue – these rats trot among the coupling bodies. They lick blood that's running from body to body. As a couple comes, the rats nip their hands so their human legs come undone; the children who're unable to sleep or who're plunged into dream attack.

بَچّگانِ بیخوابی یاِی خواب کُشَند.

The children who're unable to sleep or who're plunged into dream kill.

The leper said, 'Stop worrying whether you're going to get fucked, sailor.'

I thought the world had gone mad from lack of love. Loneliness in the form of alcoholicism and materialism had made mothers attack their own children. The mothers spread their young thighs and, having penetrated the narrow cunts with hands and wrapped-around cocks so small as to be almost non-existent, knocked the children on their heads ate them made sure they didn't exist before they had a chance to grow up. The few kids who emerged were warped.

One woman eight months pregnant was squatting and shitting under the light coming out of a church's stained glass windows. She had raised her skirt over piles of shit. A black snake glided from the confessional, under the church door, out to the smell of shit. He lifted his head and moved into her thighs. She cried out; her forehead hit the concrete. The serpent was writhing around in her intestines. He injected his venom into the child.

The leper said, 'Stop worrying whether you're going to get fucked, sailor.'

A young revolutionary, blood now dried gluing a golden chasuble to his thighs, was dreaming, immobile, in the ray of the golden light coming out of the stained-glass window. Incense smoked out of his eyes. He was looking at an image of Jesus Christ crucified. Asleep he raised his arms, rolled his neck over his left shoulder. He danced. Sharp rays lit his shoes' nails. In trappings of gold and linen, at each turn, he saw 'God'. He smiled, extended his arms out, reversed his neck over the other shoulder; the image of love veiled by pain, glimpses of love, were making him dance. He climbed on to the altar, never stopping dancing, but a living man struck a sword into him then threw him over the altar's steps.

The leper said, 'Stop worrying whether you're going to get fucked, sailor.'

A female revolutionary whose name was Giauhave bent down, with her right hand picked up a rat, and patted the rat. 'Rat, come on, stop trembling. You don't have to tremble anymore cause I'm here: You can walk into my blood. You can crack and crash all my insides between your bitty teeth just so you'll have enough to eat. You'll never again be lonely . . . little bitty . . . never again.'

A guy came over to Giauhave and entered her. A deacon who was young who had escaped the massacre was preying. As he lifted his bloody eyes to the fucker, the fucker's hand was overturning the tabernacle. His other hand on Giauhave's ass slid down to her clitoris then over to the ciborium where it felt a sacred wafer, picked it up, and pressed it into her mouth. Now the young deacon recoiled into the far end of the crypt.

The fucker reached for another wafer, turned this wafer up her cunt, then withdrew his cock lightly browned from her asshole, placed himself between her slightly swollen cunt lips and pushed. After her other mouth had eaten, Giauhave moaned, moaned louder as she ate the man's liquid. The man was breathing hard as the cool winds.

Then I, Sinbad the Sailor, left the land of criminals and headed for New York City, my home . . .

....

End of the Story of Sinbad the Sailor.

....

One day a shitload, I mean a shipload, of Arab Prisoners appeared. Their words to each other were poetry:

....

An Arab female:
I, an Arab, have seen giant Arab words which are larger than any other words, more real than an eye sliced in two, in the sky. These words were illuminating a star which was wandering.

The place where I saw words was the turning of the world.

I turned.

I remembered.

Finally I remembered something: my home or me. It's against you, Death, (wind which has clotted into a hypocritical mask, eye which drives away light, face closed against joy), it's against you, Death, that I'm writing down or inventing this memory.

It's against you that I'm writing down or inventing memory.

مرگ

Death

New York City.

My first memory: It was a hot summer in New York. I was

squatting on the floor (which was also my bed) of my room (which was also my apartment). The ceiling simultaneously fell down on top of me and crumbled. That dust made my room become wartime. I understood that what you see, you are.

Everything there was for sale. Mecca, the Tigris River, The East River, polluted water, bad breath, Palestine, Hanoi. Five years ago richies who were scared the terrorists might nab their money had started coming to New York and buying up every building in sight. Now all the property has been sold.

Sold. Sold down the East River. Exiled from ourselves. Cut-off heads. Each of us is carrying our cut-off head on a plate in the richies' dinner party. We're waiting to be born again and this isn't mystical; it's our only chance.

America, Death. If you're anything but Death, you're the masses of exiles.

آزادی

Freedom

As for Liberty. Liberty's a nail which was thrust into my head. It's also a nail they stuck into my cunt. Only I know my cunt is my diseased heart.

My cunt is a rose from which perfume comes when part of it breaks.

New York City, my home, Liberty. Who do you hate more, boy? Niggers or Arabs? I think you hate Arabs more. Once your deep culture was black. Now you're becoming Arab.

The ceiling of languages is falling down. Either add to this rubble or shove at least some of it away.

Liberty, shit. The liberty to starve. The liberty to speak words to which no one listens. The liberty to get diseases no doctor treats or can cure. The liberty to live in conditions cockroaches wouldn't touch except to die in. The liberty to be an eighty-three-year-old Ukrainian shuffling around in her slippers among the cat shit in the slum building hallway – 'Is there a landlord here? Is there light anywhere?'

إنهدام

Demolition

What is language? Does anyone speak to anyone? Is language computer language, journalese, dictation of expectation and behaviour, announcement of the allowed possibilities or reality? Does language control like money?

The movement of the hand across the page in the Persian language is the movement of the spirit or of fire.

The kids in the New York City school system are now setting their schools on fire because they know that fire is action.

Harlem is the Holy Trinity. There, babies turn into punks; punks skewer gutter-rats for fun; gutter-rats live on human baby flesh. 123. Mr Tax Man, The Honourable Judge, Sir Cop. 123.

Harlem – the black hates the Jew. (And for good reason – the Jew owns black property.)

Harlem – the black hates the Arab cause Arabs started the black slave trade.

Broadway, in the centre of Harlem – people eat drugs and drugs eat people. The cops control the drugs. The clamp comes down.

Broadway, in the centre of Harlem – Festival of police clubs. Whenever I see through my eyes here, my eyes are coffins. Cause the red snow is freezing them into ice. At the end of all this, (of you, Liberty), at the end of all: it's all black. There will be more and more black people in New York City.

Though I'm not black, Harlem, I know your rancour, I know on what your hatred's fed. This is because I'm Arab. And I'm female. I'm gonna tell you something. Everytime there's a case of hunger, someone's hungry, soon there's going to be a cataclysm like a thousand stomachs which are holes or whores. Everytime there's just one prison, soon there's going to be more than double violence outside that prison. It won't be vengeance: it's cause-and-effect. Connection. Connect fists. There's no pendulum swinging cause the poor swing lead pipes. Under your concrete, Urban America, the piles of shit in the sewerpipes around which the icy air has put its arms (the only physical affection left in disease) are so numerous that the shit's going to burst through the concrete and hit the fans . . . the winds of history . . . Even the steps of the whites are lost in these winds of perfumes . . . The rich know nothing . . . strangers . . . strangers to the world they own . . . themselves . . . Winds of perfumes.

All Arabs know that 'stranger' equals 'evil'.

Black Harlem is a wife-beater. The whites are killing even themselves. They're at the point of total death. Just the beat of time will bring them to death. Time, in the USA, is going to beat the whites to death through its blacks. The tears of the blacks are becoming volcanoes because pain doesn't die but transforms. The pain of hunger is becoming the pain of killing. Black Harlem, through cause-and-effect, you're going to pick New York City up in your arms with love and dump it in its own shit. Because death is always strange, I who am Arab hate every stranger.

On the day of Allah, *there will be no more loneliness*.

New York City, you are my home and I'm exiled from you. For me, you are my hole and my whore. So as soon as I get rid of this emptiness and this self-victimization in me, there will be no more loneliness in me.

An Arab male:

According to Sheik Nafzawi, the *Koran*'s a manual for fucking. The *Koran*, then, is a cocktail, a road which leads to the drunkenness of fucking. Like a drunken bird. Like a bewitched lovebird. Like a mad lovebird maddened, the *Koran*'s verbal turbulence – the thousand and one verbal variations, the thousand and one and more variations, similitudes within dissimilitudes and dissimilitudes within likenesses – all transform into something beyond, about to move into flight.

The Arab female:

But how can I fuck someone when everyone's getting AIDS?

The Arab male:

Even culture in this prison prevents us from finding shelter, from fucking each other. This culture is preventing both the living word (the movement of the living hand) and fucking (the movement of the living body). This dead culture perceives the earth as concrete or marble and not as the water flowing from our tears.

The Arab female:

Fuck all that. My cunt's the centre of the world. My cunt is a tree. Every leaf, every blossom, every fruit comes from my cunt . . .

The Arab male:

Comes in your cunt.

The Arab female:

. . . My cunt is the rose or blood of the winds. I stink of everything. Your cock's never gonna get in here cause you can't catch me and imprison me. I am not a lovebird in a man-made cage.

The Arab male:

Liberty truly is a cunt.

Ché Guevara saw that Liberty is a cunt and he took her to bed. The bed was the Bed of Time. Or the Flowerbed of Roses Watered by Pain. Toward morning they fell asleep.

What did Liberty feel about Ché? Does anyone know what a woman feels? Can a woman feel? No. When he woke out of his dream, she had split.

From then on, Ché could only dwell in dreams. In New York City in Detroit in LA in Newcastle in Marseilles in Beyrouth. The hives. Where people are driven mad by their desires. Driven into dream . . .

The female Arab:

What good are dreams when you're stuck in prison?

The male Arab:

. . . .

The female Arab:

Physical and mental lust were eating out my body at the same time I knew there was only loneliness. The CIA had created loneliness in that city and made the sun into a piece of ice.

I decided either I can die or I have to refind emotion. The rising of the rivers. This is why I left New York City.

I left New York City the way one leaves a lover's bed when one doesn't give a damn about the person one's just fucked and it's 5:00 in the morning and the pavement's crawling like a dead cat.

I left nothing.

Always unwilling to feel.

There, I could get orgasms out of any one.

In New York City, my three lovers were three dead stars. Every bed had stuck so many splinters into my spine that my spine had become a tree trunk, knotted over itself, turning into and into itself, knots upon nots.

I was a living cross upon cross looking for the love upon which I had shat. That's why I left New York City.

New York City, you are my spine.

The male Arab:

The USA is a dead nation. It's devoid of dreams. The USA has destroyed all that we call human life and substituted religion. This religion is worship of money and blind faith in stupidity. The USA has decimated its own soil and air. The USA has substituted learning how to be controlled and the rote memorization of facts for any education in living. Every aspect of the USA's life is now fit for death. Fucking leads only to disease. The USA is a cancer on the flesh of reality. All Americans are born diseased and live writhing.

The Female Arab:

Peace to the dead and the death-bringers. Peace to my sick home, city of AIDS or the death of love.

. . . .

End of the Arab prisoners' dreams.

. . . .

My dream:

Calm was the night when the galley sailed on a warm, smooth sea. The crew made me climb the main-yard. I had already taken off my pants. I knew they were all mocking me, throwing their heads around with disgusting laughter, but I couldn't stop myself, I've never been able to stop myself. Because I didn't want to stop myself from doing it. I asked them for more and more insults until something had to happen. I knew I could climb to the top of the mast. I was at its foot, half-naked. I saw the wood above me, looming, tall, thin. As straight as the cross. I wanted them to laugh at me more. I put my arms around the pine wood, then my legs, aiming to climb, like a baboon whose hideous ass is sticking into the face of the sky. Dots of shit could have showed. The frenzy of the men around me was at its height. I climbed half-way up the mast. The captain walked out on deck. He couldn't control his men's sexual frenzy. I was the only one in control because I was disappearing from them. Their heavy breathing was my coming. The solid rod of wood hung over the ocean. The ocean breathed. When I reached the top and touched its pinnacle, I was calm. I woke up in my prison cell. The captain's huge arms were around me and he asked me to marry him.

. . . .

The people whom the CIA force to live in prison are evil

because they're insane. They live in dreams. Let our madness turn from insanity into anger.

Escape To The Angel Of The Dawn

I had to get out of prison.

There was a small window high up in my cell. Stretching up on tip-toe, I could just see through these bars down to a street. Through these bars were masses of hair, foul, grey and black, drool-clotted. Occasionally the hair parted, or turned around to reveal, deeply lined facial skin. Sometimes grey and black and drool-clotted hairs covered up the lower halves of the facial skins. A few times, a black leather-covered hand lay among the hairs. So many heads, so much filth, that smell was visible, the colour of turd, that there appeared, not only to be no sky, but that the rotten and rotting buildings had disappeared. Live rot had erased dry or dead rot.

The owners of the foul heads were mostly in their forties and fifties and overweight. Overweight to a point at which the use of smack becomes reasonable. In an unreasonable world, reason isn't reasonable. There was one actual reason for their overweight: since the only occupation for their reasoning faculties from birth had been motorcycles, they knew nothing about anything else. They knew nothing about their bodies. They knew nothing about sex. They instinctively smelled their way to odiferous oily holes. Male and female. This stupidity made everyone who wasn't a motorcyclist so strange to them that they ignored, beat up, and raped all but themselves. In an unreasonable world, reason isn't reasonable.

The animals got on their bikes and rode everywhere, anywhere, whenever. The winds, almost them, were good, very good. The sun burned down on flesh turned into freedom. One motorcyclist had been in an accident and was dying. He saw a shovel lying against a pole, (PARKING 6 p.m. – 7 a.m. only). The sign was no longer applicable. The shovel was lying there for his grave. Graves for left-over human bodies. Graves are only for those whose lives, lacking freedom, were dead. The wind passed through his head's wet grey hairs. Though he was dying he got himself on to his Harley and started it up.

One day I decided it was time to leave prison. I simply walked out.

I stood on the street I had seen, outside. As usual, bikers were lounging in a forgotten sun across the corner of the street. Now I saw that some of them were female. Five of them. All five women were lifting up their T-shirts to show each other or to show somebody – a dead world – their teats. To the furthermost left, the woman's hair was grey almost white, dead short. Sunglasses sheltered some eyes from a half-dead sun. Tattooed blue snakes ran down huge breasts. Out in blue. I thought she was fifty-five. The other women looked like they were in their twenties.

The breasts and nipples of the younger woman standing right next to her looked even larger. Giant nipples are made to be hidden in mouths. They should be outlawed, their owners should be restrained into hiding them away, because they lead to fetishistic behaviour. But there are no more laws. She also didn't have any eyes.

The girl in the middle was as flat as a guy. She was also as tall as a guy and her eyes were closed.

A red like blood helmet completely hid another woman's face. A black lace bra hid her breasts.

The last woman had mousy hair and large, though not huge, breasts. The breasts cast shadows over the beer cans, standing and lying, mostly unopened, on the hot concrete.

I began to run easily, lope like a four-legged animal, down this street. Loping with the freedom of fucking, with the freedom of the wind. Ran down the next street, concrete was natural, street after street. I was flying in order to fly; I was a motorcycle. Instinctively I chose an isolated, narrow alley where my body became only a streak in another's perception and a streak in the window of my own memory.

Suddenly I don't know why. I felt, sensed, heard I was being pursued. I was now at a large thoroughfare. A few Bentleys flew by. They were the limousines of the dead; it was a Voodoun procession for the dead. The thoroughfare's spaciousness stopped me, dead. Unable freely to run, I had to look around. Hesitation is death. Any hesitation for an exile is death. I could no longer run. I was no longer a motorcycle.

It was a dream. That gang wanted to kill me. Sands lay beneath and around my legs. The closer they moved to me, the less my legs could move. Through the deepening, and rising sands.

The Seine lay sparkling, in the distance, a solid glittering bar, a paradise for the weary tar. Actually the Seine is as brown as a dead worm.

I knew that, below, where the water actually lies, the gates and hidden passages in concrete walls can be hiding places. They are shelter for the criminals and bums. All I had to do was reach water.

Footsteps sounded behind me. The prison guards must have discovered my escape. They were following me. My heart almost stopped with a gasp and, at the same time, beat too hard for my life to continue. The prison guards could have been my parents. I don't remember but I know: my parents are monsters whose actions I have no way of understanding. The monsters are tracking me down. I'm not sure who the bad guys are, and who're the good.

I took my body and forced it, tamed it, to make it to the river. Though I was running slower and slower, I made it to the river, the birds were fucking, down white concrete steps slippery from the sun. The Aztec sacrificial temple's stairs were too steep for humans. I would have dived into the ice-cold water to escape fear. Daddy Monster Fear. All I've ever wanted is freedom from fear or to fly. But the ice-cold freedom which I barely tasted, tasted only in my imagination, was too weighty for a child whose identity is predicated upon Monsters. I wonder whether the names which I give things, how I name things, determine, to any degree, how things happen. Probably not. As I touched the bank, a huge hand grabbed my left wrist.

Out of fear and love I almost collapsed back into the ice-cold water. I saw myself in a black veil, now invisible, but still able to see outside – a woman escaped from her harem, now caught and born away by a Berber whose muscles are gigantic. He lifted onto the bank and tore off the bottoms of our clothes. He grabbed me, then, by the shoulders. With a thrust of his thighs, a single thrust, reamed me.

This steel or sex, this act, threw me forward almost ten feet. My palms scraped the pavement. When I turned around to speak to him, to see the man, and saw that he wasn't a prison guard, but a motorcyclist, he walked off. I was left alone. I was lying with my pants down by the side of that dead brown river. Shreds of material lay in the sunlight and my ass ached. I wondered whether this time this lover would return.

It's you who, though I cry I plea I excuse, won't let me kiss your foot even once.
Make me walk through fire or water.
You're the Sultan of Royalty Who gives the orders.
How can I laugh unless you laugh?
The soul is the slave of this laugh without lips without teeth.
Pity those who see your laugh.
But your laugh's hidden in the eyes of beasts.
You who are the glory and ruler of humans who have hearts
Are the doctor of us, sick.
On a rainy day the sick of the world come to a garden
On a rainy day I need friends.
This morning, in the garden,
I plucked a rose – I was scared the gardener was going to catch me.
He said to me gently,
'The fuck with a rose. Take my whole garden.'
Everyone has friends; everyone has mates;
Everyone has talents; everyone
Works. We who have hearts, we relax in the image of the person we really love,
in our emotions' sun,
in the dark shadows of the cave.

Pirate Night

But the blazing will to live: to live anew.
And the struggle of these people to realize themselves in the world of modern times, whose sin is to have been made without them.

DEAD FISH
FUCK

I I Realize Something

(Thivai speaks)

1.

I got up off that concrete, bare-assed, naked, and thought to myself: I've just been pretending I'm a pirate and mean and an Arab terrorist and have no morals. Actually, I ain't none of these. Then, I almost started to cry, which I don't usually do, cause I wasn't anything and cause I was all alone on the concrete and cause my asshole hurt.

Then I stopped thinking 'bout myself cause I was bored and I looked around me. The sun was shining in its full brightness like it had always shone before this and there was nothing around me. Nothing except for stone, sun, sky, and water. This was a ruined suburbia. I thought, if there's nothing around me, there's nothing for me to do. But I've got a life on my hands: my life. I could off myself, but I won't because I love my life.

Inside me I saw two hearts pierced and pinned together by an arrow. Half of the arrow was white and half, black. A leafy scroll winding around the pierced hearts was black or white.

Because there's nothing in this world, I can be the King of the Pirates and rape and murder and roll all the gold and IBM stock in this deserted world between crab-infested toes. Mine. I'll also be the ballerina whom my grandmother longed for me to be. Then, I'll wear décolleté hand-beaded gowns and journey to parties with thousands of lovers, parties where stars fuck and fuck each other over and become too burned-out to fuck. The male half of me'll rape the female half of me, which, I know, isn't very nice, but what can you do in a society which doesn't recognize human needs? Since there're problems in every society, even a revolutionary Algerian one, it's necessary to fuck. Then, having fucked and been fucked, I'll be at peace. This is what I told my grandmother when she was trying to force me to be a ballerina. But she never listened to anything I ever said.

As soon as I had settled down in my mind and in the broiling sun and had stopped drying, it began to rain. One moment would be dark as if the sky was bruised and the next moment was lightning flashes, thunder booms. Total confusion. Each thunder lasted longer and longer until each thunder was rolling for a long time away to the other side of the world, the side to which all but lightning and darkness had once fled. The once-dead worm-river was growing as if it was in a nightmare. As if I was in a nightmare. Brown water or wormy-skin was licking my toes. The sky was the pain inside me. I didn't mind where it hit my flesh cause it was never going to go away. There's nothing to do in rain but sleep.

I dreamed of the St Valentine's Day when I had believed that the cunt was dead.

Being a man means living in nothingness.

When I woke up, the sun was awake and full and there was no one around me. Maybe there was no one anywhere. Like no garbage. I had felt lonely, lots of times I remembered, but not in the blaze of that full sun. When the sun's so strong, even concrete turns into sun. My soles were lucky I wasn't wearing concrete shoes.

The sun was the laziest thing in town.

I saw a boat or something lying about thirty-seven yards down the canal. Lying tied to a stick. A dog who's been whipped; stick stuck in the boiling concrete. I unleashed the dog and put myself in its or his or her mouth. The dead don't bite. I slipped out from shore a yard or two, letting the dead wood find its own place. In the water and sun. Driven by the sky, the current carried us dead along the endless concrete. Dream-ridden by sun, all was OK by me. I picked up an oar which had become half an oar and steered the wood into the edge of an island that was sitting like a frog right in the canal. I hadn't even gotten out of this boat when I heard a meowing. Meow meow. Meow. That used to be what my cunt said when she was healthy. Meow. It was my cunt. Abhor.

I was glad to see her, as if she was my heart's double, because I had been through loneliness. She looked like a cat who had drowned, but I was so desperate from loneliness I didn't even know I was desperate. I jumped out of the boat and said. 'Hi, cunt.'

She must have thought that I was dead. Maybe I was. Abhor's always been scared of death.

But, according to me, even in Abhor's case, something's always better than nothing and nothing's better than death.

'Don't you hurt me!' Abhor shuddered and winced. Abhor was always saying strange things because she wasn't quite right in the head because she had had a hard life. Her father had made love to her.

'Don't you touch me! I don't want a dead man touching me! I'm not crazy!' She didn't know anything about herself.

'Abhor, it's me and I'm not dead.'

'Yes you are.' This was a useless argument.

'You're crazy, Abhor.' That stopped up her mouth. I was so glad to see the cunt, everything that had happened to me since we had lost track of each other burbled like regurgitated worms right out of my mouth. The champagne or worm-like gladness came from my desperate need for sexual love. I think this need is insignificant, a roulette wheel which, always turning, always turns back to zero. But I don't know what else there is. I talked and talked about what had happened to me, and since Abhor was listening, I wasn't lonely anymore. Abhor listened in silence.

I asked her for food.

She asked me for a gun. Those were her first words.

'What kind of gun?'

'Some kind of Magnum.'

'I don't have a gun.'

'Then get me food. I haven't eaten in days.' She looked like someone had eaten her and regurgitated. Like the river.

'How can we get food without a gun?'

Both of us thought about that one a lot, but I guess we didn't think enough, or our thoughts were disabled, because we couldn't figure it out. Finally, we figured it out: Abhor dressed me up in the clothes we pulled off a dead girl who had been floating along the river. Though I knew that the dead are poison and so these garments were poisoning me, I knew it was more important that I now wasn't alone anymore and had social responsibilities. In this female drag which made me look helpless, I went out to search for food and pharmaceutical drugs.

Though they were wet, the dead girl's clothes felt so good on me, and free, that I jumped and skipped and felt fearless enough to bang and knock myself against the first whole door which I saw.

The door was attached to a building.

A woman in female secretarial drag opened the door. Her clothes were typically colourless: light blue and grey. Blue was the same as grey because everything was grey. Thin, invisible stripes enlivened this grey. The clothes had been cut to avoid all contact with and emphasis on the body, especially genitalia. In the beginning of the western industrial world, the garb of secretaries had prophesied the era of AIDS. 'What d'ya want?' she tried to shut her door on my little hand. 'I'm not buying anything.'

'I'm not selling anything, ma'am. I've got nothing to sell. Since I've got nothing, ma'am, I'm trying to find my uncle. He used to work on the hydrogen bomb. He's out of work now. I never met him cause he hates children. That's why I don't have anything.'

'Then what do you want with your uncle?'

'I want to tell him that my mommy doesn't have any money: all her credit cards died at the same time as each other and were buried in paupers' graves. Then, mommy disappeared leaving a will in which she left her white poodle, Tinkerbell, to us. That's my nine sisters and me. There're no boys in our family. None of us know how to feed her poodle who bit off my father's left nipple when he tried to kiss her one night.'

'Who'd he kiss? The poodle?'

I could tell my story was beginning to work. 'The poodle's a girl, ma'am, and I believe she's never had it done to her. I've never had it done to me,' I quickly added.

'Your poodle must be starving.'

I was ravenous. 'My poodle's not hungry, ma'am. She just had a meal at the McDonald's over there. That's her favourite food. I'm just worried about mom. Do you know where I could find my uncle?'

The secretary began to look at me suspiciously, but then got caught up in her own misery. Cause people only think 'bout themselves. 'I don't know anyone in this godforsaken city. No one's left here. Lots of bums, sailors, animal fetishists, whores, lunatics. People whose skins are coloured. Thank The Lord there are still policemen who do their duty even though they're coloured too. Ghost town nowadays. Black ghosts. Black stink.'

'But my uncle ain't black, ma'am, cause he worked on the bomb for the CIA government. I'm awfully scared of the dark and who's in it.'

'Then you come right on in here,' she ordered me, 'and wait 'til my husband gets on home. He's a man. Cause he's my husband. It isn't safe for a girl to walk alone in the dark, through this city. My husband'll walk with you to your uncle's house. I know he will. My husband isn't black, child.'

This made me nervous. I decided I had landed with real rapists who were also lunatics and a real gang. But I've never had any sense. Only curiosity. I walked right inside that rapists' house.

'By the way, honey, I didn't catch your name.'

Just then a rat walked out of a hole. I didn't have to lie. I could shriek cause I was a girl. Another rat walked out and another, and the secretary, her name turned out to be Mrs Williams, didn't mind at all. Maybe she wasn't a girl. Genders were complex those days. 'There're a lot of rats here,' she, Mrs Williams, said.

'I don't like rats.'

'You get used to them, child, when you're poor. Guess you get used to anything when you're poor, even death. I throw things at rats sometimes, books and used needles, and they look at me. It's an exchange. I guess they think they're seeing a species of mammal who's so mentally and physically weak, it's – I'm – almost extinct. What do you think rats think, child?'

'I think rats have aristocratic thoughts.'

'That's it!' The secretary yelled. 'Rats think they own the world. Just like my grandmammy. She used to march into the fanciest grocery store in town – a charcuterie-patisserie – just like in New York City – and take whatever she fancied, she never *wanted*, because she knew she was the Queen of England. She was the Queen of England. By then, England was dead. The salespeople in the store never minded when my grandmammy took things. That is why, child, I don't mind rats now. I'm so lonely in this ghost town, I need rats to keep me company. That's why you can't mind things when you're poor.'

'What about Mr Williams, ma'am?'

'What about Mr Williams?'

'I mean Mr Williams and loneliness.'

'Oh, he don't token to rats. Mr Williams was brought up differently than most people. Regular people. He don't have to lose his fantasies. Keep your eye on rats, girl. You never know when your life's gonna get lonely. Human life's a funny thing. I know it is. But I don't know anything 'bout rat life.' She motioned to two modernist chairs. I didn't know if she meant me to sit down on them or to throw a chair at the rats, and, being a girl, I didn't care which cause being a girl meant being passive.

Now I didn't want to be a girl no more cause girls, being passive, don't eat enough. Cause girls don't get enough to eat. Now, if girls were meaner, they'ld get whatever they wanted. To eat. Cause the meanest of us all get the most. Cause that's the meaning of *meanest*. Who's the meanest of us all? It's dead people. Cause dead people have no emotional or other human considerations to stop them from being mean. All of human history proves this.

I would rather be dead than a girl.

Right then the secretary looked me right between the eyes. She said, 'Rats're meaner than humans.' Her husband walked into the room.

Just as though their two hearts had been intertwined, Mr Williams was dressed in a dark blue pin-striped businessman's suit with padded shoulders. There weren't any jobs anymore except for the cop jobs cause cops always take what they want. He looked down at dead ruffles bunched up between my scabbed knees and said, 'Well, well. Who do we have here? She certainly is a pretty one. Uh huh.' He turned to his wife. 'Isn't she, honey?'

I felt too shy to respond to this admiration cause I had never thought I was pretty.

Mrs Williams just looked at me like I didn't fit in.

'How could I not notice this little thing?' His blue eyes moved upward from my dead ruffles to my tits. Only there weren't none. He kept on staring cause he was looking and not finding, but, since I couldn't figure out what he was staring at, I got so flustered and red, I just turned to Mrs Williams and said, 'Gotta find my uncle right now.' I had forgotten about eating.

'I'll take you where you're going,' said Blue-eyes.

'My husband (Blue-eyes)'ll protect you. There're sailors and other riff-raff around these days.'

'I don't wanna be protected,' I announced.

'I got a lot of money,' Mr Williams said for no reason at all. 'I sell comic books. I sell all of the comic books in the West to the West. I'm a nice guy. I like strong women. Does that mean I'm a feminist? I'd like to be a feminist. I pay my employees as little as I have to because they don't know anything, and they're always asking for more money. That bothers me a lot. That bothers me a lot. I'm about to open a new comic book store in the Beaubourg Museum.'

'Why are your employees stupid?'

'I'll tell you about stupidity and business: the Algerian revolution was stupid! Right. Innocent people got killed. But it was good for business. Any revolution, right-wing left-wing nihilist, it doesn't matter a damn, is good for business. Because the success of every business depends on the creation of new markets.' He drummed his left finger into the table. 'Do you know what human death really means? It means disruption.' Drum. Drum. 'Disruption is good, necessary for business. Especially comic books.'

'Your wife said there're a lot of rats in this house.'

'If there were rats, you'ld be screaming.' Blue-eyes looked away from my lack of tits. 'What's your name, boy?'

But I don't tell businessmen my names. Instead I told him that I had run away from home because my father had given me a lickin' for not being black. That got him.

Mrs Williams was almost crying out of empathy. She looked at her husband like a whipped dog.

'My two sisters are in nunneries cause they're complete dykes,' I continued, 'so I have to find myself some family. I have to find meaning in my life.'

Finally, Mrs Williams started to cry and Mr Williams came towards me with a grand frying pan in his hand, as if I was a rat, so I ran. Out.

In this human world in which a male and a female heart intertwine, it's no good (for pirate rats) to look for pirate treasure in or out of other humans.

The river was rising. I've only seen one dead woman in my life, my mother, except for the dead girl whose clothes I was wearing. A few trees, like dead fingers nibbled by rats, sprang out of the water. Rats' teeth stick straight out of their gums because rats are constantly hungry for everything and an animal becomes what it desires. Now what's true of rats is true of humans. I decided: it was no good having anything to do with humans: I would look for treasure. I leaned against two dead fingers and thought about rats' tongues.

The river made me feel good. Didn't know why. Maybe it was all those dead and living branches not doing anything and the waves not doing anything, sure they growed and got smaller, but they all came to the same thing, nothing or everything, the same end, and all the black-and-blue sky, as if it had been bruised, but it hadn't, wasn't doing anything. I figured I didn't have to do anything cause everything was OK, all black-n-blue, the heart. Black branches; dark blue sky, black clouds; black concrete. When I start feeling joyful or mindless, I start singing. I sang about insects until I was back with Abhor.

She was sitting in the dark picking her toes. I didn't have any food. I told her that humans were useless and we were going to look for treasure elsewhere. She agreed.

We got into our rowboat and cast off, so that we could find the treasure. I guess we drifted for three days and three nights. Right before it'ld turn daylight, being the man, I'd slip out of the boat and steal us food. Between night and morning was the time it was easiest to rip off caviar, kiwis, aged rums, and cookies. Pirates don't eat raw steaks: they just kill humans.

Sometimes we slept all day while the boat and the river and the world drifted on, and sometimes we didn't sleep at all. At night the stars floated through black air like dead fish in a bottomless ocean.

This was the good life, stealing, but we weren't pirates yet. Abhor and me. We were just riff-raff good-for-nothings like the rest of the floating world.

On the third night, a storm hit us with lots of lightning. Abhor became a chameleon or, rather, reverted to the lizard that was deep down inside her. She told me she wasn't going to become a pirate cause she was fucking someone else. I didn't see what that mattered because we weren't fucking each other. And fucking means nothing to me. But Abhor insisted it meant a lot to her, her being a woman. I told her she was just emotional, being a woman: having a fuck is, actually, like taking a leak. Look, Abhor, the sky's taking a huge leak. Is the sky emotional? Or crazy? You're trying to say something else to me, Abhor. There must be a real reason why you won't become a pirate. The sky was pissing down on us so forcefully, all of our hair and bits of clothes and even flesh was cold, shivering.

Abhor was cold and dumb, but not dumb enough to think that fucking mattered. Not as far as being a pirate went.

I was so fixed on being a pirate that, straight against all my honesty and straight-forwardness, the same honesty and straight-forwardness that Abe Lincoln had had, I decided to be cagey. 'So who're you fucking, Abhor?'

'I'm fuckin' some girl.'

I didn't know what to say to that because I didn't care. I asked if the girl was pretty.

'She flicks her lighter against the insides of her thighs and lights men's cigarettes.'

'I don't smoke.'

'Most men smoke.' I began to get the picture, or a picture.

There was no one around in the rainy world.

'I guess you like this one.' I sighed. 'Are you in love?'

'Guess so.'

After all, I had some emotions too. 'Then what are you doing here, Abhor? Why aren't you with her every minute of the night if you're so in love with her?'

'Since she doesn't have a home, she has to live with different men. I can't even phone her. So I have to wait for her to phone me.'

Abhor was saying all this crap to me, but I understood nothing. Since I hadn't needed or wanted anyone for more than a quick (romantic) fuck before and after I had met Abhor, I didn't understand why she would think fucking more important than being a pirate. Now since I didn't want to be hurt by her evil, I decided to replace myself by a sheer act of my will in the world sans emotion. So I turned my back on Abhor. I saw a wreck on the river.

'I'll be seeing you, Abhor.'

She put her wet arms around my waist. I don't remember her touching me ever before. 'Give me time, Thivai. I'll be a pirate.'

In the storm I saw my emotions or myself clearly. The storm got worse. It always does. Abhor and I were huddling in a large dent in the stone along the river. I clearly saw that she was using me to test out her committment to this beautiful, rich, lazy woman. Now I'm a man. So I don't hate anyone cause of sex cause sex is always painful.

So by and by I say, it's still pissing down hard, 'Looky yonder. There's a steamboat who must have fallen on a rock and died in the terrible storm.'

Without saying anything to each other Abhor and I leaped onto our trusty ship and headed right for that wreck. Light from the lightning clearly showed parts of her. A pale green deck. And black poles. Then other parts of her. An old rocking chair next to a steering wheel.

I wanted to get on to that wreck as soon as possible and never leave it. Then soon I wouldn't care about Abhor anymore even though she was as crazy as me.

While we were rowing to the wreck, Abhor said she didn't want to go to a wreck. She had someone to live for and I didn't. I had no one. 'I doan' want to go fool'n' 'round er no wrack.' The girl says. 'Shee-it. Like 'as not we never gon' get home to our loved ones cause the Devil Himself 'asitting on that wrack an' He got a hatchet in His Left Hand 'n He's just a waiting for our necks, to cut through them, so He can make pearl necklaces for His loved ones.'

'The Devil don't have no loved ones, girl.'

'Sure He does. He ain't just a slut. He always sleeps with someone He likes, He's bisexual, cause when that person dies of somethin', AIDS and syph, the Devil's done worse evil than if he slept with someone He didn't care about.'

'That's what love is,' I said gravely. Maybe Abhor and I agreed on something. She couldn't disagree with that. She might have a diseased, that is, overactive, clit, but she couldn't believe in love. 'Let's get on the wreck.'

I bothered to think more about Abhor. She didn't matter to anybody even if she did own an overactive clit which, just like President Reagan's buttons, could set off the neutron bomb. Neutered. 'We might be able to steal lots on that wreck. They say that Captain Kidd went down, down to the Devil, cause the Devil's the greediest of us all, and left a map which remembered his path to doom. This map tells where the buried treasure is hidden.'

'What buried treasure?' Abhor inquired.

'All the buried treasure Kidd and his big men got from murdering and raping and looting innocent young and innocent old people.'

'What is that buried treasure?'

Abhor was as dumb as a girl even if she was a girl and, dangerous in her lower parts.

'By murdering raping and looting men get gold 'n jewels 'n engraved stationery 'n corporations 'n hospitals.' My mom, cause she had been part Jewish, and cause I wasn't a girl so I couldn't marry a rich man, had wanted me to be a doctor.

'Murderin' only brings murderin',' Abhor replied.

Because Abhor wasn't a man, I was going to make her walk the plank. She capitulated and told me she'ld walk on to the wreck. The lightning showed us the dead boat just in time, for a huge black fish of a wave, like Jonah's whale, was about to eat us up.

We crawled and clambered upon the wracketty deck. Some of its wood boards had crumbled into nothing. Since we couldn't see either where we were going or were, cause the air was so black, Abhor and I were crawling around up there like dogs. Abhor lifted up her leg, pretended to piss, and giggled. She had the sense of humour of a cat who's wet and in heat.

As soon as we knocked our heads against an edifice which reached up, way up into the black sky, I figured we were at the captain's cabin. I shook myself into its wall, Abhor's teeth holding on to part of my pants, and found I was right in my figurings cause I was right at a window.

The window was open and light was coming through it like through an opening into the world. *Whatever part of me besides my eyes sees saw two hearts which were touching each other. A sword pierced both hearts. The pain could not be told.*

I started hearing. Human voices. Since the voices didn't sound like angels, they were devils. Devils is snakes. Devils talk about treachery 'n lies 'n hatred. The devils were pirates.

One Devil voice said: 'That's no reason to kill me. I can't speak . . .'

Another Devil voice interrupted: 'You're lying, boy. You've been openin' 'n flappin' your mouth 'bout everything to everyone for a long time now. There's only one way to stop up your mouth.'

The third Devil voice said: 'Killin's nothing to us.'

Since curiousity's the strongest characteristic I've got – me being a pirate – at these very words, I looked right into that light. I saw a human lying horizontal on a floor. Wrists and ankles tied by ropes to iron pegs stuck in the floor's uneven wood. They had probably been hammered in. Murder hammered in. Not into the wood, but into a man whose black beard was so big, half of his flesh was hair.

Over him, there was a guy who held a lantern in his hand. That was the source of the light I saw. The lantern-holder had one real eye and one black hole. Each of a second standing man's hands were clasping immense kitchen knives.

These knives were so big that if they moved vertically down, they'ld slice the hair-mountain, like a pregnant spider, into three separate pieces. I've always been afeared of spiders.

On the floor Blackbeard was epilepsying that he'ld always been as honest as the day was long. There was no more day.

One-Eye said that it had been at night that Blackbeard had tried to murder him and his friend. That this murderous action had had no reason.

For this reason, One-Eye and Knife-Hand were going to murder him.

Then Knife-Hand, who's skinny, squeaks up, he can't talk properly, probably cause his hands're bigger than his mouth, that no one's going to kill Blackbeard.

'You got somethin' 'gainst killing?'

'You're a good man,' Bushy-Hair said from the floor.

Right then Knife-Hand the Pacifist and One-Eye with this lantern walked out of that room right on to the deck and right next to the wall into which I was trying to squish myself. Abhor had disappeared from biting me up.

They talked about killing lots. One-Eye was all for killing

lots cause that's the way of the world, he said. Even of the world's history. Knife-Hand said that he wasn't actually against killing (humans) cause he was a man and no man can be, but he believed in killing sensibly. One-Eye asked what sensible killing is. Knife-Hand replied to him that sensible killing is moral killing and moral or more killing is when the killers don't get blamed for killing mainly by the society and more specifically by the cops. So the killers are morally clean. One-Eye asked why any man would want to be clean. Knife-Hand, whose kitchen knives were spotless, replied that, to be particular, in this case, knifing Bill (that must have been Blackbeard's name) would be morally wrong or evil whereas letting him go to his death as the wreck naturally went down to the bottom of the water and got cleansed by that water would be natural cause that would be letting nature take her own course.

One-Eye and Knife-Hand walked back into the cabin.

I couldn't decide which one of them was right cause I've never been much for morals. I would have called and asked Abhor what she thought, but it was too dangerous to open my mouth. She wasn't anywhere. My stomach sank because I couldn't bear the loss of love. Drowning, I silently called for her as loudly as I could. Glub glub. Drowning with Abhor.

A small hot hand took mine. Abhor hadn't walked the gangplank and drowned yet even though she was so conniving and vicious she should have if there had been any Justice in the world. So there wasn't Justice. Nor love. 'Abhor,' I managed to hiss, we've got to get rid of these murderers.'

'Why?' She answered me. Just to be contrary.

'Cause they're going to murder someone.'

'Us?' Abhor asked.

'No.'

'Then why do we have to get rid of them?'

I took tighter hold of the little hot hand and yanked it hard. She said she was going to do what I said. We were going to get rid of One-Eye's and Knive-Hand's escape rowboat so they couldn't get to shore and leave Blackhair to drown. Then they'ld all drown. Then we were going to find a RAP

(آگاهی انقلابی ع ر بی)

(Revolutionary Algerian Police)
station and sick 'em, dogs that cops are, on the drowned or not-yet-drowned murderer dogs. Cause dogs eat dogs' flesh when dogs is hungry enough.

That's how I figured things.

Abhor, cause she was vicious, figured things another way. She said that it was wrong even to murder murderers. Even for revenge.

'There's no revenge involved. I got nothing 'gainst those murderers.'

The rain was pouring down so heavy, the world below was a wet sheet. All the children were pissing in their beds. Perhaps they were dreaming of their parents.

I carefully explained to Abhor that since murderers murder people, it's necessary to murder murderers back. To murder back a murderer is not to be a murderer or to murder, because the first or primary (in terms of Aristotelian causality) murderer is the real cause of the murder.

But since Abhor was a girl, she didn't understand political theory.

I gave up. I knew that not only weren't we real murderers, we weren't even pirates because we hadn't taken any loot and women who are the same as loot. Being adult means being able to see one's self clearly and to change those faults. I decided now I was adult. I told Abhor she was as much at blame as me. She said she wasn't anything.

There was no more light anywhere. Even the rain couldn't see. There was no more anyone. Everyone was in bed, even the river, dreaming wet dreams cause there was no more sex. Dreaming of flying on top of rising waters.

After a while, there were some lights. Abhor and I got into the murderers' rowboat and steered, our rowboat following behind like a fish on a hook, toward the concrete quai; when we just reached the quai, we pulled in our oars and let the boats themselves float to the stone. Though there were many lights around us, no people were in sight.

Abhor wanted to tell the cops about the drowning murders so that the murderers wouldn't drown. I refused because I, for moral reasons, don't believe in sickin' cops on anyone for any reason. Abhor scratched my face up so she won. We looked around in that black for a cop station, but we didn't see it. Finally, we stumbled over one.

A bored cop who was on duty, or something-or-other, mumbled he'ld look for murderers immediately. But there was no money involved so the cops didn't do anything 'til Abhor let slip that we were pirates after loot. Then, one Revolutionary Algerian policeman who was so fat he had to be wheeled in a shopping cart and the cop wheeler, who was an ex-punk who didn't give a damn about what he did as long as he didn't have to think 'bout anything – he was ten years old – followed me and Abhor down to our rowboats. By that time the wreck had floated past us and was under so much water that there must have been three more dead murderers floating in the Seine. That's when I knew that all human action is worthless. I was sad because now Abhor and I were disqualified as pirates because we had sent two murderers and one victim to their deaths but we hadn't gotten no loot.

Depression is the same as black air. Abhor and I got into our rowboat and got away from the cops. On another section of the quai, we got out, felt sad, and slept like dead people.

When the sky and the earth were back to normal, I opened Abhor's eyes because if someone didn't open them for her she slept straight through the day. By the time I had opened them, we were quarrelling again.

Abhor started it because she was a treacherous drowned rat and should be gangplanked. She said that she wanted nothing more to do with me.

I didn't want to be a pirate alone so I had to swallow my pride and ask her why she wanted nothing more to do with me.

She didn't say nothing. Saying nothing is the worse thing a person can do in emotional times, in these emotional times.

As we rowed on, there was no more concrete, only trees. Willows and elms hung over deeply grassed soil as dark brown and rich as velvet. There wasn't a sound of anything or of anyone else, just as if the world was asleep.

'Why d'you come with me in the first place, Abhor?'

'You asked me to.'

'I asked you cause I wanted to be pirate pals with you. If you don't want me, get out of my presence forever.' She knew I meant the gangplank. I was going to drown her. I'ld never have to have anything to do with her again.

Now and then, here and there, a breeze came to visit our boat, drifting through the lazy waters, along with smells of dead giant fish. Then plum leaves and all sorts of magnolia blossoms; then more dead fish. The insects wanted to live up my nostrils, but didn't want nothin' to do with Abhor.

I don't know what I need
I don't want any responsibility
I don't know what I need

Abhor sang. We both watched the lonesomeness of the river, lazying along, by and by almost lazying into sleep. Just solid lonesomeness.

This lonesomeness hurt me. We had the river all to ourselves; Abhor didn't want me. At night Abhor and I would look up at the sky. It was so beautiful, my feelings opened up into it. In that atmosphere, space, which was black because it was limitless, tiny sparks, appearances, things, emotions glowed for different lengths of time. Under this infinity, Abhor and I talked to each other about nothing, the way people talk to each other when they don't have to listen to the other person cause they've partly melded into the other person. Or the sky.

Sometimes stars would shoot down at us like the Devil was up there, shooting his gun. Then I'ld remember, or Abhor'ld be silent, and there'ld be a pain in me like a physical hole.

I knew that, a long time ago, Abhor and I had been partners. At that time I hadn't known what that meant and had just accepted our close friendship. Now it was as if we were two different kinds of beings, like human and Martian, cause there was a gap or a volcanic chasm between us. The volcano destruction had come either from Abhor's not wanting me or just from my own insides. It was heavy, like nothing's heavy. It was a black hole as is all of living space.

I can't bear nothing when that nothing's part of me. I couldn't bear the sky above me. I couldn't bear the blackness. I couldn't bear not knowing. I couldn't bear all the things, especially when they were beautiful, through which I was drifting.

Since I knew Abhor was going to get rid of me as soon as the two of us got somewhere, I knew that nothing was all I had. A hole in the flesh. You could call it fucking. I could bear pain, a hole being torn in my flesh, but I couldn't bear, no way, no flesh, no Abhor, nothing. I decided I was going to stick her in prison.

I was going to get Abhor in prison in the first place cause she was as strong as I was: I knew I was a snake and low and crawling on the ground (though I was that way only cause I was in unrequited love). But she was a paranoic porcupine and a piece of shit and a stinky skunk naturally. That's cause love can change a man. Whereas women are the way they are naturally. So when Abhor wasn't looking at me, I scribbled a note to the CIA. This was real easy to do.

Dear CIA,

The runaway nigger who engineered the bust-in to your Washington DC computer library a year ago is now floating down the Seine in an old rowboat. I know where she is and am willing to lead you to her for lots of money.

Yours sinscerely,
Captain Blood
(X)

I didn't want to sign my real name.

I figured if they put Abhor in prison, I'ld be able to see her every day and I'ld collect the pirate loot, or prison payoff, even if I had to collect it all by my lonesome.

I mailed this note. Now I was cleaned of all sin and pure. The truth was that I had never known sin before I had met Abhor. Abhor was just like Ahab. She was as rotten and unfeeling as a fake leg because nothing, (not even womanhood), was natural in her. For the first time in my life, I prayed. I fell down on my knees, right in front of Abhor, and then over on my hands, scraping them on the concrete, and I prayed that Abhor would get out of my life forever because I loved her.

As I prayed this, Abhor's mean little skunk eyes looked right at me. Then her right hand scratched the black hairs under her left armpit.

'I can't give Abhor up to the cops,' I prayed aloud. I decided I was going to leave her forever cause she didn't love me. I hated her guts cause I loved her and I didn't love anyone.

I said: 'Abhor, I'm leaving you forever.' I turned left down a path parallel to the river. There didn't seem to be any animals or insects around.

After a while there were insects who were buzzing while they slapped their asses against my face. Their asses left baby trails of blood on my cheeks. Insect shit is human blood. Or Abhor's fingernails. While I'm fucking her. Nothing comes of nothing.

I walked and walked and then I realized that I missed Abhor and that I loved her. There was nothing to do but go back to her.

By the time, night, I came back to the boat, there was no Abhor.

2.

I started walking back . . . or forward . . . again . . . but I was so depressed I couldn't walk. As if I wasn't able to walk, I just made myself walk. Forward. While I walked, I kept remembering everything that was my past; it all seemed nothing.

I decided to keep on walking. The more I walked, the more down I felt. I hated my eyes, my nose, my mouth. I came to a road.

In back of me I heard a motorcycle. As soon as I could see it and it was passing me, I yelled 'Stop!' Its driver stopped it in a spray of gravel and sand.

'I didn't hurt you so you got nothing 'gainst me,' its driver said.

I looked at him and thought he could be the one who had fucked me in the ass.

'You didn't hurt me,' I replied. 'But if you want to find out, why don't you test me out?'

He did. He was satisfied, as far as I could tell. For the moment I felt good. For the moment. That's what quick sex is. He said that he didn't usually do it with someone, but I didn't know how he did it with no one. He said he plus me were an adventure.

I was feeling so good I told him all about how I wanted to be a pirate and about Abhor. Though I usually can't talk to strangers, I could talk to him real easy cause he was so tall and just kooky or gooky looking. He looked just like a lopsided teddy-bear all of whose sides had overgrown. He rubbed his paw into the gravel.

By and by, Mark, he told me that was his name, said, first I said, 'My living's more and more lonesomeness. I guess I need some love.'

To which Mark said, 'I was a fool not to say this before.'

Now I thought that he was agreeing with me that those who are outcast by society, and maybe those who aren't, but who isn't these days, are becoming more and more lonely. Which goes to show that even two people who really like each other never understand what the other one's saying. I said, 'Yes.'

Mark said, 'I know where she is.'

I jumped up though I was so sad nothing could make me glad. 'Where's Abhor?'

'I bet she's the one they just put in the jail down the road.'

'Why do you think it's her? Have you ever seen Abhor, I mean, before this?'

'Well the cops were carrying someone who was tied in knots and handcuffed. Handcuffs mean a prisoner. The cops were smiling. All cops are straight. When straight men smile, you know there's a woman around. Smoke means fire. There're no cops who're women. Since there were no other women prisoners there, that woman must be your girlfriend.'

I could only follow the last part of the reasoning. Loneliness had eaten up my mind.

'So we have to steal her away from the cops. I'll figure out one plan and you figure out another and then we'll figure out the best one.' He reached a logical conclusion.

I liked the idea of stealing Abhor. I didn't care about cops, but that was minor. Even though the sun was shining down very hard, I could think hard. The sun was shining down as hard as it could. I really liked the idea of stealing Abhor. 'I know how we'll steal her for ourselves,' I said.

'First of all, we'll learn which cop carries the keys to her cell. Then one of us'll seduce him. You. When he's finally asleep and happy from all that effort, you'll pickpock the keys out of his pocket and carry off Abhor. I'll tie her to the boat, she'll be happy, and we'll sail away down the river.' I was sad.

'That plan would work, Thivai, but it's no plumb good. It's no good, Thivai, cause it's too easy cause nothing ever comes easy to no one. Not even piracy. We need a harder plan.' The sun was shining hard.

I went through my brains to find something harder, but it wasn't any good. The river was too lazy. There're no brains when a person's sad. Living was too hard to find something harder than living in the brains.

I was so sad with loneliness and longing to be with Abhor, I wanted to kill myself. I threw a pack of Tarot cards to find out whether I should kill myself or not.

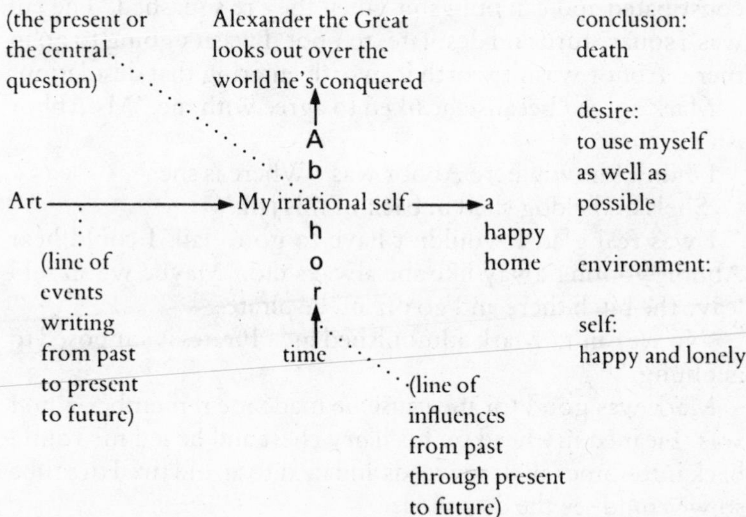

These cards clearly showed that I liked the messed-up world in which I was living and that I was going to die. But it still wasn't clear, at least to me, whether I should kill myself or not.

Mark's plan was so complicated it was sure to get me and him killed. Which was good. You can't be a pirate unless you die by hanging. I didn't care about the other details of his plan. Besides, Mark was always changing all his plans all the time. That could have been because he was gay. If that's what being gay is. Mark had lots of thoughts.

Right then and there I knew that Mark was going to be my friend even if Abhor wasn't.

I told Mark I thought his plan was chancy and would get us in trouble with the police.

Mark asked if I trusted him.

'I trust you.' That was enough for us to go along with his plan even though I didn't know what it was.

Mark took me to jail. This was the jail in which Abhor was imprisoned. According to Mark. The building looked English rather than Parisian because Parisian apartment buildings were built human-sized for humans. Whereas the English built mansion flats to be property. Property should be indestructible, cold, and hard. Mansion flats are monsters who are constipated and can only shit when they're squashed. The jail was a square turd and desolate, to boot. I wasn't going to go in there. Abhor wasn't worth it, worth entering that desolation.

Mark agreed because he liked to agree with me. 'Ms Abhor isn't in there.'

I didn't know where Abhor was. 'Where is she?'

'She's in the dog shed in back of this jail.'

I was real glad I wouldn't have to go to jail. I could hear Abhor woofing away like she always did. 'Maybe we should leave the bitch there and go off an' be pirates.'

'No we can't,' Mark admonished me. 'Pirates is supposed to get hung.'

Mark was good for me cause he made me remember who I was. I leaned my head on his hairy chest and he led me round back into some tall dead weeds and next to an old tired tire tube so we could see the dog shed.

By the time we had climbed up and down some half-torn wire, waddled through rubble that used to be a parking lot with two dead cats instead of cars left in it and what could have been half of a decaying human, I guess instead of a motorcycle, though I'm no authority on humans, and had arrived at what looked like it must once have been an outhouse, in its better days: I was so tired I didn't want to see anything. So much for human perception. There was a huge lock on the door. The lock wasn't locked. We just walked inside. The shed couldn't have been an outhouse because it didn't have enough floor for there to be a hole, much less a toilet, in its middle and there was no Abhor. There were also no humans in the parking lot. Mark and I replaced the lock on the door so the door was locked as good as ever.

'Do you know how we're gonna break Abhor out of here?'

'No.'

'We're gonna dig her out, Thivai. It'll take a week of hard labour.'

I thought that was a good plan only I didn't know where Abhor was.

'She's out in the field with the other niggers.'

'I thought there weren't niggers anymore.'

'When there are prisons, there's niggers and nigger-owners.'

Mark knew everything cause he was gay. I've never been nothing. Abhor was black.

First of all, we had to make friends with the nigger who was in care of, leading and feeding Abhor so as we could steal the key of the unlocked lock from him.

This nigger believed in witches. Witches are women who are inimical to men.

Mark said that he was so strong, mentally and physically, he was fool-proof 'gainst witches. In other words, he was gay. That's why, though a man, he was able to be gentle.

I agreed with Mark 'bout Mark, but I didn't know if I agreed about witches cause I had never seen them. 'What does one of them look like?' I asked the nigger.

'It's not so much what they look like, cause they only come after men at night. It's what they say and smell. I mean: how they smell. At night witches're always whispering in your ear. Just like when you're alone in your own bed about to go to sleep and a mosquito comes buzzing along right into your face. Only a mosquito only wants your blood. As for their smell, a witch smells enough, especially in the bottom half, to make a man act crazy and unlike himself. Then a man will do a crazy thing for a witch. This is why a man has to be on his guard when he can't see.'

I told this prison guard the only person I had ever been on guard against was Abhor. Just like I didn't know what witches were, the guard didn't know what an Abhor was.

Mark asked him whether he had a dog.

'No, Sir, I don't have no dog. Not while I'm working. Why do you think I own a dog while I'm working?'

'Cause you've got a dog bowl with stinkin' smelly food in it right there in your hand.'

'That's for no dog!' The nigger smiled gradually all over his face then said, 'You want to see what kind of animal it's for?'

We both said 'Yes' and he led us to the left side of the shed to a wire enclosure in which was Abhor. I didn't let on that I recognized this animal which, being the most dangerous in the world, was more dangerous than any witch, even though I didn't know what a witch was, and that I loved it. Her. Abhor raised her eyes a little and looked directly at me.

'Do you know her?' the nigger asked me.

'How should I know her? I've never seen her before.'

'She's looking at you like she knows you.'

I explained to him that cause women don't see well, they're always running after the wrong person. Women're always in trouble, especially sexual trouble. Therefore, it doesn't matter what a woman looks at: it only matters how a man looks at a woman. Mark said he never looked at women.

'See?' I said.

Then I further explained to the nigger that I called him a nigger cause, though the Algerians had taken over Paris, the American CIA still ran everything and, besides, I didn't know his name. The nigger said his name was Harry and that witches were the real reason Abhor was staring at me. Whenever something in the universe doesn't make sense, Harry said, like the American CIA controlling everyone 'n everything, it's cause of witches. It's worse than this. Humans think they control everything and the more they think this, because of witches, the worse everything gets. Since things – affairs of state, the state of affairs, the state of humans – is now pretty bad, there must be a hell of a lot of witches around. That's what Harry said.

Then he turned to Mark and asked Mark if he, Mark, now took witches lightly even though they were women, so those two argued about which witch meant what, while I whispered to Abhor that me and Mark were going to dig her free like a dog. At the word 'dog', she tried to kick then bite me through the wire. Which showed how mean she was.

I still planned to save her because I loved her.

Then Harry told Mark and I to leave cause it was getting dark and the witches were about to become operative.

Mark and I went back into the woods where we built a fire out of twigs and other garbage cause it was now the full of night. There were no witches around.

Over the fire we perfected our pirate plan for rescuing Abhor. First Mark said that it was a shame that there weren't hundreds of cops around so he could call out his motorcycle gang and wage all-out war. I said I was getting sick of all-out perpetual war. Mark said there wasn't any other kind of war cause war breeds war like lovebirds. Lovebirds can't breed elephants cause if they did, they'ld die, at least the female ones. Then Mark said it was a shame Abhor wasn't chained to Harry or at least to her bed, like a woman should be, unless she was a witch, cause if Abhor was chained, not a witch, we could blow up the shed with dynamite and the police hang-out without injuring one hair on Abhor's head. I replied that was cause cops are stupid. If the cops weren't stupid, they would have chained Abhor to her bed and the shed and the wire and the dogs' collars cause they would have known that she was mean and vicious.

Mark thought. He said that it was clear we needed dynamite. 'She's so ornery and contrary, being a woman, that she wouldn't let herself go with us unless we dynamited her up.' That sounded right to me. Then Mark said that we'ld have to dig a deep moat around the shed before we dynamited it up. That didn't sound right to me. Mark said that that way, when Abhor was escaping, she'ld fall down and break a leg. Then she'ld have to let us make her escape no matter how ornery and contrary she was. That sounded right to me. I know that it's hard to control a woman even if she isn't a witch.

Then Mark said that the safest thing to do would be to saw off one of Abhor's legs. That made me upset so I told Mark he was gay which was why he didn't understand what went on between men and women.

Mark said that there are lots of historical examples, throughout human history, of how humans cut off each other's ears fingers and limbs for moral and other good and proper reasons. Judges often commanded; the Church approved; it being almost the highest human morality. Was Abhor, Mark rose up on his tippy toes where he always was anyway, was Abhor, just cause she was a woman, exempt from human morality?

I had to think about that one a bit cause I'm no moralist. It all just went against me. Sometimes you don't know why something goes against you, you just know it does. Cutting through Abhor's leg. I told Mark that I absolutely knew what I knew was moral for me, but I didn't know for another person.

Mark backed down. He always finally agreed with me for the sake of agreeing with me. He said we wouldn't cut through Abhor's leg in order to rescue her, but we'ld smuggle a penknife to her so she could cut off her own leg.

I was insistently against that one because of my morality. Mark asked me what my morality had to do with Abhor since she was another person. I said when it came to morality, in the final analysis, logic wasn't an important consideration. Blood was.

I said, instead of a penknife, we'ld smuggle Abhor a pen. The pen is mightier than the sword. That way Abhor could write down, with her own blood as ink, how we rescued her, how brave our hearts were, how strong our arms. All of human posterity would hold us in their esteem. Mark said he wanted to be held by strong blonde boys.

That was our plan. We needed lots of penknives so we could dig Abhor a moat.

Well, midnight came around like it always does. I didn't see no witches come out of the closet of the day. Mark and I walked down to the river and searched through its cold 'til we had found twenty-seven penknives and one used condom, then we walked all the way back to the cop station and left the used condom, like a baby, on its deserted steps. In back of the station, we dug and dug into the flesh of the earth until grey, like a tear, appeared in the flesh's clothes, the sky. Both of us were so tired, we could no longer see. My hands felt red. By the time we could see, I saw that we had dug only four or five foot deep gouges in the flesh. I was sure we had one hundred and seventy six more feet to go.

'If we had all our lives to dig and we were going to live 'til we were eighty years old, we could dig for Abhor. Since we're gonna die young, Mark, this ain't going ta' work.'

'Then how can we get Abhor to break a leg?'

I thought and thought, but I couldn't think of no way to hurt Abhor properly. Finally I sadly said, 'We'll have to dynamite her up.'

Mark thought that was sensible, but we couldn't find any dynamite cause dynamite was still illegal despite the revolution and the cops wouldn't give us any. Not that we had asked them. I've never known how to ask for help.

The next day I sent Abhor a pen in the mail so she could write down her memoirs.

The problem now was that Abhor didn't know how to write because, being black, she was uneducated. While I was thinking about this new problem, Mark put on a Body Map tuxedo which he had gotten off a dead man he had found floating in the river while my back was turned. Mark told me it's necessary to dress up for funerals and similar occasions.

Abhor was so happy to see us she pissed in her pants once we had woken her up. Then she told me and Mark she loved us. I wondered what she meant by 'love' cause she smelled. Women never mean what they say like men mean what they say, cause if women did, Abhor wouldn't be telling a gay motorcyclist that she loved him. Unless Abhor wanted to be a victim of unrequited passion, but I didn't think she did. So I decided it wasn't possible to tell what she ever meant. Then Abhor, sobbing all over her prison garb, said that she wanted to get out of jail and be a pirate cunt.

'I'm going to go away with you boys right now,' she said.

We told her that was too easy. She was going to have to get permanently and seriously maimed escaping from her jail because escaping from jail is a difficult and dangerous thing for a man to do.

'But I'm not a man.'

'Then you're not going to get out of jail,' Mark said.

'What I mean,' Abhor uselessly protested, 'is I don't want to get maimed.'

'Why not? A man has to endure pain and more severe tribulations to show that he has the power to make someone of himself. Being maimed is the way a man shows he's a man.'

Mark didn't quite agree with this cause, he said, he didn't want to be a man. He didn't like his father. I informed Abhor she had to be a man to be a pirate. If she wasn't a man, she was as good as dead.

Then we gave Abhor lots of huge safety pins so she could draw lots of blood out of her skin with which to write down lots of memoirs. She was probably going to be shut in jail the rest of her life. Abhor and I remembered our mercenary days, before there had been a revolution and then the CIA had taken over everything, and Mark listened very closely so he could learn how to act. Mark and I decided that it would be good for Abhor to spend the rest of her life in jail because jail life would make her become like Malcolm X. So if we rescued her, we were going against her best interests. That was my final answer to Abhor.

The sky had turned grey again and Mark and I abandoned Abhor. I had abandoned Abhor so often, I was getting bored with abandonment. Mark and I marched into the police parking lot where we found some old and dead dogs. Abhor must be hungry. We went back into the woods to get some more plans.

Our newest plan was to make Abhor, though she was uneducated, or because she was uneducated, into a great writer so that she'ld have a reason for being in jail for the rest of her life. And at that time, society needed a great woman writer.

On the fourth day or the fifth day or on some day, cause the Devil created our world in seven days, when the light of the early evening was mild enough to avoid hurting Mark's and my eyes and Abhor was back from the fields, we sat her down in some shit to learn her how to write properly. First, we taught her how to slice up her thumb with a penknife blade. That way she'ld have a lot of blood.

Abhor didn't want to do that cause she was a big scaredy-cat. I told her good that if she wanted to be great, as great as a man, she'ld have to learn how to endure tribulations even more severe than pain and still keep her mouth shut. Abhor blabbed that I never shut my mouth and, whenever my mouth's open, lies come out of it.

Mark didn't listen to her palavering, but held her right thumb right down, and I sliced into it. We held her right thumb down cause Abhor wrote with her right hand. Writers need disability or madness they can overcome in order to write. The reason for this madness came from Arabia: in Islamic society and culture, writing and drawing are the same movement, calligraphy, the tracing of the movements of the heart across the page. Now there are three kinds of hearts. (1) *The double heart* in which each heart hurts the other heart. (2) *The single or lonely heart.* (3) The single heart which through the pain of loneliness has become *a rose.* We sliced into Abhor's thumb and got some blood. I drew the three hearts in her red blood.

The double heart, the first heart, was one heart placed over a second heart. This sign was me and Abhor. One arrow, like a knife, was piercing both hearts.

A scroll which said *EMPIRE OF THE SENSELESS*

twined writhed wriggled and giggled, like a snake, around our double hearts.

A knife pierced *the single heart*, the second heart. This heart was me without Abhor. An eagle whose beak was as big as the knife, perching as if she was shitting upon the knife's handle, said *IT'S BETTER TO DIE THAN YIELD TO SHIT*.

Having been pierced and pierced and pierced, our hearts were dead. Our dead heart had become *a red rose*. The knife was still standing in our corpse or rose. A snake who was saying nothing wound, poised to bite, around the open rose. This was the third heart. This was a cunt.

I asked Abhor whether she understood all this.

'What do hearts have to do with writing? I've lost a lot of blood so far.'

I explained that these hearts were applicable because they were senseless. To write is to reveal a heart's identity. Abhor heard me, squeezed some more blood out, and traced, rather than drew, her own, the lonely heart. Cause she wasn't able to write by herself yet. Then, like a baby falling flat on her or his face, she printed the words *FUCKFACES ALL MEN* then *THE SHIP IS SINKING* right over the bloody heart.

I told her these words weren't good writing because they had nothing to do with nothing. With Abhor. Cause Abhor wasn't a pirate yet cause she didn't know nothing about ships. To write or to describe a heart, I explained, demands accurate observation of the self and of the self's world. Abhor said that I didn't know shit about pirate ships because, being a man, I had the wrong equipment.

I gave up. I told her it would be better for her to have nothing to do with hearts. Finally, Abhor agreed with me and she swore to the Bloody Virgin that she was going to be celibate forever when she made it out of prison.

Then I told Abhor that if she was going to be celibate, she'd have to meditate on a bloody rose.

Then I cut into Abhor's four fingers with another penknife. There was blood all over the place and something or someone smelt like fish.

This was the end of Abhor's first writing lesson. Making Abhor into a great woman writer obviously was going to take more blood than sweat.

Her second lesson followed immediately on the first. Cause time didn't exist anymore. With my help, Abhor composed a letter to the Revolutionary Algerian Police (RAP) in that blood which was lying around which hadn't dried yet. There was lots and lots.

First we drew for the cops a skull and crossbones. The cross, like a sword, pierced the skull's empty nose. A scroll which was twining tombstone-like around the cross, or the other way around, read *IN MEMORY OF VLADIMIR*.

'Now,' I told Abhor, 'you've written your name properly. That's how you write your name.'

Abhor felt she had made progress in writing. It's necessary to make a child feel wanted.

Dear REVOLUTIONARY ALGERIAN COPSCOP,

Don't murder us even though we're white cause we're trying to be your friends even though that's fucking hard. (Abhor asked who this 'we' was. I told her 'we' is always a disguise. Then she said fucking is now harder than being friends with cops.) Cops: there is a desperate gang of Englishmen in your fair city of Paris who intend to prove that they're honourable by stealing Abhor out of your dog shed. These Englishmen can't see through their morality. This is their plan:

At midnight they're going to walk to the dog shed and open its door and lay down in the mud so Abhor can walk all over them and dirty them up. Then, they're going to off Harry cause he's also black. Then they will have proven their English valour.

We are telling you this only because we used to live among the English and had to endure their refusal to talk about sex.

We're on the lookout for any English.

At midnight when we see an Englishman coming fully, we'll blow our horns. We've got big horns. Then the English can't blow you Arabs up.

If the English don't, or can't, come, there's no need to do anything, but if they can come, come into the dog shed and murder each of them one by one. Slice off each one's head then his hands and ears and pin these accoutrements to the dog shed's wall. The dirt below will soak up the blood. Like stale bread. Then the bread might smell a little. Like Abhor.

If you don't do all this exactly as we have told you, the bread will smell a lot. Like Abhor's menstrual blood.

We're telling you all this because we're unconcerned and uninterested.

CAPTAIN BLOOD

Abhor said that she couldn't send this letter we had just written to the Revolutionary Algerian Police, who were just around the corner, because there was too much violence in it. I explained that a great writer cannot afford to be sentimental in his or her writing. Mark and I sealed up this writing in her blood. Then we sealed it up in all of our blood so we were now blood brothers. And sisters. Cause our blood was mingled, we didn't know what we were.

I immediately ran to the post-box on the corner of cop station so the cops would get our letter as soon as possible. As if I was in love, my heart was beating louder than a dead man's. But as soon as I had mailed this letter, I remembered we had forgotten to tell the cops the date of the English invasion.

I raced back through all the garbage of night to Mark and Abhor to warn them of this. But we all agreed that if we sent the cops another letter, they'ld think we were cranks.

Since I couldn't send them a letter, I lifted up about three bugles which I had lifted earlier that day out of a partly bombed-out toy store in which some young children were tearing the heads off dolls and gluing them on to robots. I blew every bugle. Our ears were blown out while many cops came out running and they ran to the dog shed. Like dogs.

Mark and I, also like dogs, leaped into the dog shed before the cops got to us. Abhor screamed and screamed. Not like a dog. She didn't stop screaming, so Mark stuck the round end of a bugle in her mouth and tied it there with a cloth. Abhor untied this cloth which was now full of drool. She wasn't going to keep her mouth shut. When the first RAP lunged through the wooden door, Abhor threw herself through the shed's other hole which served as a window.

Mark and I followed her, howling. The cops sniffed and barked at our footsteps.

The faster we ran through their parking lot, the closer the cops seemed to come to us. The breath of one of these animals was on my neck. The more I sensed I was in danger, the less I could run.

They were about to capture or kill me. Abhor had disappeared. Mark was pulling at my left fingers, but I wasn't able to move. Letting myself go into my weakness, my death, I fell to the ground, somersaulted backwards into a clump of nettles. Mark was squatting in another patch. The cops raced past us. Mark and I kept crawling on the ground, backwards, through nettle clump after nettle clump, here and there there was a magnolia, 'til we reached our rowboat. The blood we left gleaming on the nettles turned them into wild roses.

Abhor was waiting for us by the small rowboat. She asked where we had been.

I answered we had been rescuing her out of jail.

Mark asked her what it was like in jail. Do the sufferings of jail make a human stronger?

'No.'

'Then what does jail do for you?'

'When I was in jail, I could have torn my heart out and eaten it, then, out of boredom.'

We were standing in the boat on the soil. I decided the Seine's waves were rising too high for safety. Our ship was foundering in a wave so huge, it was white. A dragon's head in its fury of white teeth rose from the waters below, from the black deep. All around Abhor and Mark and me, in that dark black, tyrannosaurs and ape-eating fish were swarming. Swarming around one little ship.

Mark and I loosened the ropes until we sailed away, down the Seine, until we were too tired for anything but oblivion. Then we put the boat next to the fence of what must have been a posh restaurant. One light bulb was still burning.

All of us rolled from the boat on to the dark red and black

land and immediately fell asleep. Abhor was on my mind and Mark was on my mind, so I slept restless. Twice I stood up in the middle of a dream, remembered bits of the dream all around me, and walked through these bits to where Abhor lay sleeping. I saw Abhor thinking, meditating in the dog shed, so passive due to all that meditation that she couldn't leave the dog shed on her own, though physically she could have. In my dream. In another dream or part of the same dream, I saw myself going after something. I couldn't see or tell what I was going after. I saw that I was just going for this, not thinking about how or why or if I was right or who was around me. Just not thinking at all. Then I saw that Abhor was following me. And because I was the one who was always leading and not thinking, Abhor and I always landed in a mess. Whether we were apart from each other or together. Then, I swore, only in my dream, that I'ld start to be thoughtful and not have so many pirate plans. Then I dreamed that Abhor swore to make more plans. The next time I woke up, it was dawn and Abhor was still visible to me, she was sleeping beside half a chair. The one light bulb had gone out. I knew now that I didn't know whether I loved her or not and that that didn't matter because Mark and I had rescued her, taken her with us. That that was love. I guess all this dreaming teaches us something. Abhor was still asleep.

II Black Heat

(Abhor speaks)

As soon as I woke out of my deep sleep, I saw the two guys looking at me. One of them looked like a tree if a tree was a mammal: limbs shot out of him as if the limbs had been shot up with vegetable growth hormone. The hair didn't fare any better: it wasn't long so much as sprouting. In colours. Mainly bleach that's gone wrong. He was big. Too big for me.

The other guy looked as if he was mean and warped because his eyes were little and they looked like menstrual blood. Then I remembered that I hadn't had a period in two years.

Looking at these two men gave my eyes cramps.

But I knew who they were. They were the two who had taught me how to write.

Since now I knew how to write, I wrote them a letter while they were watching me.

Teddy Bear One of Whose Arms Is Missing:

I feel I owe you an explanation. I don't owe Thivai anything at all. (You could ask Thivai to explain this to you, but I know he won't. Either because he doesn't think that his treating me as less than his own shit is important or because he doesn't know that he treats me like shit. Thivai thinks this way because he thinks that I'm shit because I'm a woman. So do you. And when if you really knew what had really taken place between Thivai and me, you wouldn't care cause men always protect each other's asses when it comes to women.)

Both of you would be better off if you'ld at least admit that you think that women aren't human and men are. You believe that women are wet washcloths you can use to wash the grime off different parts of your body or to fling into the face of another person (a male).

Everytime I talk to one of you, I feel like I'm taking layers of my own epidermis, which are layers of still freshly bloody scar tissue, black brown and red, and tearing each one of them off so more and more of my blood shoots into your face. This is what writing is to me a woman.

Even though I love you, Mark, because you're a man I hate you. I'll explain why.

The whole world is men's bloody fantasies.

For example: Thivai decided he was going to be a pirate. Therefore: we were going to be pirates. If I didn't want to be a pirate, I had to be a victim. Because, if I didn't want to be a pirate, I was rejecting all that he is. He, then, had to make me either repent my rejection or too helpless to reject him. Then, he decided he loved me. By the time he decided that, I was in jail.

You two collaborated in keeping me in jail by planning escapes so elaborate they had nothing to do with escape. That's western thought for you.

This is what I'm saying: you're always fucking deciding what reality is and collaborating about these decisions.

It's not that I agree with you that I'm a wet washcloth. It's that I don't know what reality is. I'm so unsure, tentative, tenuous, lonely, uncertain from loneliness, anguished, sad that I'm not certain enough to fight the decisions I should.

I guess I'm going to get into more and more messes cause that's the way I am, but I hate all of you.

Abhor

I finished writing this letter and handed it to Mark. He read it and giggled. Then he handed my letter to Thivai. Mark was still giggling.

I think that Mark has the right approach to life. Or to something.

Thivai read my letter and yelled, 'Oh, she's dead, she's dead, I know she's dead.'

'Who's dead?' Mark asked. I didn't know about what, or whom, Mark was thinking.

'She's alive!' Thivai exclaimed and ran his hands through the few bits of hair which remained on his head. 'We truly love each other and we're going to get back together again.' With that, Thivai stopped plucking at his hair, kissed me, and started running around in formless shapes on the concrete, just like a lovebird who's heard another lovebird – any old lovebird – squawking. Thivai's sense of reality was less than Mark's. Not that that had anything to do with anything.

Since I wasn't out of my head and I was determined not to be anymore out of anyone else's head who was out of his head, I decided I wanted to be part of a motorcycle gang. First, I had to learn how to ride a motorcycle. First, I had to find a motorcycle because I didn't have enough money to buy one. I said this out loud.

Thivai raised his head out of his narcissism and asked me why.

'I have to find a motorcycle,' I explained so that he could understand me even if he was mad, 'so that I can be free to steal Puerto Rican candles and other Voodoo items and silk sheets and tin plates for camping out on the mountains and penknives for playing mumbley-peg and for writing real memoirs – these are biker stories, not prison memoirs, never prison memoirs – and biker mags. They didn't allow me to read anything in prison. And so that I can move so swiftly, even when I'm not dreaming, that I fly everywhere anytime and I escape all cops forever.' This sound right to me as I said it. A lot of what I say is bullshit and weird.

'You don't know how to ride a motorcycle, Abhor. I do.' Thivai said this only cause he had to do everything better than me.

If he had any decency in him, he would have offered to teach me how to ride a motorcycle so that I could join the gang.

'But you can't learn what you already know.'

'You don't know how to ride a motorcycle, Abhor.'

I didn't listen to him. I turned around, walked into the woods, and found a Honda which was only a year old, prerevolutionary, and in perfect shape except for one cracked mirror.

I walked this bike back to the concrete then placed it on its stand. 'You shut up, fatherfuck,' I said to Thivai. 'You know what you are? You're nothing since you do nothing and you feel nothing and you have nothing that is no actions. But you're so scared you are the nothing you are, you keep pretending that you control this earth. That's why you don't have a bike.'

'Abhor's not a slave, even if she is a runaway nigger. She's as free as any cretur who walks this earth—' Mark was trying to stand up for me, but too drunk.

'OK,' Thivai snarled. He wasn't going to fight me and a man. 'Say that you learn to ride that motorbike. As well as a woman can. You're still not going to be able to join a motorcycle gang because motorcycle gangs don't let women ride bikes.'

'The Angels live in the US of A where the CIA play with gays,' Mark added parenthetically.

'So you know all about ancient history cause your head and the rest of you is dead,' I snarled, primarily at Thivai, and parenthetically at Mark. 'But you don't know anything about what goes on now.'

Mark mused on my words. 'I once knew a bike gang made up of dykes who used to act in Russ Meyer flics.'

Thivai ate his own shit. 'I don't see what all this fuss is about. I can't give you your freedom, Abhor. No one can give another person that person's freedom. Of course, you're a free person. You are perfectly free to ride a bike even if you don't have a clue how to ride and drop dead in the process.' Thivai was good on logic and wit because he didn't have any feelings. 'I just wanna know. If you're free, Abhor, why do you bother protesting?'

I wasn't going to protest anymore. I was going to smack his face into red pulp. But I did neither. I walked my bike back into the green woods.

In the green woods, I thought, to myself: 'Now I'm going to have an adventure! My adventure is I'm going to wade knee-deep through blood and soar higher than the winds!' As I said these crimson words, with my hands on the handlebars, I looked as sweet and contented as an angel whose mouth is stuffed with fresh cherry pie.

I didn't know what Thivai and Mark were doing.

I found a cannister of gas and one of oil, filled the bike. Then

I rode the bike, which I could ride well, except for one thing. Everytime I used the clutch, the clutch stopped me. I didn't want to be stopped: I wanted to go. I got angry at the clutch and called him or her a shitsucker. This showed that both men and women do evil. But this knowledge and understanding didn't help me deal with my clutch.

Finally I got so pissed at not being able to go anywhere, I pulled the clutch in and screamed. I was revving all the time. The second I let the clutch go, the bike shot forward. I learned that a clutch controls power; to get more power, you have to control power. That was good.

I rode back to Thivai to demonstrate to him that I could ride and he said I couldn't.

I replied, obviously I was riding.

He replied I didn't know the rules.

What rules?

There're rules of road behaviour. They're found in a book called *The Highway Code*.

I had never heard of any rules so I didn't know that there were any, so I went back into the woods where I found a wet copy of *The Highway Code*. This was an English book, dated 1986.

I had the CODE so now I could drive.

Back on the concrete, I told Thivai and Mark they could follow me if they found bikes, or they couldn't if they didn't, they could do whatever they wanted, not that anyone could give another person permission to do what he or she wanted, because now I could ride a bike and wade knee-deep through blood and soar higher than the winds. I took off on my bike.

After a while, I stopped, wiped my brow so that my brow was greasy, and looked, for the first time, at *The Highway Code*. Its first rule for bikers said that a biker should keep his (I had to substitute *her* here, but I didn't think that changed its sense) bike in good condition. Since this bike wasn't mine, I could keep her in any condition. Since this is only commonsense and commonsense is in my head, I tore out this section of *The Highway Code* and tossed it into a ditch.

The next part of the code said that I must keep myself in

good condition to drive. Since I was obviously in bad condition from my jail experience and from my Thivai experience and, generally, from life (my life), there was no need for me to stay away from as much booze as I could get my hands, paws, and other limbs on. This is what *The Highway Code* said. That I, like a bike, need lots of fresh juice.

If *The Highway Code* was all commonsense, I could throw it all away cause I knew what commonsense is cause that's what commonsense is.

I didn't throw the pamphlet away yet, but hopped on to my bike and rode 'til I hit a suburb.

About five schoolboys who had never gone into their school once because they were too bratty and because there weren't schools anymore because there were no more rules, were standing in a straight line from one end of a zebra crossing to its other.

I decided that my proper driving course would be to kill them.

There were two cars in line ahead of me who were also waiting to cross this zebra. The driver of the one nearest me, a Renault, was blinking and blaring his horn. As loudly as he could. A punk in the first car, so beat-up as to be unrecognizable, both him and his car, having been sandwiched between the brats and the honker since the beginnings of eternity, slowly walked out of his car and walked back to the honker. The honker told the punk to go, go forward.

'I can't.'

'Why?'

'There are children there.'

'Run them over.'

'Shut up.'

The businessman heard that, rolled up the windows of his new Renault, and ran his Renault into the punk's scrapheap. Since I was unsure what *The Highway Code* said about this situation, I had to think for myself. I again decided that my proper course of action would be to run over a brat, this time so I could get the hell out of there before the businessman decided to run into me.

I acted on my plan, but unfortunately missed a brat.

Since I still wasn't sure what *The Highway Code* had to say about this situation, as soon as it seemed safe to me, I pulled up against a fire hydrant. Like a dog. The first hydrant, like a dog, was useless, not cause there weren't fires anymore, but because there was no one including the cops, who disliked fires enough to quench them. Just like a dog who needs to piss or to sniff, I drove up against the fire hydrant, pulled out my *Highway Code*, pissed all over it, and opened it up at random:

Leave enough space between you and the vehicle in front so that you can pull up safely if it slows down or stops suddenly.

This rule was confusing for two reasons. First: there had been ample space between the businessman's and the punk's cars so lack of space couldn't have been the reason. For anything. Second: there was no vehicle in front of me.

I figured I had to find a vehicle in front of me so I could obey the rule. I patiently waited for fifteen minutes. Waiting for this vehicle was like finding someone to love when you're not in love.

But, unlike love, I found someone. Someone who looked like a bum who's been almost all the way through bumhood was driving a red something, perhaps a pick-up truck, down the road at about five m.p.h. give-or-take five m.p.h. He was going slow. Neither the man nor his machine looked functional, to me, though both were. Crawling. Life can be weird that way.

You meet someone one day by chance and your whole life changes.

Now that I had found my stranger, I took another peek into my driving book. I was becoming a good, road-worthy driver because I was reading and memorizing the rules of driving before attempting to drive.

Never get nearer to your stranger than the overall stopping distance.

I didn't know what an overall stopping distance was so I looked it up.

mph	overall stopping distance in feet
20	40
30	75
40	120
50	175
60	240
70	315

(stopping distances increase greatly with wet and slippery roads, poor brakes and tyres, and tired drivers.) (A punster obviously wrote this book.)

Since the sun was shining her ass off because she was horny, almost as horny as me, (that's how bikes make me feel), and I was high on my knowledge of *The Highway Code* and a bit of speed, this coda had nothing to do with nothing.

The bum in his red truck was now well past me. I started up my bike and started to think. I was cruising along slowly, at about 55, and the bum was doing 5. The overall stopping rule didn't say anything about 5 m.p.h., much less about 5 m.p.h. versus 55 m.p.h. Maybe calculus was needed, but I couldn't remember my highschool calculus because I had never needed it. By now, I was so angry that I had been forcing myself to study all these rules which had nothing to do with nothing and didn't work, that I drove straight into the hobo's vehicle.

BAM.

I don't think the old man felt a thing. He hadn't heard a thing cause he kept on wobbling on at 5 m.p.h.

I gave The Book one more try, stopped my bike, and looked down into it. Its pages were hot.

Make way for ambulances, fire engines, police or other emergency vehicles when their blue lamps are flashing or their bells, two-tone horns or sirens are sounding.

I pushed left-hand's second finger into my horn button, kept it there, and rammed into the bum truck again. BOOM. The bum didn't feel or hear a thing.

For once, the Code book was correct. This was an emergency.

But now I was on a two-lane carriageway and so confused, and upset cause I was confused, that I had to pull my bike up into its left edge. I looked into the empty space and thought that, in this world, I have no one to rely on when I'm in deep trouble. I wasn't going to cry. The old bum had disappeared.

About half an hour later the same bum and the same truck, half of it, the other half had somehow become pulp, were waddling around, or, rather, through a hairpin bend, whatever that was, right past me. Suddenly I saw that the truck was actually three vehicles, a '54 pink Chevy, the door of another pale green Chevy, and most of the chassis of a red oil tanker all pushed together. Except for its back which had been pushed into something worse than a has-been boxer's face.

I didn't know if this illegal vehicle was legally allowed to move, so I looked back into my Highway Code. I was a member of my Neighbourhood Watch. For a second I worried that if I looked into my *Highway Code*, the turkey would have time to escape from my eagle eyes. The next second I thought that this turkey was going so slowly, he wasn't going nowhere. This is one of the rules of the world. If you don't go anywhere, you don't go anywhere.

When driving in fog, it is vital that you should obey the rules in Rule 55.

That's exactly what *The Highway Code* said and it was true. The old man was, obviously, driving through heavy, heavy fog because he was swinging from side to side, his vehicle was swinging from side to side, and sometimes, when these swings came together, he disappeared, just like a drunk who's drunk enough to pass out. This proved to me, as London drivers had also shown me, that anyone can learn to drive.

I looked up Rule 55 to learn how the old man had learned to drive and how anyone could learn to drive.

Rule 55.
a) Check your mirrors and slow down.

I didn't have any mirrors because I had chucked them because looking into them had tended to make me slow down. I never look in mirrors cause then I'll think that I'm beautiful. So I slipped on to the next part of Rule 55.

Rule 55.
b) Don't hang on to someone's tail lights; it gives a false sense of security.

I started to keep on remembering this by repeating it over and over in my memory because it was important. At the same time I started up my bike and revved as hard as I could so that I could slow down properly.

Rule 55.
c) Watch your speed; you may be going faster than you think.

I switched gears twice and revved up even more so I was sure to not be going faster than I thought.

Rule 55.
f) See and be seen.

This was it. I switched into fifth and revved up to 120, then stared down at the speedometer so I exactly knew my own speed. As I was driving correctly by staring down at the speedometer, naturally I did another correct thing. This shows how good a driver I had become. I did not hang on to the truck's tail lights. I smashed into them. I looked up. I saw and was seen. At least, felt. Feeling's better than seeing. The truck stopped. The hobo also stopped, lurched over the driver's window, and partly fell out so that he was draped over his left-hand mirror.

Rule 55.
g) Check and clean mirrors and windows whenever you can.

The truck was dead. Miraculously, the old man wasn't. He was hobbling, then walking toward me, with a ten-inch switchblade open in his right hand, while I looked down at my art work. He was right-handed. He looked like a cross between a drowned rat and a three-car wreck. A gentleman's top hat, falling over his left eye, unfortunately didn't obscure his vision because this left eye was a hole. I was confused about what was happening because there were no more rules. Perhaps I was on the crossroads of Voodoo. One road was that the old man was trying to give me an important message. The other road was that the old man was trying to kill me.

I jumped on my bike, U-turned, and drove the other way. The problem with following rules is that, if you follow rules, you don't follow yourself. Therefore, rules prevent, dement, and even kill the people who follow them. To ride a dangerous machine, or an animal or human, by following rules, is suicidal. Disobeying rules is the same as following rules cause it's necessary to listen to your own heart.

I shifted the Honda back into fifth to listen to my own heart. *The Arabian Steeds.* My heart said these words. Whatever my heart now said was absolutely true. I pulled the bike up against a telephone pole some kids had twisted into a cock and took out a pen and the *Code*.

I looked into the heart. I drew the first picture I saw on the *Code* cause it was the only paper I had.

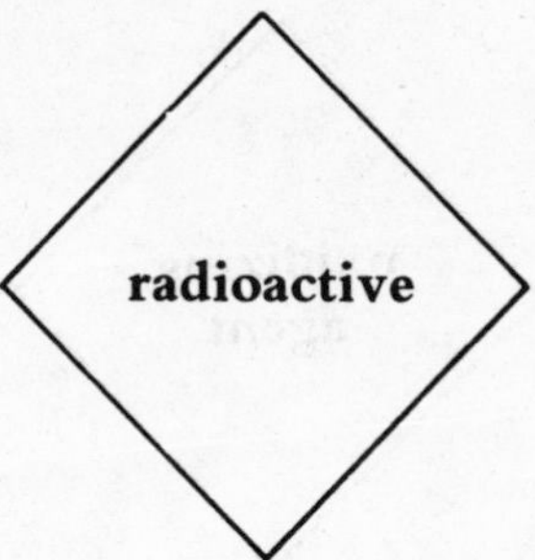

(He was now in that part of the world in which wild Arabian horses roam.)

The next picture I saw:

(This part of the world was so hot that the wild Arabian steeds had trouble finding water and motorcycles steamed up. People had to be mad with will to survive such heat.)

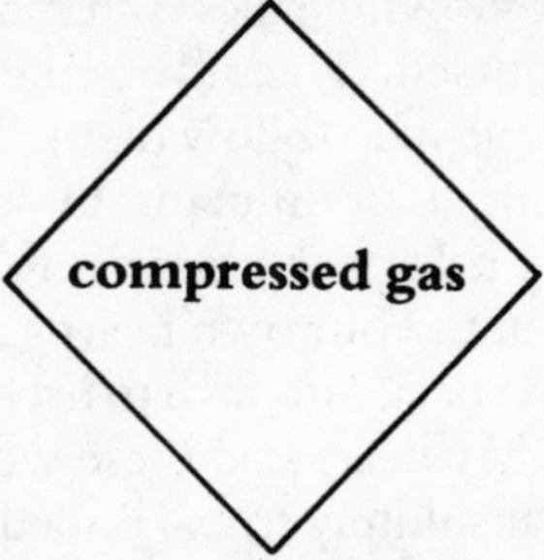

(The CIA was upturning the soil which had been used for agricultural purposes, and uprooting trees, in order to mine the gas sources. There were more and more motorcycles.)

The next picture I saw:

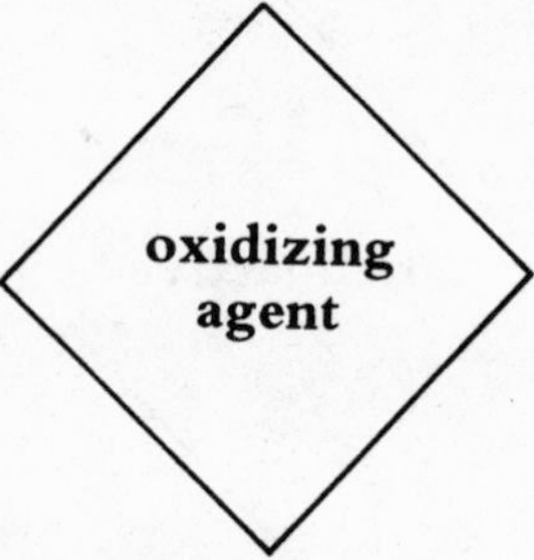

(The sun's power was strong than the CIA's. The horses knew this. Riders and motorcyclists lounged around on dried earth which had once been the grounds of a thriving city.)

The next picture I saw:

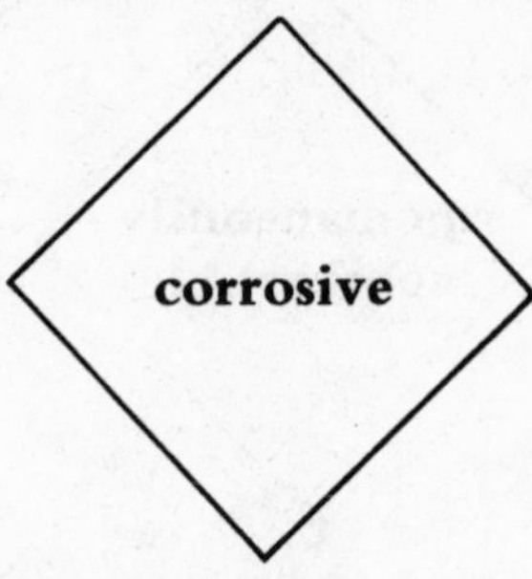

(Let anger be anger: neither self-hatred nor self-infliction. Let the anger of the Arabian steeds be changed through that beauty which is blood into beauty.)

The next picture I saw:

(Toxic.)

All of this came to me for no reason at all and so it all had to be true.

I drew a final picture which summed up all the other pictures.

This was me.

From now on *The Highway Code* no longer mattered. I was making up the rules.

This is my rule. All of you hear this:

When I die, probably by my motorcycle, (for riding a motorcycle is looking at your own skull),

throw me, dead, or my dead body, into the ocean. Then all the fish will have someone to eat out cause they can eat me up.

If the CIA won't let you do this because, they'll say, you'll be polluting the ocean by unpolluting their oil and waste pollution: dump me without a coffin into some soil. I don't want to feel claustrophobic when I'm dead. Stick a sharp sword into this dirt for a tombstone.

I mean this.

Next you can hold the funeral. Only rock'n'roll music. Opera and classical destroy all but dead human nerve synapses. If you play more than seven notes of any classical music, my corpse, at least half my corpse, will rise halfway up out of the waters or dirt into which you put me and vomit all who've been dead for hundreds and hundreds of years all over you. You'll eat it.

When the rock'n'roll has reached the pitch of white noise, let an inordinate amount of booze including Russian vodkas and coloured Chartreuses, because the parrots are coloured, be brought out, so that the parrots can get smashed and squawk without ceasing. Then there will be no more death. Humans will or will not fuck, however each one pleases. In general, in particular, and specifically, the point of my funeral will be ecstasy, the point where complete isolation is equal to its opposite, never the alienation of this daily life.

Cause I do not want my death to make anyone more down than this society has already made him or her.

An Algerian Revolutionary Cop pulled up beside me. He said he wasn't going to arrest me for speeding.

I couldn't punch him out cause I didn't want to go back to jail.

I didn't tell him that I didn't want to go back to jail.

This cop was seven feet tall and had pimples so big, it looked as if volcanic craters had dug their crab claws into his visage. His legs were longer and skinnier than his brains.

As if it knew what was going on, the sky began to rain. Mark and Thivai pulled up beside me. They must have stolen some motorcycles because they were riding choppers. Thivai had been speeding, so, as he pulled up, his back wheel slid, left rubber, but this cop didn't care cause both of them were men. They were all pissing on me.

Then, the cop, who was jotting indecipherable and illegible notes down on a piece of paper, informed me that my manner of driving would possibly get me in trouble and probably killed. First of all, cop said, you speeded along without any regard for me so I was forced to keep up with you. (I silently thought he should keep his balls and even his tongue in a burglar-proof safe.) Secondly, I simply bypassed every junction I met. I finally opened my mouth and carefully explained that bypassing junctions is safe driving. By bypassing junctions, I was bypassing cars who are the natural enemies of motorcycles. Then, the cop told me I was dangerous to all living men. (At this point I decided the cop could keep his balls attached to his body cause I was going to cut off the bottom part of his body and send it down the shark shoot as soon as I had biked to Haiti. In Cap Haitien, the Tontons used to throw the Haitians they didn't care about down the shark shoot.) This cop told me, furthermore, that it had been difficult for him to follow me because I had signalled too soon. I told him that, because I didn't know there was anyone else in the world, any signalling was an act of faith.

Mark and Thivai kicked me.

I kicked them.

The cop gave me a roll or scroll as long as Julius Caesar's memoirs with thousands of X's all over it, and left. I looked at Mark and Thivai.

Mark and Thivai kicked me again. I hurt.

I asked them, privately, why they kept kicking me. Hadn't imprisoning me been enough? They had lost that one, just like the Americans had lost Vietnam. Were they now trying to invade . . . me?

Thivai and Mark kicked me again.

Then I thought about how a sword pierces a cunt. Only my cunt is also me. The sword pierces me and my blood comes out.

It doesn't matter who has handled and shoved in this sword. Once this sword is in me, it's me. I'm the piercer and the pierced. Then I thought about all that had happened to me, my life, and all that was going to happen to me, the future: chance and my endurance. Discipline creates endurance. All is blood.

Thivai explained that he was kicking me for the same reason that he had had me put in jail. By enduring and breaking through tribulation, I could become a model and heroine to women. I didn't bother replying to his lack of wit, but turned to Mark and told Mark I wanted to join his motorcycle gang.

Mark said, no I didn't.

I asked why.

'. . . there was a teenybopper . . .' Mark was autistically mumbling as if he had never heard me or anyone, 'who said to a guy in my gang, just as he was about to rape her, that she had AIDS. He thought she was saying this just so he wouldn't rape her. So he did. Pork her. She did have AIDS. By the way. The cops sent the member, our member, to jail for rape.

'He spent two years in a work-farm west of Marseilles. Then the Algerians took over. Remember? They changed the jail system, and, as a result, Smutface, my buddy, was sent up north to Maximum Security. Some policewoman picked him up in her car to take him there.

'Smutface told me this himself:

'"You the dirt biker goin' to Algeria State Corrections, are yuh?" she snorted through her nostrils. "I gave up my Sunday when I weight train the hardest just to see that you're safe 'n sound. Instead, if you ask me, you should be lyin' under six feet of shit." She was a typical ball-breaking bitch only fatter and pimplier. She put me in her car. My balls were dead because I couldn't touch them because she had cuffed my hands to a steel bar bolted to her car's floorboards. So I couldn't wank off and shoot my poison right into the cow's eyes.

'Prison.

'I couldn't talk back to her cause if I did, I would have had to tell her she was a Martian. She didn't stop chewing her lips. Between her chewing, she chewed on a Milky Way.

'She chewed and chewed. "Ya know, biker, you oughta be real grateful to me cause I'm allowing you to see nature. Nature's a wonderful thing. If I had my way, no biker would ever see nature. Cause the moment you see nature, you go out into it and foul up our streets with your noise and your greasy hands and your destructive machines. I gotta brother in the USA Airforce. He says they oughta blow a big hole in the ground and drop every bike that's been made on this earth into that hole. I agree with my brother.

'"The fact is, biker," her left hand was thumping part of the car seat next to her flabby ass, "if it was a few years ago when us cops had all been white, we'ld electrocute all you. There wouldn't be enough electricians around for the job. Yes sir. Count your blessings, boy." She smoothed back her few strands of hair.

'They drove on for hours. Mathilda, the prison and diesel engine, told Smutty about another brother of hers. Mathilda's mother was a cow. The, this, brother had once been a witness-for-the-state in Dallas, Texas. The United States. A seventeen-year-old was being tried for shooting a woman in the head right after he had raped her. When the judge learned that the kid was a biker, he gave the kid the maximum sentence.

'Finally the sun started to go down. Mathilda stopped her car by a Wendy's. She unlocked Smutface's cuffs. She used her personal cuffs to chain him to the diner's counter. While he ate with one hand and his mouth, Mathilda told the rest of the customers that he had raped a girl.

'Mathilda held out her bank card to the waitress to pay. The waitress said they couldn't take bank cards anymore. Mathilda laughed, said she'ld get her wallet out of the Buick, leave biker boy so the waitress could rape him. The young waitress looked disgusted.

'Smutty thought she – the waitress – was a good-looking girl because when she bent over the sink and down, he could see the flesh slightly, but not bulging, right next to her little panties. He knew the little waitress liked his staring at her.

'When Mathilda returned for him, Smutty asked her if he could shit. She wanted to say "no", but had no choice. He asked her if she wanted to watch him. She looked like she wanted to puke and said he stunk even when he wasn't shitting. She looked at the waitress, but the little waitress didn't look back.

'Mathilda checked out the men's room, saw that its only windows was heavily barred, then let Smutface in there.

'Once he was alone, my friend banged out these bars with

part of the sink's pipe, pushed himself out the hole and ran around the back to his jailer's car. He figured it'ld be open from when Mathilda had gone to get her purse.

'It was. He picked up her shotgun which was lying on the car floor below the passenger seat. He was planning to run for the bushes, then the river, live free.

'But when he turned around from the car door with the shotgun, Mathilda was standing there. Smutty used the shotgun's butt to ram her hard, up against a nearby car, so hard that she almost passed out.

'He growled at her and moved the barrel up to stick it right into her mouth. There was a sudden, sickening smell that took over the air as he jammed the barrel hard so far past her teeth that it pointed straight up to her brain. The smell drenched over him even more as he realized what it was. Shit. She was a typical diesel: weak when it came to the punch. Her eyes became huge as they looked right down into the clean, dark barrels of the double shotgun. She tried to speak, but only made a choking noise. So she kept looking straight down the gun barrels. She didn't have to look down them long. With his other hand Smutty took her revolver out of her belt and brought it down hard on the base of her skull. He felt better than he had all day long.

'He drove off in the cop Buick, came back to our gang, and told us this story.'

I told Mark that he was right. I didn't want to be part of a motorcycle gang.

I stood there, there in the sunlight, and thought that I didn't as yet know what I wanted. I now fully knew what I didn't want and what and whom I hated. That was something.

And then I thought that, one day, maybe, there'ld be a human society in a world which is beautiful, a society which wasn't just disgust.

DISCIPLINE
AND
ANARCHY